BROTHER to DRAGONS, COMPANION to OWLS

Tor Books by Jane Lindskold

BROTHER to DRAGONS, COMPANION to OWLS

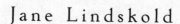

Jane Lindskold

ORB

A TOM DOHERTY ASSOCIATES BOOK
New York

BROTHER TO DRAGONS, COMPANION TO OWLS

Copyright © 1994 by Jane Lindskold

Previously published in 1994 by Avon Books.

An Orb Book
Published by Tom Doherty Associates, LLC
175 Fifth Avenue
New York, NY 10010

www.tor.com

Library of Congress Cataloging-in-Publication Data

Lindskold, Jane M.
    Brother to dragons, companion to owls / Jane Lindskold.— 1st Orb ed.
        p. cm.
    "A Tom Doherty Associates book."
    ISBN-13: 978-0-765-31481-9 (trade pbk.)
    ISBN-10: 0-765-31481-9 (trade pbk.)
    I. Title.

PS3562.I51248B76 2006
813'.6—dc22   2006040049

First Orb Edition: August 2006

Printed in the United States of America

0 9 8 7 6 5 4 3 2 1

BROTHER to DRAGONS, COMPANION to OWLS

ONE

◞◞◟

"MORNING FALLS ON THE JUST AND THE UNJUST," I OBSERVE, and the nurse smiles politely and continues brushing my hair.

Betwixt laughs from where I clutch him in my hands, the other head, Between, snores. He is not a morning dragon.

"Turn us over, Sarah," Betwixt coaxes, and I do this carefully, balancing the four stubby legs on my pant leg just above the knee.

Betwixt growls approvingly, "That's a good girl. Now, be a love and scratch in front of my left horn, right above the eye ridge."

I do this, studying my friend as I do. Betwixt and Between are a two-headed dragon. They are small as dragons go, standing only seven inches at their full height and running only ten inches long from barrel chest to tail tip. They also have blue scales, red eyes, and smell faintly of strawberries.

The nurse interrupts my thoughts and turns me to face the mirror, "There, now, don't we look pretty this morning?"

I look, pleased as always by the effects of my weekly bath. Hair straight but thick, shaded the yellow-white of cream, falls shining to well past my shoulders. My skin is fair and touched with rose. My eyes are the pale green of milky jade.

Smiling, I borrow Bacon's words, "There is not excellent beauty that hath not some strangeness in the proportion."

When I finish dressing, I "run along" as the nurse tells me, firmly holding Betwixt and Between. Breakfast for ambulatory residents is being served in the cafeteria. I get on line, place my dragon on my tray, and accept what is handed to me.

"A day without orange juice is a day without sunshine," I say to Jerome, whose dark face parts with a bright smile.

"You've got Polly well trained," another worker says.

"Sarah," Jerome replies. "Her name is Sarah."

"Polly'd be a better name," the other laughs. "The loony who never says what but anyone else teaches her—just like a pet parrot."

Jerome gives some soft reply. He is a Witness and always turns the other cheek.

I see something in his eyes, though, and whisper softly, "Beware the fury of a patient man."

He nods once and I move on and find a seat at one of the tables. Between is awake by now and with Betwixt is eagerly awaiting his share of my breakfast. First, I dip my index finger in the juice and place a drop on each dragon's tongue. Then I take the plastic jelly packet, break the blister, and squeeze a tiny dab of jelly into each of the dragon's mouths.

A shadow falls over the table and with a scraping of chairs two people join me. Both are men. Both are like me, insane. Ali is schizophrenic. Often he is drugged so heavily that he shuffles like a zombie. He must be throwing his pills away again, because his tiny eyes in his swollen, porcine face glitter with malice.

Francis is manic-depressive. I do not need to see his bright, mismatched clothes or the nervous way that he flutters his long-boned hands to know that he is currently manic. The way he laughs as he takes his seat and nudges Ali, who "accidentally" shoves my tray, spilling my juice onto my toast and eggs, tells me.

I suppress tears and hear my dragons hiss. Then I cut the ruined part from my toast and squeeze the remainder of the jelly onto it. The eggs are beyond saving, the juice mostly gone. Because of my grooming, I have missed the early service and already the food line is closing down.

Ali and Francis don't like that I am ignoring them. Ali reaches to grab Betwixt and Between. They hiss warning as my free hand flashes out, faster than Ali's flabby paw. I tuck the dragons onto my lap and finish my toast.

"Hungry, Sarah?" Francis asks.

I nod slowly, wondering if he is sorry for what he made Ali do.

He sniggers. "Then you shouldn't feed your breakfast to a rubber dragon!"

Seething, my temper hisses. I see that lined up on his tray are three linked breakfast sausages. They are cold, and white grease congeals on their edges, but they look better than my soggy, orange-juice-flooded eggs.

Again, my hand flashes out and I seize the sausages. Jumping from my chair, I laugh.

"The line between hunger and anger is a thin line."

Then, my dragon in one hand, the sausages in the other, I dart away. I finish my breakfast in the ladies' room, carefully washing my hands after. I am finger-combing my hair into order when the five-minute bell buzzes.

Seizing Betwixt and Between, I scamper to the sewing workshop. Ali and Francis will not follow me there. By evening, they will have forgotten—I hope.

I am ruining a zig-zag stitch seam when a group of people come into the workshop. Nani, the workshop moderator, rises from the machine where she is sewing a fine seam and goes to meet them.

I immediately recognize Dr. Wu, who supervises my Wing at the Home, but the woman accompanying him is a stranger. She is tall and curvaceous, with golden hair and a sunscreen-pale complexion.

The buzz of conversation from those patients closer to the front alerts me that something interesting is going on. I stop my machine and remove the shirt I am sewing. Picking up my ripper, I begin methodically removing what I have sewn, all the while stretching my ears to hear what the visitors are saying.

"I think you are distorting the definition of functional, Dr. Haas," Dr. Wu is saying angrily. "Yes, some of these patients can walk and feed themselves after a fashion—if someone supplies the food—but they are not fit for mainstream society."

"Come now," Dr. Haas says in measured, reasonable

tones that make me shiver. "Certainly you are being over-cautious in your diagnosis. I see nearly twenty adults in here, all busily working. If they can work, they can get credits; with credits, food can be found."

"Don't be ridiculous!" Nani snaps. "Work such as these patients are doing here has been done solely by machines for centuries. There is no market for these skills. What we make here is cycled back into the Home to help defray costs."

Dr. Haas's cool smile turns predatory. "Cost is the bottom line here. The beds are needed to take care of completely nonfunctional patients. Those you are coddling will be reclassified and discharged. Perhaps some of the borderline cases can be given work as orderlies."

Their progress through the room has brought them up beside my table. Trembling inside, I quickly feed the shirt fabric back into the machine. Dr. Haas pats me on the shoulder, but her attention is for Dr. Wu.

"Tell me what's wrong with this lovely child," she purrs.

"Sarah was diagnosed initially as autistic. She is hardly a 'child' either. Her records list her as nearly thirty. That innocent expression you mistook for youth reflects her utter inability to relate to her environment."

"She does not show the withdrawal characteristic of autistics," Dr. Haas challenges.

"No," Dr. Wu hesitates. "That was the initial diagnosis. In the past five years, she has become more responsive to external stimuli, but hardly in a constructive fashion."

Dr. Haas interrupts him and turns directly to me. I shrink away from her bright green eyes, cuddling Betwixt and Between for comfort.

Baring perfect teeth at me, Dr. Haas asks, "How are you today, Sarah?"

I stare blankly.

"'Sarah'—That's your name, isn't it?"

"What's in a name?" I manage.

The golden eyebrows shoot up as Dr. Haas turns accusingly to Dr. Wu. "Shakespeare?"

"Sarah shares a trait common to autistics in that she has a nearly perfect memory for the oddest things. We had a patient here several years ago who read a wide variety of works—especially Shakespeare and other literary classics—to Sarah for hours on end. Sarah appears to have retained a great deal of what she heard."

"Can she communicate, then?" Dr. Haas seems anxious.

Nani replies, "Poorly, after a fashion. If she attaches importance to some phrase, she will recycle it."

Something in her posture tells me that she is already defeated, despite the brave smile she gives me.

Dr. Haas's smile is broad, but unauthentic. "Well, I think Sarah is a fine candidate for reprocessing. With her looks, she can find work as a model very easily. We're doing her a favor, helping her out of the nest."

They move on. I sit unmoving at my machine. No one seems to care.

"HISTORY?" THE STERN MAN AT THE TERMINAL ASKS WITHout turning to face me.

I stare, poised in the doorway for flight.

"What is your history?" he snaps again.

"What is history but a fable agreed upon?" I ask.

He swivels his chair and studies me. "Oh, yes, I was warned about you. Give me that disk."

I extend the piece of plastic and he drops it into the terminal.

"Patient's History—Review—" he tells it.

"Sarah. No surname. No precise date of birth," the disembodied voice announces. "Admitted from Ivy Green Institute, private facility."

A light begins to flash and the voice states without change of tone, "Classified! Classified!"

The man studies me for a moment, then shrugs, his face falling into lines of habitual boredom.

"Don't matter," he says, punching a button. "Computer, reprocess patient as socially functional and discharge her."

The computer grunts and he hands me another plastic disk. "Here's your walking papers, Sarah. Go out of here and turn left. They'll send you on your way."

I stand frozen. He repeats his instructions more slowly. I turn and walk to the door. Betwixt and Between mutter comfort, ignoring that in my unhappiness I am swinging them upside down.

The normally sepulchral discharge area is in chaos. Myra Andrews, who usually spent her days watching the soaps, is frantically processing orders. Her subjects are panicked men and women who, until that morning, had been cloistered, in many cases for most of their adult lives. Various flunkies drafted from other areas try to keep order. I recognize Jerome from the cafeteria. He waves but is too busy to stop.

Another flunky takes my name and gestures me into line, where I find that both Ali and Francis are in front of me.

Too numb to be surprised and welcoming them as something familiar on a day too full of change, I smile.

"So, you're getting out, too?" Francis says. He's clearly verging on his depressive phase.

"They can only set free men free," I reply.

"You're right, sister," Ali agrees, seeming to have held on to his belligerence. "We were long ready to get out of here. They aren't throwing us out. We're leaving!"

We huddle together: frightened, defiant, numb. Orderlies arrive and take charge of us. My flunky is a lady I faintly recall from the Library staff. She is chatty and kind.

"Come along, Sarah. First, we'll get you your medical clearance."

She takes the hand in which I do not hold my dragon, leading me like a child. We go to a temporary bank of medical scanners. They are easy to use, but a bored-looking tech drifts over to assist.

"If the patient checks out clean," she explains to my escort as they match my body to the human silhouette on the chair, "then press this tab. It'll give her a whole host of immunizations and a five-year sterilization."

"Five years?" my aide seems concerned. "That's quite a while, isn't it? What about the patient's civil liberties?"

"Flip 'em," the tech replies. "If I had my way, we'd sterilize them permanently. What good can a crazy contribute to the gene pool? Anyhow, check the chip when you finish the outprocessing. Technically, these folks remain the wards of the state for the next decade. Loco parentis."

She laughs at her own joke as she helps me to my feet.

Next, my aide takes me to a supply heap. Digging through various stacks—much of it clothing I recognize as having been made in the sewing workshop—she packs a nylon travel bag.

When she hands it to me, I realize that it is so light that it couldn't possibly contain more than a single change of clothes and possibly some extra socks and underwear. I sling it from my shoulder and let Betwixt and Between perch on top. They have been very quiet, but I feel that their ruby eyes have missed nothing.

The last thing my aide gives me is a plastic credit card, not unlike the ones we use in the Home for merits and demerits. She points to the glowing numbers.

"This is your money, Sarah. It's not much, but if you are careful, you should get by. Do you understand?"

I don't, but I nod.

"Good. Can you read?"

I shake my head. She frowns and puts aside a list she had been about to give me. For a moment, I think she will say something. Then she takes my arm and leads me to the exit door.

"Good luck, Sarah," she says and pushes me gently through the doors that open before me.

I step and find myself facing the busy street I had often watched from the windows. Newly processed patients huddle singly and in groups, uncertain what to do. I see Ali and Francis and hurry toward them, the enmity of the morning forgotten.

They only nod and we stand and watch the traffic hiss by.

Rain has fallen recently and the streets are still wet. Evening darkness is filling in the gaps left by the parting clouds. Here and there, automatic lights flicker on.

Ali holds Francis by the arm. The other man has retreated into a depression more paralyzing than any of the drugs he has taken in the past.

"See ya, Sarah," Ali says. "We're off."

He shepherds his friend off, muttering confidently. Neither spares a glance for me.

"Parting is such sweet sorrow," I whisper after.

Looking around, I find myself alone and for the first time in memory there is no one to tell me what to do or where to go. The doors of the Home are locked behind me.

Staring out into the darkness, I start to cry.

TWO

~

FOR MANY HOURS I WANDER THE DARK, WET STREETS, COM-
forted only by Betwixt and Between's witticisms. At last,
hungry and wet, even the little dragon falls silent, and I huddle disheartened in a doorway. The cold metal security bars
press against my back and the damp pavement seeps
through the soles of my shoes and the seat of my pants.
Still, I am tired enough that I drowse.

In my dreams, I hear chattering voices. Only when they
persist and grow shriller do I begin to suspect that I am not
dreaming. Reluctant to relinquish sleep's shelter, I open one
eye. Quickly, I open the other, for I cannot believe what is
before me.

A girl crouches on the sidewalk, her head level with mine.
Her hair is shaved short and dyed flaming orange; her lips
are iridescent blue. She wears tight pants of bright purple
leather and a short cape of the same material. When she
leans forward to prod me again, her long, silver earrings

jingle and I see that she is not wearing a shirt—instead a wolf's-head tattoo peers out from between her small, round breasts.

I stare at this harlequin, so amazed that I forget to be afraid. Her blue lips curl in a smile both innocent and merry.

"Hey," she says. "What's your name?"

"Sarah."

"I'm Abalone."

She looks as if she expects me to question this. When I don't she goes on, "I haven't seen you before. Are you new on the streets?"

Confused, I can only shrug.

She tries again. "Is this your home?"

I shrug again. "The foxes have their holes and the birds of the air have their nests, but the Son of Man hath not where to lay his head."

Abalone grimaces. "You're not a preacher, are you?"

I shake my head.

"Wolf's Heart!" she exclaims suddenly, touching her tattoo. "I've got it! You're from the nuthouse, aren't you?"

I tilt my head inquiringly.

"The Home, right?" Abalone's glee is apparent.

"Yes," I say, happy to please this merry miss.

"Great! Beer and pizza for me," she says, leaping to her feet. "And Head Wolf will be proud of me. Come on?"

I hesitate.

"C'mon, you don't want to sleep in the rain, do you?" she asks, putting out her hand to draw me up.

I am familiar with following other's commands. Taking her hand, I get to my feet. Abalone is shorter than I am. I wonder how old she is. From their place in my travel bag, Betwixt and Between study Abalone.

"What a piece of work is man!" Betwixt chortles.

Between hisses. "She said beer and pizza. It's better than being cold, wet, and starving."

I let my guide hustle me away. As she takes me down side streets and alleys, I quickly lose whatever bearings I had. Finally, she pauses before a dark, narrow concrete arch.

When she has unlatched a door, she looks up at me, her face somber. "Walk where I do; step as I do. Do you understand?"

I nod.

She slips through the arch and I follow. The building is empty, the interior dimly lit from a streetlight outside that shines through a broken window. I follow Abalone, matching her step for step as she walks directly down the center of the room. A few steps before the center, she makes an abrupt right turn and continues in a straight line.

Now that we are deeper in, I can see that the floor is cracked and worn. There are many holes from which the bitter mustiness of dampness wafts up. A misstep would land me in the pit, followed by a shower of concrete.

Abalone leads the way through several more turns in this markless maze until we come to an apparently blank wall. Now she finds her grin again and pushes aside a heavy canvas curtain. I gasp—it is so perfectly painted that I must touch it to reassure myself that she has not somehow transformed stone so that it will bend.

"Head Wolf made it," she says, again with the touch between her breasts. "He calls it tromp le eye."

She gestures me past her and I step onto a narrow platform that extends over Chaos. Abalone is beside me in a moment and she gestures down.

"That's the Jungle—Welcome home!"

I cannot move. I cannot speak. I can only look down and, as I do, the colors resolve themselves into shapes and people.

Abalone has brought me to a great cylindrical room made all of metal welded along lumpy seams. Electric lights ring the middle heights, illuminating all but the highest curve.

There are holes scattered randomly and some of these are patched. Others lead to wooden platforms like the one on which we perch. Ladders of rope and wood and metal cling more or less firmly to the sides. Heavy ropes and cables web the cylinder's heights. From some of these, hammocks are suspended, with people asleep in them or swinging gently back and forth.

On the ground level more people mill. Some are eating; others are singing around a small camp stove. Along one edge, a three-quarters-naked couple wrestle, oblivious to the action around them. I guess that there must be three or four dozen people within the cylinder and that most are adolescents.

To one side, with a cleared area around it, is a small domed tent, beautifully painted with lush jungle foliage and bright, impossible flowers.

Abalone tugs me and half leads, half drags me to the nearest ladder. Knees shaking, I follow her to the floor. She does not pause to praise me, but simply walks directly toward the painted tent.

Overwhelmed, I clutch my travel bag and, with my eyes downcast, walk behind Abalone. Even so, I see little things that tease my curiosity: an ebony recorder with the loving polish of hundreds of hands, a worn doll, a pair of new shoes with the tag still on them, again and again, the wolf emblem. I hear soft comments as we thread our way to the tent, but no one addresses us directly. Sometimes, only Abalone's strut tells me that we are the center of many eyes.

We halt before the tent and Abalone motions for me to keep silent.

Then she squares her shoulders, thrusts out her little breasts, and proclaims: "We be of one blood, ye and I!"

Her words have barely been completed when the tent's door-flaps open and a young man walks out. He is dark-haired and dark-eyed, with brown skin and fine features like those of a Hindu doctor at the Home. He wears nothing but a loosely wrapped bit of cloth around his slender hips. His skin is lightly beaded with sweat and I smell clean, male musk.

He is trailed out by a petulant-looking girl with pure white hair and slate grey eyes, wearing nothing at all but a wolf tattooed on one buttock. As she walks across to get water from a tap, I see that the wolf chases a doe tattooed on the other buttock.

But this is peripheral, for the man is speaking to Abalone and with his words, chatter and song melt into silence in waves around us.

"What have you brought to me, Abalone?"

"One of the people from the Home. A woman. Her name is Sarah."

"Sarah," he tastes my name, "from the Home. What do you have to say for yourself?"

His black eyes meet mine and something like lightning flashes through me. I have seen such eyes time and again in the Home. Always the clear, piercing gaze was dulled sooner or later by drugs. The Head Wolf is mad—utterly and completely mad, but it is a glorious madness.

Almost too late, I recall that he has demanded a response from me and I struggle to find one.

"I celebrate myself, and sing myself, and what I assume you shall assume, for every atom belonging to me as good as belongs to you."

As Abalone had, Head Wolf stares at me. Then he smiles and gracious lips curve in a gracious smile.

"A fine reply, Sarah. Do you mean what you say?"

"Head Wolf wants to fuck you," the white-haired girl snickers. "Do you know what that means, fruitcake?"

Without turning, Head Wolf backhands her. His eyes never leave me.

"Edelweiss is correct. I would like to fuck you. You are strangely beautiful, Sarah. But I think that you need food and sleep more. I will wait, for now."

His too-brilliant eyes leave me and turn to Abalone.

"You have done well, sister wolf. You may have beer and pizza enough for you and Sarah. Let her sleep in a hammock near yours or if she fears the Heights, you may claim lair rights for her on the ground. Guard her well and bring her to me next twilight and we will teach her the Law of the Jungle."

He reenters his tent. Minutes later, Edelweiss follows him, the handprint still bright against her pale cheek.

Abalone brings us pizza and beer. She doesn't laugh when I feed some to my dragon.

I find that I can sleep in a hammock and with daylight the electric lights are turned off and the Jungle lapses into a sleepy lull. Despite the novelty of sleeping twenty feet above the ground, I am exhausted enough that I sleep until the electric lights come on again.

When Abalone sees me moving, she climbs over and takes me below, where I can wash. She even helps me to comb my hair. Then we climb back into the Heights and study the Jungle while we await the time to meet with the Head Wolf.

"Careful, Sarah," she cautions me when I get overbold. "We're up a bit and there's no net to catch you."

"Life," I say with a shy smile, "is performed daily without a net."

She smiles her blue smile. "That's the spirit, Sarah. You'll like it here in the Jungle if you really think that way. You must be burning up with curiosity, but can you ask questions?"

"Curiosity killed the cat," I offer hesitantly.

"Right, but cats like it in the Jungle. Cats and dogs and children, all of us strays, but we're happy here."

She sits next to me and shows me how easily the hammock becomes a swing. I put Betwixt and Between on my lap so that they can see the panorama of the Jungle come to life.

"Hey, Sarah."

Abalone's voice is tentative and already I know enough about her to feel surprised. I turn to look at her face and realize that she is blushing. I raise one eyebrow and she blushes more.

"Sarah, about sex—fucking. Do you understand it?"

I search for a reply.

I am hardly a virgin. The first man to empty himself into me was a psychiatrist brought in by the Home to discover if I really was mute. When he decided that I was, he raped me. It was easily done—all I was wearing was a paper gown. He finished, cleaned himself up, and then me. When someone commented that I seemed distressed after the session, he dismissed it as trauma related to the testing. I was twelve.

Later, other men and a few women discovered what can be done to a mute. When I learned to speak—in my fashion—the assaults diminished some.

Abalone, I realize, is fearful for my presumed innocence. I wonder what this fire-haired girl has seen.

"Man, biologically considered," I reply at last, "is the most formidable of all the beasts of prey, and, indeed, the only one that preys systematically on its own species."

Abalone laughs. "Oh, it's not that bad."

"The evil that men do lives after them," I parry feistily.

"Yeah, I guess you've seen a bit," she says after a moment's reflection. "Head Wolf isn't too bad and he won't fuck you unless you ask him. Some of the others . . . They know the Law, but still, watch out."

Motion from Head Wolf's tent distracts her. She begins to climb to the nearest ladder.

"Follow me, Sarah. We can't keep Head Wolf waiting."

I follow, afraid to go again before those mad black eyes, yet tingling with anticipation. This time, when Abalone stops before the tent there is no shouted challenge. Head Wolf is waiting and with a toss of his head he gestures us to a cleared open space where many of the other Jungle residents are gathering.

"This is our Council Rock," Head Wolf says. "Here we give our Law. Some of the Pack must go out and hunt, but the rest have stayed this little while to help me teach you."

He puts out his hand and a tattered green book is put into it. The oversized cover is dark, forest green, painted with a beautiful young man seated beside a wolf, a black panther, and a bear. Head Wolf holds up the cover so that I can see it.

He smiles. "What do you see, Sarah?"

The Jungle becomes silent. I can sense that how I answer will shape all my interaction with these people. Frightened, I tighten my grip on Betwixt and Between until the spikes along their back dent my hand.

"Mirror, mirror on the wall, who's the fairest one of all?" I stammer.

Someone chuckles. Abalone kicks out. My eyes never leave Head Wolf. Will he understand me?

"What is the mirror, Sarah?" he asks softly.

I point to the book, my finger just touching the beautiful boy.

"And what does the mirror reflect, Sarah?"

I move my hand and gently brush his face.

"Very good," he purrs, "very good. This Book holds our Law. Listen. We will tell it to you."

He faces his people and I turn with him. For the first time, I notice that each one wears the sign of the wolf. Sometimes it is a piece of jewelry, others a patch on clothing, a few a tattoo proudly displayed.

Head Wolf raises his hand and like a conductor signaling a downbeat drops it. A chant rises.

"Now this is the Law of the Jungle—as old and as true as the sky. And the Wolf that shall keep it may prosper, but the Wolf that shall break it must die."

They go on, verse after verse. Abalone's eyes are wide and serious. The boy who kneels next to her screws his eyes shut with concentration. A tall black girl beats her hand between her breasts. I search futilely for one face that is less than impassioned. The words burn themselves into my mind. By the end, I know them all perfectly.

"That is our Law," Head Wolf says with a proud smile for his people. "Can you learn it, Sarah?"

I hesitate. Edelweiss already does not like me. Perhaps I should take care not to gain Head Wolf's favor.

"Go for it, girl!" Betwixt hisses.

"That memory of yours is the best thing you have going for you," Between adds.

I draw a deep breath and begin: "Now this is the Law of the Jungle . . ."

Silence greets my conclusion. Then there is a rustle and a chorus of yips and barks and howls shake the metal walls. Only when I see Abalone's proud smile do I realize that the powerful cacophony is meant as applause.

The Head Wolf's brown face is lit with a fierce smile.

"Very good, Sarah. Do you understand the words that you just recited?"

"We know in part, and we prophesy in part," I say, hastening to clarify. "When I was a child, I understood as a child."

"You understand some, then." Head Wolf awaits my nod before continuing. "Fine. The Law ends with 'Because of his age and his cunning, because of his gripe and his paw, in all that the Law leaveth open, the word of the Head Wolf is Law.' I am Head Wolf and so I have ruled these two additions to fit our Jungle Law. Chocolate, tell Sarah."

A pretty black boy with dreadlocks stands and bows. "No one shall have sex with anyone, anyway that one don't want it. Lest they die. No one pushes drugs here. Lest they die."

Head Wolf grimaces slightly. "Without poetry, but the sense is there. Pretty good, Chocolate."

"Sarah, since you don't understand all the Law, you'll need a Baloo, a teacher. Is there anyone who you would like?"

Betwixt whispers, "You were worried about Edelweiss, Sarah. Here's your chance to make friends with her."

I nod, but I am hearing the memory of Abalone's triumphant cry "Beer and pizza!" She is looking hopefully at me and I point to her.

"Those having torches will pass them onto others," I state.

Her bright smile is my reward.

After asking for Abalone and me to wait, Head Wolf walks among his people.

Some of the Pack members are clearly dressing—or undressing—for a night turning tricks. Head Wolf pats this one on the exposed cheek of her ass, straightens that one's hair, sends another to change her blouse. Nor does he shirk the boys. Most of these are groomed to maximize their youth. Head Wolf carefully rouges one fair-haired boy's cheeks. He sends another to redepilate his beard.

Across the Jungle floor, small teams are donning leather and spikes. I see the flash of blades and hear the dull clank of metal on metal. Many of these are as flamboyantly dressed as Abalone. While the prostitutes wear their wolf signs discreetly, this group has them blazoned on jackets, armbands, and jewelry.

My observations are halted by the return of Head Wolf. He gestures us into the tent.

"Come inside, Sarah. I need to explain to you how life in the Jungle works."

We duck under the painted flap. The tent floor is thickly carpeted with rugs piled on each other. Pillows are heaped around the edges. Despite fresh air through net windows, the small space smells of sex.

My heart begins to beat faster and I am honestly not certain if what I feel is fear or anticipation. But Head Wolf merely lounges back on some of the pillows. Abalone sits cross-legged on the soft floor and I follow suit, placing Betwixt and Between in front of me.

When we are comfortable, Head Wolf begins his lessons. "In the Jungle, we follow the Law, as you have seen. And like any wolf pack, we must hunt to provide for ourselves and our people. The Law has several provisions for distribution of the kill. I have simplified these somewhat for our different circumstances."

Abalone touches my arm. "Is he going too fast, Sarah?"

I shake my head.

"Even if I am," Head Wolf replies, "Abalone will teach you."

Abalone nods solemnly, her silver-and-shell earrings rattling softly as she does. Head Wolf continues.

"Simply, each of us must support our own needs. Moreover, I take a payment from each member to maintain the Jungle. With this I buy necessities, bribe police and social workers, and give rewards. New members are carried by the Pack for a week—although most begin to contribute sooner. After that, they must hunt for the Pack."

My head is swirling with questions that I cannot ask. I want to be part of this Jungle, but how? I still fear the madness in Head Wolf's eyes. Now he is the gentle teacher, but I sense brutality enforces his Jungle Law.

Abalone pipes up. "I checked her travel bag, Head Wolf. She has one other set of those awful clothes, a bit of soap and stuff like that, a slip that says she's had all her shots, and this."

She holds out my credit slip. Head Wolf takes it, inspects the numbers, and hands it back.

"Print coded," he says. "A fair amount, but not generous. The Pack will carry her for the remainder of the week. After, if you pool your resources with hers, the next week's fees can be handled. By then, you should find her something to do."

Abalone nods. "Fair enough."

Something flashes in the dark eyes at her words and she shrinks back.

Fawning, she rolls onto her back, exposing her throat and her bare breasts. Head Wolf straddles her and bites her throat, worrying the fragile skin. As he does so, he closes off her nose and mouth so that she cannot breathe.

I see Abalone's hands curl, but she doesn't whimper.

After a terrifying minute, he releases her. As she rolls upright, gasping for air, I see blunt teeth marks on her skin.

Head Wolf growls at her. "I am always fair."

"You are always fair," she agrees.

Trembling, I realize that she believes this.

THREE

~

MY EARLY DAYS IN THE JUNGLE FLIT BY. ABALONE IS A GOOD
Baloo, teaching me the customs of the Jungle. One of my
favorite lessons is how to travel the Heights without fear. I
am fiercely proud of myself the day that I graduate from the
cubwalks to the lines and pulleys that the Wolves use.

Yet, many evenings she must leave me to hunt. All the
Jungle awakens in the evening, its coming alive heralded by
the chirping of the 'Tail Wolves,' as the prostitutes are
called. Their preparations take the longest, but soon after
they awaken, their protectors—the Four they are called, although there are more than four—also rise, donning leather
and weapons.

The Tail Wolves and the Four share each others' profits,
but each pays individual fees to Head Wolf. I see he is careful that they do not become a Pack within his Pack.

Others of the Pack make their way by selling drugs.

Some of these fall prey to their own wares. Head Wolf deals with such harshly. When he repeatedly cannot pay his fee, one young man gone into designer dream is declared a hanger-on by Head Wolf from the same Council Rock where he taught me the Law. From my place in the Heights, I watch in horror as Head Wolf strangles the boy in his sleep.

Abalone is neither a Tail Wolf nor a member of the Four. She tells me she has turned tricks only when she has had no other way to earn her keep; something in her voice tells me that this is not often.

What she prefers is stealing. Her flamboyant exterior hides the soul of stealth and her special prey is vehicles. One good strike in a month and she is comfortable. Still, she takes a long time preparing each strike. All I understand of her craft is her oft-repeated phrase: "The days of hot wire and go are gone. Today, more than half the theft takes place in a computer."

Tonight she has left almost before dark falls to take care of some business. I swing alone above the near silent Jungle, Betwixt and Between in my lap.

"From each according to his abilities, to each according to his needs," I say softly aloud.

"Wondering what you can do?" Betwixt asks. "I thought so."

"Me, too," Between adds, then recites, "Don't want to be a Tail Wolf/ Don't want to be a Four/ But no matter what you name yourself/ You're nothing but a whore."

"What's that supposed to mean?" Betwixt retorts. "The Tail Wolves are whores, not our Sarah."

"They're selling sex honestly," Between snaps. "Sarah just sits here leaving half the Pack panting for a chance at her. You both know that Head Wolf took her so fast because he wants her."

They bicker, but I do not interrupt. They have framed my dilemma perfectly. I have seen that not all who come to the Pack are so quickly welcomed. Most must prove themselves first—living as hangers-on, doing the filthiest chores.

Soon I must decide what I will do. My choices seem limited. Either I must become a Tail Wolf (The Four will only take proven brawlers) or be a beggar—a Tabaqui, in the lingo of the Pack.

The Tabaqui are barely tolerated and I have heard debates as to whether begging is really legitimate "hunting." My choice seems clear—either I must choose a path that will disgust me or one that will disgust others.

I have not yet reached a decision when the welcome buzz of a pulley on wire signals Abalone's return to our roost. She skids down to my hammock and drops lightly next to me.

"Good Hunting, Sarah!" Her eyes are bright and her blue lips curl with mischief.

"Good Hunting," I reply.

She leans close, so that she is whispering in my ear. "I have a heist ready. Want to come?"

I nod vigorously. "If it were done when 'tis done, then 'twere well it were done quickly."

"That's the spirit, I think." She hugs me. "I don't understand you half the time, Sarah, but that's okay, too."

. . . .

Reaching for a guide rope, I stand, scooping Betwixt and Between up with my free hand.

"Can't you leave the dragon?" Abalone asks, a resigned expression anticipating my reply.

"I am a brother to dragons, a companion to owls," I say stubbornly.

She shakes her head. "Put your brother in your shoulder bag, then at least it'll be out of sight."

We make our way outside by the same route that Abalone first used to bring me into the Jungle. There are other ways, but this one, which requires memory, lightness, and grace, is her favorite. The few times she has taken me out, however, she has been careful to show me other ways.

Outside, I gulp the night air gratefully. The Jungle is one cylinder among a score which once held chemicals for a factory. It is vast, but by necessity it is enclosed and the air, seasoned by many bodies, is pungent and hot.

Abalone touches my hand and at her bidding I trot down the aisles. We walk into another deserted portion of the factory, cross through an underground tunnel, and emerge in a subway station that is deserted now, but once, Abalone assures me, was a busy place built to deal with the factory's traffic.

From there we walk down the service walkways to an active station and catch a train uptown.

In the near-empty station where we disembark, Abalone unlocks a closed rest room with a key card. Inside, she opens a backpack, fills a sink with warm water, and proceeds to transform herself.

Skintight trousers and T-shirt go into a heap on the floor.

She replaces them with a neat business suit—skirt, vest, and frill-trimmed blouse. Blue lips are scrubbed clean and tinted pale peach. Cheeks are discreetly rouged to highlight fantasy cheekbones. Eyes are resculpted with liner and shadow. A final touch dusts a couple of incongruous freckles across the bridge of her nose.

She winks at me and skins a wig over her fiery buzz and the fire is banked under a crop of close, dark curls.

"What do you think?" she asks with a proud smile.

I shake my head with amazement. "I have heard of your paintings, well enough. God hath given you one face, and you make yourselves another."

"*Hamlet*," she replies to my surprise. "I did some drama before I left high school."

She scoops up the clothing from the floor and into her pack, fighting down some emotion. When she looks at me, whatever it was is gone.

"Never make known what you have seen tonight," she says, and I sense the nervousness behind her smile.

"The rest is silence," I promise.

"Good. Now, in those jeans and that sweatshirt, you'll be practically invisible if we cover your hair and you keep the dragon tucked down in your bag. I've brought you a baseball cap."

Motioning for me to bend down, she tucks my hair up under the cap. The brim even shadows my pale eyes. Stepping in front of a mirror, I preen—this is one of the few times I've seen myself in the street clothes Abalone gave me and I like the look.

Normal. Mainstream.

"When we go up to the street, walk a little behind me," she says, extracting a notebook computer in a slimline clutch from her pack. "If I get in a car, keep walking straight. I'll pick you up. Otherwise, just follow me."

"Thou shalt not steal," I say, striving to make the words express my concern for her rather than condemnation of her craft.

The wicked smile blossoms, incongruous on peachy lips. "I'm not. If the work I've been doing with my tappety-tap here has done the trick, I own the car. I just need to find where the former owner has parked. C'mon."

I follow and the world outside is one I have never known. Here the streets are straight and smooth. Well-kept shrubs and slim-trunked trees grow with metal grids at their bases. Tall buildings, threaded to each other with glass tubes as the Jungle is with rope and wire, make cliffs that threaten the sovereignty of the sky.

Abalone walks confidently onto the sidewalk and I wait a moment before daring to trail her. Although the hour is late, there are still some pedestrians on the night streets. We become fish in that stream and no one gives either of us so much as a casual glance.

When Abalone turns to claim a car parked in a metered space, only a warning hiss from Betwixt and Between reminds me to keep walking. I do, but now all the things that had seemed benign, even mildly amusing when I knew that Abalone was there to deal with them, become frightening and threatening.

A man looks my way. I tense and prepare to run. He goes

by and I realize that his glance was for the clock in a shop window.

Thumping music announces a juvee gang. As I remember how the Four treat trespassers, a damp sweat prickles across my skin. I don't even dare to scratch lest they look my way. But they pass me without even a rude comment.

By the time Abalone hails me from where her new vehicle idles in a cross street, I am almost too weak with fear to climb in the passenger side.

She gives me a grin and we swoosh off above the dark streets. When she leaves me in an all-night diner with food and tokens for the video game built into the table, I am almost over my fear. Leaving Betwixt and Between in my bag, I slip them French fries and drops of oversweet orange soda.

Abalone taps on the window an hour later. Her hair is again the color of fire and her lips shimmering blue. We take the subway back to our turf, but, though dawn is a mere hour away, she does not take me to the Jungle.

Instead, we go to a strip of concrete and crabgrass that has been dubbed a Park by a municipal blueprints maker. We sit on a wall and Abalone lights a lovely little pipe made from copper tubing.

"It went really well tonight, Sarah," she says after she has it drawing. "I made good money on that piece. Of course, time'll show it was floated, but flip 'em. If a kid like me can bust the codes, anyone can. They should write better codes."

I gesture confusion. She puffs smoke rings, considers, then gives me one of her sparrowlike tilts of her head.

"Sarah, I told you that car belonged to me when I drove it away. That's true—I made it mine. A cop could have pulled me over and everything in the computer would have said that flitter belonged to 'Abby Shane,' the name on the ID I was carrying."

She breaks one of her smoke rings with her index finger. "Setting that up took me a month, but I'm rich now. I can pay my fees to Head Wolf until the next 'repossession' is ready. And I can pay yours, too. That is, if you want a job."

I nod vigorously. Not to be a Tail Wolf or a Tabaqui!

Seeing my excitement, Abalone holds up a hand. "The job doesn't ask much—on the surface. But you're going to need to learn a whole lot to swing it."

"When the strong command, obedience is best," I reply.

"Fine, briefly then. I want you to help me steal vehicles. I've been at the job long enough that before long someone is going to get wise to me. I change my appearance, use false names and prints, and forge IDs. Still, I'm the same general height and build and if anyone started really checking . . ."

She shrugs. "I want to start using you to pick up the cars and sell them for me. We'll split the profits, say seventy/ thirty."

A host of protests race through my mind. I can't drive. I can't bargain. I can't even talk! My worries choke me and my hands flutter to my throat.

Abalone pulls them down and holds them.

"Easy, Sarah. I think you can do it. If you don't want to, there are other ways to stay in the Jungle"—she looks away—"maybe even better ways."

I tilt my head inquiringly. Abalone lets go of my hands and starts thumping her heels on the wall. I wait.

"Head Wolf may not like that I'm giving you work— especially since he doesn't quite know what I do. The Law states that adults should be able to hunt for themselves. You know the part."

I nod. "The Jackal may follow the Tiger, but, Cub, when thy whiskers are grown. Remember the Wolf is a hunter— go forth and get food on thy own."

"Exactly, your Baloo is proud of you. I may be able to make Head Wolf see this as part of your training. Sweet Mike, you're innocent enough. I think he'd go for it." Her voice drops to a whisper. "Especially, if you're willing to make him feel good about it."

Even in the dawn's early light I cannot interpret the expression on her face. Shame, pity, even jealousy seem to vie for dominance before she is again my weird, wild teacher. I touch her shoulder and point to the sky.

"Remember the night is for hunting, and forget not the day is for sleep."

She stretches and hops off the wall. I stand and we walk back toward the nest of chemical tanks. We are almost there before she turns to me again.

"I'll speak to Head Wolf as soon as the Hunters have left tomorrow evening. Do you want me to?"

My heart is in my throat, but I manage, "Yes."

ABALONE HAS BEEN IN HEAD WOLF'S TENT FOR A LONG while. I try hard not to wonder why.

Betwixt and Between can tell that I am worried, so to distract me they tell me what has happened while I was sleeping.

Betwixt starts. "Chocolate came running in here wearing this lovely leather biker's jacket. He was just starting to strut it around when what do you think happened?"

Between answers him. "What?"

"Shut up, stupid. I'm asking Sarah."

Lest the dragons start sulking, I politely meet the ruby eyes and look interested.

Satisfied, Betwixt continues, "We hear police whistles and sirens from the way Chocolate had come."

"The idiot not only propositioned a cop," Between snickers, "but stole his jacket."

"You can bet that Head Wolf wasn't pleased," Betwixt says. "He had the Jungle sealed and members of the Four on each doorway. Everyone who was awake had to keep silent."

"The cops never found any of the entrances," Between adds with a wondering shake of his head. "And when they were gone, Head Wolf beat Chocolate until the kid looked like the worst side of a sadist's fantasy."

I barely hear the end of the story. Below, the flap of the tent is moving and Abalone emerges. She waves for me to come down and I scramble with lines and pulleys.

In my month and more in the Jungle, I have gotten beyond sore muscles and fear of falling to where I move through the Web as easily as the long-term residents. I am at her feet practically before she has lowered her hand.

"Head Wolf was—receptive—to my suggestion."

She nervously licks her lips. I realize that she must have done this frequently in the last hour, for the blue eyeliner with which she paints them is nearly worn away in some places. I scan her for bruises or teeth marks and find none.

She continues. "He wants to speak with you alone and make certain that you really want to do this. It's up to you to prove to him how much you want it."

I nod, my options thinning into one line. My heart beats wildly, as I know what I must do.

"Go on." Again Abalone gives me the strange look she had in the Park. "Head Wolf wants you."

I hardly hear the snickers from the few Pack members still lounging around the camp stoves. With a hand I hope is steady I scratch the tent door as I have seen others do. The painted surface looks smooth, but is ridged and uneven to the touch.

"Who is there?"

"Sarah."

"Enter, Sarah."

Lifting the flap, I duck and enter. Once in, I kneel on the cushioned softness and wait.

"Make yourself comfortable, Sarah. I only have a few questions for you."

I look up and move to sit on the cushion he has indicated. The dark eyes seek for and hold mine. I can only bear to hold their gaze for a moment and am grateful that Abalone has taught me that a Cub must never hold the gaze of a senior Wolf, nor any Wolf the gaze of Head Wolf. But when I look away, it is not from courtesy, but from a sense that if I look too long, I will be swallowed.

"Abalone tells me that you are learning well, but that you have much to learn. Did you always live in places like the Home before you came here?"

I nod.

"So you cannot read or drive or even work a simple terminal?"

I blush and shake my head, ashamed.

He quizzes me further about what I can and cannot do, always thoughtfully phrasing his questions so that a "yes" or "no" will do and so that I will not need to struggle for an answer. His kindness relaxes me and I find that I can look at him as we talk.

Finally, he says, "I can see the reason for what Abalone has suggested. With your current assets, however, you could still do very well as one of the Tail Wolves. Surely, you do not scorn that way of hunting."

I do, but I shake my head, knowing that the Tail Wolves are the most reliable providers in the Jungle.

"Sometimes I think that Abalone does," he continues. "I hope she has not passed that attitude on to you."

His eyes say more than his words and my heart knows it is time. Words swim in my head in a chaotic pattern. My hand reaches out and touches him lightly on the cheek.

He waits with dark eyes hooded. I stretch out my other hand, hold his face between them.

Words I know are not needed for this form of communication. I make him as mute as I am, cover his mouth with mine. When next he speaks, there are no words at all, but I know perfectly what he desires. With only a small sorrow, I give in to him.

Indeed, he is glorious in his madness.

FOUR

❧

THE NEXT DAY, AS ABALONE BEGINS MY LESSONS, I CAN hardly keep from touching the ivory wolf's head that dangles from a silver loop in my left ear.

The ceremony promoting me from Cub to Wolf had been simple yet moving. Head Wolf and Abalone shared the cry "Look well, O Wolves." The Pack members questioned Head Wolf and were satisfied as to my fitness. Even Edelweiss was more friendly after the inspection was passed and the token presented.

Yet, I realize that I still must prove myself more than a hanger-on. Thus, I bend my head over the model control panel that Abalone has cobbled together for me. The letters and numbers mean nothing to me and have a disconcerting tendency to squirm and move upon the surface.

Abalone deals with her frustration with my inability by focusing the lesson on developing manual skills. What I will do with them comes after.

My determined concentration is shattered as if it is a smoke ring when a thin voice pierces the Jungle with the Stranger's Hunting Call: "Give me leave to hunt here because I am hungry."

I have dropped my practice panel into a holding bag and am sliding to the floor even as Head Wolf's deep voice answers, "Hunt then for food, but not for pleasure."

Thumping to the floor, I race across and embrace the little, bent woman who has entered the Jungle and stands before Head Wolf unintimidated by the Four who hover over her.

She embraces me in turn, "Easy, Sarah, love, in all things moderation. You will strangle me."

"Professor Isabella! Professor Isabella!" I repeat over and over.

"Dear child," she says. "Certainly I have taught you to speak better than that. But I won't leap you through *Othello* and Chaucer quite yet; this charming gentleman with lupine pretensions wants to speak with me."

Head Wolf has watched me greeting Professor Isabella, amusement replacing his initial anger at her invasion. Abalone has joined us, those few members of the Pack who are not out hunting circling round.

Professor Isabella pats me and I sink down to sit at her feet. From this familiar post I study my old teacher. I had believed her unchanged from when I had known her in the Home, but now I see differences.

She still has snow-white hair and delicate, tissue paper skin faintly threaded with blue veins. But her frame is more bent and her hands are swollen, the knuckles shiny with arthritis. My initial joy had numbed me to the fact that she smells strongly, as if she has not bathed in weeks.

The Law of the Jungle insists, "Wash daily from nose tip to tail tip." I wonder why Professor Isabella is not taking better care of herself.

"Professor Isabella." Head Wolf cocks an eyebrow. "May I call you that?"

She twinkles. "Professor Isabella Lacey, once of Columbia. I quit during the budget crisis of the nineties. Met Sarah in the Home where I was 'resting.'"

Head Wolf nods. "You don't look like a professor."

"She's a Tabaqui," chirps one of the new cubs, a little boy called Peep. "I seen her by the train station."

Professor Isabella smiles, but I see a flush underneath her weather-worn skin. The truth hits me suddenly.

Head Wolf is speaking. "I recognize the lady, Peep. I simply did not know her distinguished credentials. I recognize you, Professor Lacey. But why have you found hunting in our Jungle necessary?"

"Eloquent." Professor Isabella shakes her head wonderingly. "I would have enjoyed you as a speaker in some of the meetings I have been bored through. I am here because you have one of my students, my last student."

"Sarah." Head Wolf nods. "Lovely Sarah. If you wish to speak with her, you are welcome, but after this, meet her elsewhere."

Head Wolf steps back, the interview over. The Pack disperses and when Abalone would drift away, I reach out and snag her cape.

"Stay a while, that we may make an end sooner."

Abalone stops at my lightest touch. Professor Isabella studies her quizzically. Abalone's return gaze is cool.

"So, you are Sarah's friend," my teacher asks.

"I'm Abalone. Yeah, I'm her friend."

Their words are calm; their tones are even, friendly. But their budding animosity comes to me as a strong scent, like urine in a subway tunnel. My heart tears. I cannot bear that these two, at least, will not love each other, will torment each other over their possession of me.

I step between them, touch Professor Isabella's arm, then Abalone's. They let me turn them like dolls. I take Professor Isabella's hand.

"Thou wert my guide, philosopher, and friend."

"Pope," she says. "Yes, I was and am, Sarah."

Now I take Abalone's hand in my left. "Those friends thou hast, and their adoption tried, grapple them to thy soul with hoops of steel."

"*Hamlet,*" she says, but the look that she flashes Professor Isabella is playful. "Act One, scene three."

"Spoken by Polonius," Professor Isabella concludes. "Sarah has surrounded herself with people of sophistication and culture, it appears. I would be a fool not to listen to her judgment."

"It's still just a bit after dark," Abalone says. "Let me take you both to a diner."

I smile, feeling genuine curiosity flavor their new accord and dissolve the jealousy. When we are out in the cool night air, I walk between my friends and listen to them talk, taking pleasure that one can tell the other what I lack words to explain.

". . . so when the word came that the Free People had adopted a peculiar, lovely woman who spoke only in strange fragments and carried a rubber dragon around, I knew she had to be Sarah. I tried to stay away, but I finally gave in."

We arrive at the diner and Abalone takes a corner booth, where our conversation will go unremarked. She slides me a jelly packet for Betwixt and Between.

"Ah, I see you know Betwixt and Between," Professor Isabella chuckles.

"Is that its name?" Abalone giggles. "Neat. She always feeds it, so I've given in."

"You and me and everyone else," Professor Isabella sighs. "Sarah is amiable but she turns mean if anyone tries to take Betwixt and Between away. She will leave them for short periods of time—if she must—but heaven forbid if they are not where she left them when she returns."

Between comments, in a dreamy voice, "Remember the goons who hid us in the linen cupboard?"

"How can I forget?" Betwixt retorts. "You wouldn't stop whimpering and I knew we would need both of our heads to yell loud enough for Sarah to hear us."

"Me whimpering?" Between is indignant. "You whimpered! I planned how to get Sarah to us!"

"Did not!"

"Did so!"

"Not!"

"So!"

Abalone and Professor Isabella keep talking as if they cannot hear the dragons.

"You seem to be Sarah's protector," Professor Isabella

continues and Abalone swells a little. "Have you kept your Head Wolf from prostituting her yet? I know that you personally don't streetwalk."

Abalone seems at a loss before her bluntness. "Head Wolf isn't any common pimp."

"Certainly not." Professor smiles wickedly.

Aware that the words have somehow offended Abalone, I interrupt.

"If it be possible, as much as lieth in you, live peaceably with all men," I say in agitation.

"Blessed are the peace makers," Professor Isabella replies, patting my hand. "Abalone, Sarah seems to want us to be friends. Forgive me for my assumption, but Sarah's beauty is extraordinary. I could not help but believe that she would be encouraged to sell that beauty or at least trade on it to gain Head Wolf's protection by becoming his mistress."

"Half-right," Betwixt chortles.

Blushing, I swat him.

Abalone keeps some poise. "I'd be lying if I didn't agree that Head Wolf is hot for Sarah—but so are half the guys and girls in the Pack."

Professor quirks an eyebrow at her and Abalone colors.

"Not me, I don't go for girls and, anyhow, Sarah is like my kid. I'm her Baloo. I don't have any place messing with her that way."

"I *do* like you, girl," Professor Isabella says. "You are almost as weird as Sarah. Can you tell me what you do have in mind for Sarah?"

Abalone bites her lip. "Better if I didn't, but I'm not going to pimp her unless she really wants to be a Tail Wolf. And the same goes for begging."

"I'll rest with that for now." Professor Isabella suddenly looks tiny, frail. "But I hope you'll let me see her."

"We are the Free People and she is a Wolf of our Pack. No one will stop her." Abalone laughs at her tone. "Sure she can see you—every night if she wants. I'll bring her to you even."

"Blessed are you among women!" I glow, squeezing her hand.

Professor Isabella finishes her coffee and scoops all the sugar packets on the table into her pockets. Almost as an afterthought, she takes the remaining jelly packets and the crackers left from Abalone's soup.

She stands. "And thank you both for the best meal I have had in a long while. I had best get some sleep if I'm to be up for the commuter rush in the morning."

My earlier suspicions return and I struggle to find a way to ask. We are just outside the diner when I find something I hope will do.

"Oh woe is me, to have seen what I have seen, see what I see!"

Both she and Abalone stop and study me. Fearing I will fail, I pluck Professor Isabella's sleeve, tug at her layers of tattered and mismatched clothes, pat her pockets with their hoarded treats.

Professor Isabella presses her lips into a thin line. When she opens her mouth, the blood rises into them, making them seem painted.

"They threw me out, too, Sarah. Earlier than you, but just the same. Did they tell you that I had returned to Columbia?"

I nod, tears running down my face unchecked.

"No, dear, they lied. I have been living on the streets."

"Oh, it was pitiful!" I manage between my sobs. "Near a whole city and she had none."

Abalone is clearly troubled. "I would ask you into the Jungle, but . . ."

"I know, Abalone, 'Feet that make no noise; eyes that see in the dark; ears that can hear the winds in their lairs, and sharp white teeth, all these are the marks of our brothers, except Tabaqui and the Hyaena whom we hate.' I know the scorn Head Wolf has for beggars. He would rather see an eight-year-old boy reamed by perverse business executives than have the lad stay a beggar. I'll go my way, but please bring Sarah to me."

Abalone grows solemn. "By the opened Lock that freed me, Professor Isabella, I promise."

I hug Professor Isabella once more and trot beside Abalone to the Jungle. Once I look over my shoulder and see my teacher trudging away, her shoulders bent against a wind that I don't feel.

FIVE

⌒

I CONTINUE LEARNING TO DRIVE AND ABALONE TAKES ME
regularly to visit with Professor Isabella. In various diners
and occasional by-the-hour hotels, once again the professor
reads to me, her passion for various lines and phrases brand-
ing them into my memory.

Abalone often sits in a corner with her "tappety-tap,"
working out some complex forgery problem. When we
grow weary, we rest and my two friends talk.

"You say that Head Wolf told the Pack to look for people
from the Home?" Professor Isabella asks one near-dawn.

"Yeah, he did."

Abalone tenses some. Head Wolf is still a sensitive topic
between them, especially since Professor Isabella has somehow learned of my occasional visits to Head Wolf's lair. She
blames Abalone, which is unfair. She may be immune to the
hypnotic power in those dark eyes, but he draws me like a
hummingbird to a new-blossomed hibiscus.

"I wonder why he wanted them?" Professor Isabella muses, "Were any others found?"

"A couple, I think." Abalone's restless fingers trace the outlines of her notebook computer. "I think he spoke with them and sent them on. Did Head Wolf ask you anything, Sarah? What do you talk about when you've been alone?"

She blushes suddenly and bites her lip so hard that she leaves a thin blue line on her top teeth. Professor Isabella chuckles and Abalone sputters helplessly. My dragons giggle in duet. Over the prevailing flood of mirth and embarrassment, I find an adequate reply.

"Of shoes—and ships—and sealing wax—of cabbages—and kings—and why the sea is boiling hot—and whether pigs have wings."

"Lots of nonsense," Professor Isabella translates.

Yet, even as I accept her interpretation, I wonder. There have been many questions that I have struggled to answer, yet these are diminished beneath a vivid flood of nonverbal memories.

Head Wolf has his favorites. I am one. Edelweiss is another. A black/Asian mix Tail Wolf called Bumblebee is another. He is so generous with his attentions that he often mock-complains that he is worn out.

Yet, I have learned that many who share his tent do so for more than sex. For Head Wolf has a gift he gives beyond sexual pleasure—he cuddles, strokes, and comforts. His greatest talent is tenderness. He is never too busy to pet or soothe any of his Pack and for this a Tail Wolf may come to him although a night of turning tricks has left her numb.

I enjoy his tenderness, but I have often known kindness.

For some of the others in the Jungle, Head Wolf is the only one who has ever listened to them, cared for them. He admires their finery, settles their quarrels, and suggests what they should do when in trouble. Sometimes, he scolds; often he punishes. Always he cares.

Once, I believed fear and the Law bound the Jungle. Now I believe that what binds it is safety and compassion.

Although we enjoy our nights in diners and hotels, we cannot always loiter in these havens. Abalone explains that this would cause resentment among those of the Free People who lack her extraordinary skills. And Abalone's supply of money is not endless, especially now that she is stretching to supply three.

So, often we go to charity soup kitchens and stand on line with the other homeless awaiting something hot, cheap, and nourishing. Abalone looks at the miserable addicts and drunks who swarm around us, cursing under her breath.

Occasionally, I recognize other outcasts from the Home, but they do not seem to know me. Most are buried in the morass of their own minds.

Our favorite of these kitchens is called "When I Was Hungry." It is run by Witnesses.

"They're good people, on the whole," Abalone says as we wait at the end of a line. "They'll preach and pray, but their hearts are without that . . ."

She struggles to describe the emotion we so often encounter in the public dole lines.

"Scorn?" Professor Isabella suggests. "I agree with you. The Witnesses pity me for my religious ignorance and unredeemed status but they are without scorn. And even if Sarah here has a better comprehension of the Bible in its glorious contradictions, I can take their preaching."

"You sound as if you think Sarah's flipped short on the brains side," Abalone says, and there is a growl in her voice. "You ever notice how much sense she makes? And I couldn't remember like she does."

"Nor I," Professor Isabella agrees, "but there is something 'short' in her brains, something is missing that would let her reach in and make her own sentences."

I am uncomfortable, as always, when they discuss me this way. Even my best friends seem to forget that I am able to hear them. Recently, I have noticed that Professor Isabella addresses Abalone as another adult, but speaks to me as a child.

Frustration bubbles in my throat as it has so often before. I want to claw away the bars of this cage built by my mind. My hands, as always, reach and find nothing to grab onto.

I move along the line, sliding my battered tray and accepting a plastic spoon, a napkin, a cup of weak coffee. As I look up to accept the wide plastic bowl heaped with some noodle-filled casserole, delight thrills through me and I stare. Words come quickly.

"A day without orange juice is a day without sunshine?" I ask, afraid that I am wrong or that he has forgotten me.

Jerome's head jerks up from his mechanical task. "Sarah? Sarah! What are you doing here, girl?"

The line has backed up behind us; only a few of the people that I am obstructing are alert enough to care about anything more than the simple fact that their one meal of the day is being delayed.

Jerome shoves my bowl to me. "Go along now. We're almost done. You wait and I'll come and speak with you. Hear?"

I nod, beam, and hurry on.

Abalone and Professor Isabella are curious, but I cannot find words to explain. I eat, feeding Betwixt and Between who, like me, are nearly too excited to eat the starchy stuff. Yet, I do, for I have learned that wasting food is a crime on the streets.

Jerome comes soon after the food line has closed down. He carries a pot of weak coffee in one hand and a few nearly fresh sweet rolls on a plate in the other.

"Sarah," he pecks me on the cheek, the odors of tuna fish and mushroom soup not completely covering his own scent of scrubbed skin and after-shave.

I motion for him to sit and squeeze his hand. I rock a little on the bench, hunting for words to introduce him to the others.

"Jerome—A friend of publicans and sinners," I manage at last.

Jerome jumps, surprised. "Sarah, you praise me."

He turns to the ladies. "My name is Jerome—I guess you are friends of Sarah's."

He speaks softly and slowly, as if he is uncertain that they will understand him. Yet, courtesy is there, too, as true as if he were addressing his peers.

Abalone smiles. "Yeah—I'm Abalone and this is Professor Isabella. We kinda watch out for Sarah. You know her from the Home?"

"Yes," he nods, then chuckles. "I work there—in the cafeteria. Always tell my Balika, my wife, that surely I can do the Lord's Work elsewhere. After shoveling food all day there, I'd rather not come here, but today she was ill and I came to take her place. The Lord does work in mysterious ways. I've been worrying about Sarah since the big Exodus and now I have an answer to my prayers."

He bows his head for a moment. "I'm forgetting my manners. Coffee? Sweets?"

We all accept and with an almost sheepish smile Jerome drips the last of the pot into a little plastic scrap about the size of a thimble and puts a shred of pastry next to it.

"For the dragons," he explains. "I think that's what caught me about Sarah, back at the Home. Her always carrying around that toy and always so careful to feed it."

"Don't leave home without it," I add, blowing on my coffee. "I am a brother to dragons, a companion to owls."

"And to these folks here," Jerome says. "May I request that you two ladies fill me in on what Sarah's been doing? Poor child would be here 'til Armageddon looking for the words and I need to hustle on home to Balika."

Abalone and Professor Isabella supply him with a very-edited version of the past month and a half. Jerome seems relieved when he learns that I am neither turning tricks nor doing drugs. He is wise enough not to question where we live and seems to assume that our food and clothing come from charity.

When we are leaving, he stands for a moment with the empty coffeepot dangling from one hand, his dark face suddenly creased with puzzlement.

"Funny," he says. "I've only seen that golden-haired doctor who made such noise during the Exodus but once since. I made so bold as to ask her if she knew what had become of Sarah. She knew who I meant right off, said that she'd arranged to have her become a model, even promised me some pictures. Wonder why she'd go to the trouble to comfort me like that?"

"Guilt?" Professor Isabella answers.

"Who knows." Jerome smiles. "Come back soon, now. Let me know how you are."

He speaks in a general way, but I am warmed. The night seems more pleasant, the stars brighter, as we walk through the dark streets.

After leaving the soup kitchen, we head for one of Abalone's many safe holes. Tonight's is an abandoned building; it still has power, water, and, most importantly, phone service.

Abalone is intent over her tappety-tap. Professor Isabella drowses openmouthed on a pallet made from a few blankets Abalone has stashed there. I patiently play with my practice panel.

"Got it!" Abalone cries, waking Professor Isabella and startling me.

"What?" Professor Isabella yawns.

"I'm ready to let Sarah earn her keep," Abalone says. "We can move as soon as tomorrow evening."

Excitement and trepidation war within me. I am certain I can mechanically manage what Abalone wants, but doubt my nerve. Nor has Abalone yet confided the details of her plan to me; now seems a fit time to ask, while she is flush with her victory.

"The best laid schemes o' mice and men gang aft-a-gley. An' lea'e us nought but grief and pain, for promised joy," I say.

"Huh?" Abalone's eyes are wide as I roll out the words in the Scottish accent of a sailor who had resided in the Home for a time.

"I believe she wants to know what you have in mind for her," Professor Isabella says, shaking her skirts down. "I must admit, I've been sitting on my own curiosity."

"Lumpy seat, that," Betwixt snickers. "It's been popping up more than Head Wolf's . . ."

I pinch his mouth shut while Between laughs. Silently, I resolve that the dragons may wait in the Heights next time I visit the Lair.

Abalone has been considering Professor Isabella's question and, lifting the window curtain, she sees that we have some time left until proper daylight.

"I'll fill you both in," she decides. "I think I've thought of everything but . . . You must have guessed that I break programs, Professor Isabella."

Professor Isabella nods, her eyes lively as she sips from a cup of almost viscous coffee.

"Well, a while back, I found the way into the Vehicle Registration Banks. With some work, I can reregister anyone's vehicle to anyone else. What I do is usually cruise the streets until I find a nice piece or two habitually parked with either an electronic guard or none at all. I get the external ident data and then trace it in the VRB. After I craft a new ID, I register the target to me."

The smile on Professor Isabella's face encourages Abalone to go on with barely a break.

"When I pick the vehicle up, I'm not stealing it. Even if I was pulled over, all the data would agree it was mine. The 'real' owner would be hard-pressed to prove otherwise. Then I go to a dealer and make a quick sale."

"Let me guess," Professor Isabella interrupts. "You've done this often enough that your plan is to set Sarah up as the 'owner' and have her sell the car. Have you decided how to get around her rather distinctive appearance and way of talking?"

"I thought of several," Abalone replies, just barely bragging. "At first, I figured she could just memorize key responses to the questions. Funny, for all her remembering odd quotes, she couldn't get any of this."

Professor Isabella shrugs with a theatrical sigh. "Sarah's memory is a mystery to me. What and why she chooses to remember or understand anything is a miracle. She apparently didn't speak at all until she was somewhere in her twenties."

"Well," Abalone continues, "when that didn't work out, I thought about fitting her with a voder and speaking through it. That was too crazy and complex. What I settled on is so simple that I can't handle it."

"Go, on, Shellfish," Professor Isabella exclaims. "Dawn is coming and won't Head Wolf turn you into a pumpkin if you're out past curfew?"

Abalone rolls her eyes. "She'll pretend that she's lost her voice and come in with a prepared sales offer. The guy I have in mind speaks English real good but he doesn't read much English, just Korean—he voice notes his sales—He'll scan the offer into his computer, maybe dicker a little. Sarah can nod 'yes' or 'no' and I'll tell her the acceptable range."

"Won't he wonder why she's selling while she's sick? Why she doesn't wait until she's better?"

"Nope." Abalone flips onto her stomach and drums her heels in the air. "Not when he sees the registration and loan stuff. He'll see she's got a payment due the next day and realize that she needs to sell to cover it."

"Clever," Professor Isabella admits. "Simple and elegant. Of course, you'll disguise her more-distinctive features and all the dealer will see is another pretty Anglo. What are you doing on the street, girl?"

Abalone freezes up, burying her face in the pillow. Slowly, Professor Isabella inches across the floor to her and pats her shoulder.

"Sorry, Abalone, I should know better than to ask. God knows, every day I fear that one of my former students will recognize me. How could I ever explain? Not all of them would be as fine as sweet Sarah."

"Thanks." Abalone rolls onto her back. "Do you think you can do it, Sarah?"

I ignore the tears she's wiping away and settle for nodding my agreement.

We part that dawn, quiet and reflective, promising to meet Professor Isabella when the deed is done. In the Jungle, I worry that my tension will keep me awake, but I fall asleep as soon as I have climbed into my hammock. In my dreams, I drive down streets of the deserted financial district. My car mirror shows me a face with golden hair and bright emerald eyes.

The next evening, we go through the secret subway and end in the locked rest room. This time I change my clothing as well, putting on a tidy maple jumpsuit. Abalone fits an ash blond wig over my hair.

"Your eyes will do—no one will believe that color is natural anyhow, but combined with cream-colored hair you are just too memorable." She shrugs. "When you first came to the Jungle, I kept waiting for it to grow out, but it's real, isn't it?"

Watching the stranger in the mirror move, I nod.

"Strange color," Abalone muses, pulling on her own non-descript outfit. "I've only seen it on palomino horses and cats. Cream and jade."

We head out, Betwixt and Between in the neat pseudo-suede bag swinging from my shoulder.

The damp sidewalks seem to stick to my shoes as we walk. Once again, I am following Abalone; this time I know what we are seeking. I don't need Abalone's slight nod to tell me when we have reached the target.

A sign with a painted ideogram tells me that we have reached where the car is parked in a small garage. The first test of Abalone's skill will be here. Without a glance at her, I turn, fumble in my bag past Betwixt and Between, and find the brown Moroccan leather wallet Abalone had given me. Nervously, I pull a plastic slip out and slide it into the guard door. It swallows it and then the door slides open. On the other side, I retrieve it.

A fruity male voice says, "Thank you, Ms. Rena."

. . . .

As the door closes behind me, the aloneness that had left when Abalone picked me up from the street rushes back, chilling me. I know I must move quickly, yet I turn slowly as if wading in icy slush up to my knees.

It waits for me: sleek, predatory, silver and black, seeming to drift on parking jets. I wade toward it and am sliding the key strip into the lock when I come up short. A woman is already in the car—her gaze meets mine and when I see pale green jade the picture falls into place. The woman is me.

I know this, but my hand still is shaking nearly too hard to match the flimsy slip and its slot. I manage and step in, feeling the car bob on its jets.

The dashboard is different than the one I have been so patiently studying. I cannot find the start button; I cannot find the acceleration shift; I cannot find the brake. Only the steering crescent is familiar.

When I place my hand on the soft curve, perception chimes. The brake is beneath my right foot as Abalone had promised. Now I find the start button—a few inches higher than I had been taught. The acceleration shaft is snapped into a recess right of the driver's seat. I find the release tab, press it, and the shaft rises beneath my right hand.

Abalone has written a navigation program and I drop this into the consol. The silver-and-black shark bites and I can drop, shaking, into the padded seat while the program reels us to our destination. Outside, rain on the tinted windows stars the streetlights and headlights, beginning to shoot as the car picks up speed.

When the car idles to a stop in the driveway of a used ve-

hicle lot, I am enough in control to steer us to a fairly graceful park outside the sales office door. The shark has barely
fallen quiet when the office door slams up and a small Korean man emerges.

Touching my throat, I hand him the note Abalone has
written for me. He takes it, wrinkling his brow as he reads. I
see confusion, amazement, and, finally, greed travel across his
features. The face he turns to me is bland and gently friendly.

"I am sorry to hear," he chuckles at his own joke, "that
you have lost your voice, Ms. Rena. Do you have a copy of
your license and registration? I need to check them before
we negotiate a possible sale."

I nod and dig again for my wallet and pull out the paper-
work.

As I drop the wallet in Betwixt and Between puff reassuringly at me. I notice as I snap my bag shut that they have
gotten into a roll of breath mints and curls of silver paper
roll around their stout, stocky ankles.

Mr. Joon invites me into this office, pours me coffee, and
offers me a selection of magazines. Then he disappears behind a burlap-textured screen. I strain and hear the snap as
the forged identities are run. Beyond fear, I wait in confidence of Abalone's skill, sipping coffee and leafing through
a magazine. Blushing, I realize that I have it upside down
and flip it over just as Mr. Joon reemerges.

Pushing shiny black bangs from his forehead, he smiles.

"All looks fine, Alice," he says.

I almost look around, but remember that the name on the
car's papers is Alice Rena. Instead, I nod and gesture with
my head toward the shark.

"I'll need to run a diagnostic on the vehicle itself," Mr. Joon says, taking an oval box from a cabinet by the door, "but if everything proves in as good shape as it appears, I am interested in making you an offer."

We walk outside and he plugs the oval into an aperture in the dashboard. Abalone has explained to me that this small computer will talk with the shark's computer and provide a systems analysis. Mr. Joon will combine this with his own visual inspection and certain trade standards will set his price.

I watch as he caresses seat covers, fingers the wear on the floor mats, and plays with the sound system. The whistle from his oval box blends into the sound pouring from the vehicle and Mr. Joon ignores it until he sees the amber read-out flashing a completed operation and pops it free.

Face professionally neutral, he scans the readouts and then courteously shows them to me.

Biting my inner lip to keep from revealing my growing insecurity, I wait a moment as if studying the figures and holodiagrams and then nod, looking at him with what I hope is a decisive expression.

Mr. Joon's patter about the shark's condition flows over me. Caught in the crosscurrents of his voice and my own fears, I wait for the numbers Abalone had promised me would come. I know what is acceptable and what is not—or did when I left the Jungle. I pray inarticulately that I will not forget.

He names a figure. Resisting the urge to grab at it as a life-line, to nod "yes" and flee, I weigh it against Abalone's lessons.

. . . .

I do not even need subtlety. The number is far too low. Extending my hand, I shake my head and gesture upward with my thumb.

The next figure Mr. Joon names is better, but I hazard one more raise. He does, not as much as I might wish, but within the range Abalone had set. I nod agreement. We close the deal and I walk away with a slip showing that Alice Rena is thousands richer—as am I.

I walk quickly toward the subway entrance and find Abalone lurking where she promised to be. We vanish down into the smelly tunnels and in ten minutes Alice Rena is gone and only Sarah and the thousands remain.

Abalone waits until we are safely away to ask me how things went. "Were you scared, Sarah?"

"True nobility is exempt from fear," I reply, winking at her.

She throws her arms around me and together we laugh until the laughter shakes away all memory of my fears and leaves only the triumph of my success.

SIX

꘎

A FEW DAYS AFTER THE HUNTING OF THE SHARK, HEAD WOLF lets me know that he would be pleased if I wanted to spend some of the day with him in his lair. I gladly agree and, after informing Abalone where I would be, I go. As I had resolved previously, I leave my dragons behind.

I return to my place in the Reaches somewhat sooner than I had planned (Bumblebee had decided to join us and while Head Wolf welcomed her, I was not interested in female honey).

Abalone is gone. Searching quickly, I find that her tappety-tap is also gone. Around me, the Free People sleep, so very softly I whisper to the dragons.

"Abalone?"

"We're not Abalone!" Between says indignantly. "Where is little blue lips, anyway?"

"Weren't you staying to screw Head Wolf?" Betwixt asks, his red eyes shining.

I can tell that the dragons are hurt by my abandoning them, so I hold my questions until I have fed them some jelly and crackers from my hoard. The food sweetens them.

Betwixt finishes the last crumbs of his share. "Scratch my eye ridge, would you, Sarah?"

When I do so, not neglecting Between, the dragon relaxes. The ruby eyes seem to glow amiably rather than burn.

"Soon after you left," Between says, "Abalone got bored with her magazine. She didn't seem sleepy and I heard her mutter something about going to the Park."

"That was a while ago," Betwixt adds. "I guess she'll be back soon."

I try to relax and agree. Abalone has done well without me; certainly I must be a trouble to her—a constant shadow. I stretch out on my hammock and set myself gently rocking. Balanced on my stomach, the dragons drowse.

"Go to sleep, Sarah," Between says soothingly. "You're beat. We'll take turns watching and wake you when Abalone comes back."

I can feel exhaustion stealing through me and yawn nodding my acceptance of the dragon's plan.

"For some must watch, while some must sleep: so runs the world away."

Pulling my blanket over me, I position the dragons so they can watch. My last sensation is their claws, like little needles, gripping for purchase as we gently swing.

I do not awaken when Abalone makes her stealthy return, but true to their promise, the dragons hiss me awake. Even in my pleasure at seeing Abalone safely returned, I do not miss that they are more agitated than seems warranted.

"Say 'Hello' quickly, Sarah," Betwixt urges, "and don't let her drop off yet. We've got to tell you something and I think she should hear it, too."

"Abalone!" I call, reaching out across the space between our hammocks. I struggle, but I cannot find words for my irrational concern for her safety and my joy at her return and must settle for smiling.

"Hush, Sarah," she whispers. "You'll rouse all the Jungle. I didn't expect to see you here so early."

"Hide me from day's garish eye," I comment softly, hoping she will read my grimace into my words, "while the bee with the honied thigh . . ."

"Oh," Abalone chuckles. "Bumblebee came calling. She's been watching you, my friend. I'm surprised she waited this long."

She begins to snuggle into the down-filled sleeping bag that lines her hammock. Betwixt and Between hiss urgently at me.

"Tell her we heard Edelweiss saying that someone is looking for you. Someone from the Home from what she said. We heard her telling Tapestry while you were sleeping."

My mouth opens and shuts like a clam in an old cartoon. There are no words in my mind for this fragmented message. Still, I reach and shake Abalone.

She yawns at me. "Yeah?"

"I am a brother to dragons, a companion to owls," I start.

"Sarah, I'm tired," Abalone sighs. "I know about the dragon."

"Charity begins at home!" I try again, my voice breaking above a whisper.

. . . .

"Hush!"

"'Tis ever common that men are merriest when they are from home," I mutter futilely to myself.

Abalone falls asleep. I lie swinging, too awake and hunting for words.

"You'll never take me alive," I murmur as I finally fall asleep.

In the evening, Abalone sleeps past the time the Tail Wolves and the Four rise and leave. Their activity awakens me and I lie in my hammock watching them dress and depart, a nighttime rainbow. My mind tries to find words to tell Abalone of Betwixt and Between's warning, wishing for not the first time, that my friends could talk to the dragon.

When the commotion below has thinned, I slide down to the floor level and go to wash. I am soaping in one of the showers rigged in a curve of the Jungle tank when I hear soft cursing from down by my feet.

"Damn, damn, damnety, damn!"

Tilting my face into the gentle fall of water, I rinse my eyes and look down. A small stuffed rabbit sits in a puddle half-hidden by the edge of the shower curtain. The water has soaked into the plush and one ear is limp and bedraggled.

Recognizing that it belongs to Peep, who has recently left begging to become a Tail Wolf, I scoop it up and wash off the soap scum before wringing out what water I can.

"Ouch!" the bunny yells as I wring one ear. "*Madre de Dios*, that smarts!"

"And in this harsh world draw thy breath in pain," I

BROTHER *to* DRAGONS, COMPANION *to* OWLS

chuckle, hanging it by the ears to drip while I continue rinsing myself free of soap.

"You heard me?" the bunny says incredulously.

I nod, reaching for a towel and wrapping my hair.

"How did you do that? No one ever heard me before except for Peep sometimes." The soggy bunny appears to sag. "And he hears less and less these days, now that these buggering hedonists have him by the *cojones*."

I shrug and finish drying, but am pleased to have found another friend. The things that talk to me have never done so in the condescending fashion that even the best humans do. Betwixt and Between get bossy, but that's different.

Once I am covered, I take Peep's bunny and ascend to the Heights. Abalone is only starting to stir, so I sit on the hammock swing-style and wrap the bunny in the drier of my two towels. Betwixt and Between express lively interest in the soggy toy, especially when it refuses any breakfast.

"What's your name?" Betwixt asks.

"Conejito Moreno," the bunny replies. "Do you belong to this strange *señorita*?"

"We watch out for her," Between says. "We took up with her first back in the Institute. One of the other patients had us first and talked to us all the time. Like Sarah, this fellow could understand us, but he was wilder than her. He could talk to almost anything, even people. It ripped . . ."

Between halts, suddenly aware that I am listening, Betwixt hesitates, then takes up the story.

"It ripped his mind up sometimes. I think he might have

gone crazy, but they moved Sarah to the Home and he gave us to her before she went, so we never saw him again."

When the conversation drifts to more general things, I stop listening. I barely remember the Institute; something like cotton is wrapped around the memories. Still, I know that it was different than the Home. Since I couldn't talk at all, I was pretty much left alone.

My few memories of the place are a jumble of corridors and things that sometimes spoke and erratic sessions with intense people whose words said less than did their actions, whose favorite pen or lucky coin might warn me to never ever speak with them or they would drive me as mad as they had Dylan.

Dylan. I had not even realized that I knew his name, but now I recalled him. Skinny, eyes full of fear. Ears full of voices that he could answer in a way I could not.

I bite on the knuckle of one balled fist, fighting a certain urge to scream. For in that moment, everything in the room is talking to me—Abalone's tappety-tap, the hammock beneath me, the walls, the painted tent from which Head Wolf is emerging, Edelweiss's pillow.

Clamping my hands over my ears, I scream, "Much learning doth make thee mad!"

Abalone comes awake so suddenly that only habit keeps her from falling. Those of the Free People who have not gone hunting grow silent and then their eyes turn to me, the buzz of their voices rising.

Head Wolf grabs a ladder and swarms upward. He lands beside me, gesturing the eyes away, but it is Abalone's shoulder on which I weep, burying my eyes and aching senses in her sweet-smelling skin as if it will smother this sudden awareness.

As she pats me, muttering soothing nonsense, the voices fade until all I hear are hers and Head Wolf's. Concerned, Betwixt and Between whisper softly to each other and Conejito Moreno.

Grabbing a guide rope for stability in a way I have not since I graduated from the cubwalks, I finally sit up, wiping my eyes on my shirt. Neither Head Wolf nor Abalone ask me to explain what happened. Perhaps they know I could not find the words.

"She was stressed out when I came in this morning," Abalone offers, searching for an explanation. "Did something happen to her while I was gone?"

"Bumblebee made a move on her, but she handled it well." Head Wolf considers, swinging back and forth, his feet anchored on a cable. "You have been working her hard. Give her a rest—I'll absorb the fee."

"Thanks." Abalone's tone is threaded with emotions I am too drained to reach after. "Beer and pizza."

That dawn, we are heading back to the Jungle after spending the night with Professor Isabella when Peep intercepts us. He draws us away into the trash-filled alcove between two rusting tanks with a conspiratorial jerk of his head.

Something in me hurts as I look at the transformation the Tail Wolves have wrought in him. He has been poured into a skintight yellow tank top and a pair of matching pants that hug his little boy's ass. His sun-bleached brown hair has been styled so that his bangs drop coquettishly over his left eye and his M&M eyes have been ringed with eyeliner. The pupils are wider than they should be, even in the dim light.

"Edelweiss said keep quiet and the Tail Wolves, they say so, too. The Four, they not so sure, but I make up my own mind."

He smiles at us, an innocent boy's smile from which the streetwise cynicism vanishes for a moment. Then he draws us closer.

"I decide for me"—he pokes himself in the chest—"I hear you saved my *conejito* for me, when I left it this nighttime."

I nod, quivering at the memory of what Betwixt and Between's talk with Conejito Moreno had released. Abalone steadies me.

"She did," she confirms. "You thanking her?"

"Yes, I pay my dues." Peep hesitates, then, "The Home is hunting Sarah—they want to take her back."

Inadvertently, I tense, but Abalone is still holding my hand.

"How do you know this, Peep?"

"The word's out." He shrugs. "The Home has room and wants back those that they let loose—like her. Some might be real happy, but I don't think she'd be—she's one of the Free People, like you an' me."

He touches the running wolf that fastens his belt and Abalone raises a finger to her tattoo.

"Yes, Sarah's one of us," she agrees. "Thanks, Peep, I'll check this out."

"We be of one blood ye and I," he confirms, and with a brotherly grin for me, moves out into the street.

Abalone and I wait to let him get clear before following.

"The Tail Wolves never have liked that you didn't join them—but don't take that personally," Abalone says. "They're still your Pack. We'll sleep on this—no one'll find you here. In the evening, we'll go and see if Professor Isabella has heard more. We can also speak with Jerome or Balika and ask how hard the Home is looking or if this is just a gesture to make peace with the public for throwing nutcases out into the streets."

We duck into the halogen-lit tangle of the Jungle, alive with the Pack returning from the night's hunting. Music dins from a dozen sources; lithe bodies with hair and skin in every color planned by God, and many never anticipated, hang from the Web. Laughter and joking compete with the music.

Peep, Conejito Moreno snuggled under his arm, sucks his thumb in his hammock while Bumblebee rocks him. Deep in conversation with Midline of the Four, Head Wolf pauses from painting a denim jacket. Edelweiss and Chocolate arm wrestle near a camp stove.

An ordinary dawn before sleep stills the Free People. I climb to my place, loving the colorful chaos with my eyes as I cannot with words.

Abalone tucks me in with a tenderness she has rarely shown since her earliest days as my Baloo. She makes certain that Betwixt and Between are near at hand.

Despite her tenderness, fear that I will lose all of this makes me shudder.

"You okay, Sarah?" she asks.

"There's no place like Home," I say, struggling for her to understand.

. . . .

"Don't worry, Sarah. I won't send you back unless you want to go."

Reassured, I drift off to sleep, hearing the Jungle settle in around me. My dreams are peaceful.

When night comes, with amazement Betwixt and Between tell me that Head Wolf had spent the day perched in the Reaches near my head, unmoving, but ready to battle my demons should they trouble my sleep.

That evening we go out into a night already dark, crisp, and cold. Christmas lights shine from windows and reflect off the ice and dirty snow that clumps in corners and potholes in the streets and walkways.

Professor Isabella is late to meet us and when she does, she is uncommonly quiet. Finally, Abalone coaxes from her that she had been at the funeral of another street person, an older man who had frozen to death when the damp from the grate on which he typically slept so saturated his clothing that the faint heat was not enough to keep him from catching pneumonia.

"They buried him in a pauper's grave—unmarked except for a code number in case anyone ever traces him and matches whoever he was to his file. Only a few of us came and . . ."

She trails off.

I reach and touch her arm. "Now with his love, so his colde grave, alone withouten any compaignye."

"Yes, Sarah," she says. "You do understand, don't you?"

As we hurry to When I Was Hungry, Abalone tells Professor Isabella about Peep's rumor.

"Odd," she says when the report is finished. "I've heard

nothing about this, yet I'm certain that at least two of the Tabaqui who are usually by the Station are from the Home. No one has come looking for them."

Troubled, Abalone starts to slow, but a cold gust of wind pushes her along. We talk little more until we are at the table in the steamy soup kitchen, seated a bit apart from the rest. Jerome has noticed our arrival, but it will be sometime before he can join us.

I am wiping the extra cream sauce from Between's jaw when Jerome comes over. He carries a coffeepot and seems relaxed.

"Evening, folks," he says. "Getting too cold these nights for man or beast, so we're going to be staying open with hot coffee and tea and a space for those who'll doss on the floor or tabletop. Pass the word to those who might need it."

Delicately, he does not speak as if we need this help. I wonder if he will ever learn that Abalone has been anonymously dropping the kitchen supplies—a case of coffee last time. Suddenly, it occurs to me that her generosity may be the reason that the place is staying open later and I feel good.

"Speaking of getting the word," Abalone says, "we hear that the Home is taking back some of the nutcases they pitched out."

Jerome's dark face creases. "I haven't heard any of that, Abalone. Rumor runs the other way—that we may lose more bed space. Your source good?"

"Thought so, spoke as if worried for Sarah, like they'd make her go back."

Jerome pats my hand. "No, you're safe, Sarah. Odd company you keep, but you do seem to be doing just fine. Not like some. I saw two of your old pals. Remember Francis and Ali?"

I nod, wrinkling my nose in distaste.

He laughs, but memory stills the laughter in his throat.

"They looked terrible. Ragged and filthy, hungry, sick. It tore me to send them on with just a meal."

"Were they here?" Abalone asks and I know she means to find them.

"Yes . . . No, wait!" Jerome looks puzzled. "It was at the Home—a week or so ago. I remember because I slid them both double portions of pancakes and we never do anything that fancy here. Sorry, one chow line runs into another after a while."

"Strange," Professor Isabella says. "Very strange. There may be something to your rumor, Abalone."

Abalone nods slowly. "Yeah, Jerome, could you ask, quiet-like, about why those guys were brought back in and maybe about this rumor? Please."

She bats her eyelashes at him and with her fiery buzz and blue lips is such a ludicrous parody of the little girl that we all burst out laughing.

"I'll do what I can," Jerome promises, "but I'm not exactly in Admin Center."

Professor Isabella smiles, almost wickedly. "Do what you can, Jerome, but don't get yourself in trouble. I may know someone in the Admin Center."

We finish our coffee and step into the cold. As we hustle along toward one of our safe spots, I search and find almost the question I want to ask. When we pause at a crosswalk, I ask Professor Isabella.

"Who are you? Are you nobody, too?"

She looks at me, deciphering. "Who am I? Am I nobody, too? Ah! Clever, Sarah."

We cross and she continues, "Yes, I am nobody, Sarah, but I still know someone in the Admin Center. So do you."

Puzzled, I review the sea of faces, most without names, from my years at the Home. Most of those I knew well enough to beg a favor of—if I could make them understand me—were like Jerome or Nani, my sewing teacher, staff, not administration. I shrug.

"I'm nobody," I admit. "Who are you? Are you nobody, too?"

"Yes"—she nudges Abalone who has been listening with lively interest—"but I know someone who can get us into Admin Center's very heart. Abalone here, with her skillful tappety-tap."

"Hmm." The blue lips curl. "Yes, let's rent a room." We check into an automated facility, Abalone resisting the urge to reprogram the computer to give us our room for free. Once in, Professor Isabella goes to shower and I sit and whisper with Betwixt and Between so that I will not disturb Abalone.

She mutters to herself as she secures us from tracing and then starts into the Home's systems. If I try, I can hear her tappety-tap answering her—cursing back when she swears, cheering along with her as they break a security code, sniffling indignantly at the slovenly programming.

When Abalone was teaching me to drive, I learned that she heard nothing but the flat synthetic voice used by some programs. Now, I try not to hear because it seems like eavesdropping on lovers, but sadder because the beloved is deaf to the whispered endearments, encouragement, and support.

My dragons have been unusually quiet since the previous evening's conversation with Conejito Moreno and the events following. I wonder if they are still worrying that I will freak out. Surely that would be terrible for them, because they have already lost Dylan. I scratch Betwixt's eye ridge, rubbing in front of Between's nose horn at the same time.

Both seem to stretch and lean into my fingers.

"In much wisdom is much grief," I say softly, breathing mute thanksgiving to those mad-folk who raved in passages from the Bible, "and he that increaseth knowledge increaseth sorrow."

"Think we're sad, Sarah?" Betwixt asks.

I nod.

"Yeah, we are but—Hey! Don't stop scratching!—You scared us. We thought we'd hurt you."

"I am a brother to dragons, a companion to owls," I repeat.

The red eyes sparkle gratefully.

Between says, "We do know stuff from when you were little, back in the Institute. You're a success, Sarah. The only one who ended up crazy and out of there. We lost Dylan; we don't want to lose you."

Questions for which I lack words flutter into my throat and get trapped there. My hands rise to shake them free.

"Easy, Sarah." Professor Isabella has reemerged, wrapped in a towel. "Calm down."

I let my hands fall and the dragons look at each other, sighing simultaneously so that they blow up each other's noses. Unable to help myself, I giggle. Professor Isabella shakes her head with concern and retreats to dress. I realize that she too, is worried that I am losing control.

Between nods thoughtfully. "We can't explain it, Sarah. We're just us and the Institute people weren't exactly chatty."

Betwixt interrupts. "You know the Bible quote? 'Eyes have they, but they see not. They have ears, but they hear not'? Someone wanted people who could hear and see what most people can't and that's you and that's Dylan and that's too much for any human."

I nod and hold up my hand, signaling "enough." I need to think, to reflect. Memories without words are rising up and I know if I do not carefully handle them, I will be drowned.

When Professor Isabella returns, coifed and wearing only one skirt and sweater, Abalone ignores her questions and keeps working. She does nod thanks when the professor supplies her with cocoa from a vending machine. Then the two of us withdraw to a corner and Professor begins to read to me from the collected works of Mark Twain.

We are both so immersed in the essay she is reading that when Abalone lets out a long whistle of amazement, we both jump.

"Found something?" Professor Isabella asks, flipping off the portable library screen that Abalone had bought soon after our first meeting.

"And something," Abalone confirms, rumpling her unrumpleable hair. "The outer programs were a breeze. I could have gotten through them when I . . . I got through them easily. When I started on the records for this latest 'purge' and some Dr. Haas who was in charge of Sarah's case, well . . ."

She shakes her head in amazement.

"So you didn't learn anything?" Professor Isabella asks.

Abalone raises her eyebrows indignantly, "I didn't say that. I just said it wasn't easy. C'mere."

"I didn't want to be too direct about this," Abalone begins once we have positioned ourselves so that we can see her screen. "If someone is really looking for Sarah, her files might be flagged so that unauthorized entry would be noticed. So I went on a less obvious tangent."

She pauses to sip her cocoa, grimacing when she finds it has grown cold.

"I knew about when Sarah appeared on the street, so I worked backward through the files, looking for when the orders came down. When I found them, I cross-checked by matching not only Sarah's name, but Ali and Francis, those two fellows Jerome mentioned. Then, when I was sure I had the right group I checked who the controlling authorities were. There were three physicians or psychiatrists, Doctors Davidoff, N'goya, and Haas, who came in from outside. I found next that Haas had been the one who selected Sarah as one of those to be pitched into the cold cruel."

This time she looks at the cold cocoa before sipping.

"Let me go pee. Will you get refills, Sarah? Maybe some chips or other junk?"

She tosses me a credit slip and I head out, proud that I can do this without panicking. Behind me, Betwixt and Between call for me to remember a treat for them.

When I return, Abalone is back in her perch on the bed. I am pleased that the story has waited for me. Once we are settled with cocoa and cake and chips and the rest of my loot from the vending machines, Abalone continues her report.

"Well, the next jump was a leap of faith. I still didn't want to try Sarah's file or code a search with her specs, not until I knew more. Then it occurred to me. Someone may want Sarah back—it may be a private individual even, but whoever it is is using the Home. This is where the faith came in—what if someone screwed up letting Sarah out? I decided that made sense, since that would clear up why someone was trying to get her back. Well, the candidate for prime screwup was this Dr. Haas, who cleared Sarah to go."

Abalone pauses, swigs, and hits an icon on her screen. The screen shifts, but the pattern of numbers and letters remains unintelligible to me. Professor Isabella leans forward, though, scans and grunts.

"Bingo, Abalone. Bingo!"

Beaming, Abalone continues, "With the Haas name as a tracer, I did some more snooping. Not only does she have permission to readmit Sarah if she's found, but she was the one who had Ali and Francis dragged in. I bet they were questioned and then junked when they couldn't say where our friend here was."

"Did you ever go after Sarah's files?" Professor Isabella asks, her hand clasped tight around her drink.

"Yep, I couldn't give up, not when things were going so well. Something might have made it tougher for me later."

"Pshaw," Professor Isabella chuckles.

I giggle.

"All right, I'm curious. This gets weirder the more I look. I expected to find either that Peep was exaggerating or that a simple recall had been issued. I find neither one nor the other, a mixture of both."

She touches a few icons and this time I recognize my face up in one corner of the screen. The words mean nothing, but I remember the computer in the outpatient processing center reciting: "Sarah. No surname. No precise date of birth. Admitted from Ivy Green Institute, a private sanatorium."

I tense, waiting for the flashing lights, the warning "Classified!"

Nothing happens and slowly I let my muscles unknot, realizing that Abalone has failed to alert the warning.

"Ivy Green Institute," Professor Isabella muses. "Yes, that's where Sarah was brought from. I remember hearing something about it. Did you check them out?"

"Not yet. I wanted to see if I could get into Sarah's file at the Home. I avoided a Classified flag—it was pretty plain, meant to keep out peeping staff grunts."

"What did you find?"

Abalone's smile vanishes. "It's been rewritten, look."

The screen flickers. The same picture is there, but in the

swimming characters is information that makes Professor Isabella gasp.

"To be ignorant of one's ignorance is the malady of the ignorant," I hint, tired of being ignored.

"Sorry, Sarah," Professor Isabella apologizes. "Ignorance may be bliss, here. Abalone's right, the file describes a young woman of about your age and appearance, but nothing else is the same. The woman is not listed as a possible autistic, but as a probably dangerous paranoid. Your little identifying traits—like speaking in quotes—are completely missing."

I look with puzzlement at Abalone and she wrinkles her brow. "I don't know, Sarah, but I got out of that file as fast as I could. I checked the recall on Ali and Francis—not much help there except that Dr. Haas issued it. I think she's behind the search for you—well, at least involved with it."

Professor Isabella is still looking at the altered file.

"This frightens me, girls. The woman depicted here is dangerous—if she was 'accidentally' killed or, worse, doped to the gills, there aren't many who would question the wisdom of the action. By then, she could not defend herself."

"Wolf's Heart!" Abalone cries, kicking a chair leg. "Can Sarah, anyhow? You really need to listen to follow her as it is. She could be dragged off before anyone could understand her and decide to step in."

"That he is mad"—I point to myself—"'tis true: 'tis true 'tis pity; And pity 'tis 'tis true."

"Sarah, honey"—Professor Isabella pats my hand—"there is a method to your madness but Abalone is right, not many will take time to find it. Abalone, how long until they find she is in the Jungle?"

"Peep says Edelweiss knows someone wants Sarah. That means others do, too. My guess is until Sarah gets more time with Head Wolf than the others like. The Law doesn't forbid Pack members to fight, just demands that the fight is 'alone and afar.' "

"'Lest others take part in the quarrel and the Pack be diminished by war," I finish, remembering with a pounding heart the conversation Betwixt and Between had reported.

"We may not have much time." Professor Isabella looks sharply at Abalone. "I may be asking too much, but Sarah needs to be taken away from this area. The city is large. We can lose ourselves easily and yet keep tabs on the search. When the interest dies down . . ."

"We can move back into our old hunting grounds." Abalone nods. "I'm with you. She's my Cub still, even if she has won her wolf. I'm not leaving her now, but will she go with us?"

"Ask her," Betwixt and Between hiss together, unheard as always.

Professor Isabella looks at me.

"You've heard all of this, Sarah. Will you leave the Jungle and come with us to a safer place?"

Memories of the musky Jungle, warm even in winter's chill, of swinging free above the Pack, of Head Wolf's hands and dark mad eyes engulf me, but I know that the Jungle is no longer a safe lair for me. I know, too, that a search there may threaten the Pack and provide an excuse for our enemies.

I square my shoulders and manage a smile. "Elysium is as far as to the nearest room, if in that room a friend await felicity or doom."

"Brave words." Abalone smiles. "Head Wolf needs to know this, but it is best we move quickly and without alerting the Pack. Leave it to me. You two rest. I'll be back."

She flees before we can protest. Reluctantly, I wait, pacing the confines of walls that did not bind until this moment.

SEVEN

THE APARTMENT IS A BEAUTIFUL PLACE. ABALONE HAS DIS-
carded the sky-reaching metroplexes as too institutional and
has chosen instead a refurbished older building. We each
have our own bedroom and share a living room and kitchen.
There are even two bathrooms.

Despite the lovely old brick walls that whisper to me as I
relax into sleep, the building has modern computer security.
As an added measure against our standing out from our new
neighbors, Abalone no longer paints her lips blue and has let
the flame-tone of her hair fade somewhat. Without her
paint, she is changed. I cannot tell if she looks older or
younger, but she looks sadder—a spring flower wilted and
bleached by a late frost.

Professor Isabella does not ask how the rent is being paid
but once. Abalone meets the inquiry with silence and then
walks out.

I touch Professor Isabella's arm. "Can the Ethiopian change his skin, or the leopard his spots?"

"And would we want her to?" Professor Isabella replies. "No, as long as she is careful. Sarah, that girl is nearly as great a mystery as you and, yet, perhaps none at all."

She shakes herself and straightens the neat skirt and blouse that have replaced her ragged layers. I like her better this way; she smells sweet, like roses, but she radiates tension.

I remember that, like me, she has been insane. I wonder if the retreat from the streets and relief from the daily battle for food and heat have left her with too much to reflect upon.

"He who can, does. He who cannot, teaches," I say, balancing Betwixt and Between on the window ledge so that they can see the sparrows eating bread crumbs on the crusty snow below.

"Are you twigging me, Sarah?" Professor Isabella looks astonished, then amused. "You have become sharp. Fine, if Abalone is going to support us, I will teach you—and her if she wishes. Perhaps if I get enough into your pretty head, we'll have the monkeys, typewriters, and Shakespeare."

I puzzle over the last, but do not worry about references. Professor Isabella is happily opening her worn poetry anthology and the crisis is over for now.

Later, when she has nodded off over the book and Abalone has vanished out into the night, I lie on the floor with my dragons on my stomach.

Head Wolf had come with Abalone when she had returned to our hideout in the motel. He bowed to Professor

Isabella and embraced me. Strangely, I wanted to weep. There was little discussion, nor did he seem angry.

"The Law says 'For the strength of the Pack is the Wolf, and the strength of the Wolf is the Pack.'"

I nodded, wishing never to leave those arms.

"Do you want to go, Sarah?"

The dark eyes overwhelmed me. The ache I felt was loneliness, love, and lust. His skin smelled of cinnamon and salt. Hurting, I managed to nod. Then I pushed myself away.

"If it were done when 'tis done, then 'twere well it were done quickly," I managed, fighting tears.

"Well, then." He hugged Abalone, bowed again. "Good Hunting!"

The memory hurts no less now for having been reviewed a dozen times. I rock to my feet and pace from wall to wall, in and out of my room, the kitchen, each of the bathrooms, and around again. When I am weary, I needlepoint a pattern I am making for Professor Isabella. Abalone has promised me that she will take me hunting again soon.

I drift off and dream of sharks with golden hair and hard, green eyes. They smile with pearly teeth and sing a deadly requiem.

Some days later, the weather turns with one of those warm spells that January brings, teasing with forty degrees and sunshine as a stripper tosses away a thigh-high stocking. Not even Blake, who has delighted me until now, can keep my attention. Abalone is asleep and so I whine like a puppy at Professor Isabella.

"Well, I suppose we could go walking in the Park, perhaps over to one of the museums. Would that suit you?"

I nod, clapping my hands. Then I dart off for my shoulder bag and winter coat. Neither Abalone nor Professor Isabella seem to mind Betwixt and Between as much if I keep the dragon covered.

Professor Isabella takes longer to get ready, pausing to write Abalone a note. When we are out in the fresh air, she perks up and trots next to me.

Pointing across the grey-brown lacework of barren treetops, she says, "We'll walk that way, take a look at the museum, and then be rested to come back."

Although the walk invigorates me, the museum overwhelms me. From the moment we walk through one of the vast doors that empty into a cathedral-like hall, I hear voices whispering to me. I must remind myself that I am insane, that nothing is wrong.

This first visit, we go into a central gallery that smells of spice and dust. The exhibit is a Christmas tree decorated with angels in flight, their draperies fluttering with unfelt winds, their serene faces strangely passionate. Although they seem small against the spreading evergreen's boughs, I realize that each is larger than Betwixt and Between.

Professor Isabella draws my gaze downward to the figures at the base of the tree. Animals and people, exotic and so ordinary that they seem to be people I have seen, all travel to visit an infant Jesus who beams beatifically from his manger, sheltered beneath the prayerful gaze of his parents.

"The museum will leave the crèche up until after the Feast of the Three Kings," she notes. "Aren't the little people wonderful? Look at the detail of Mary's face."

I nod agreement. The Holy Family is beautifully done,

but I find myself drawn to the ordinary figures: the almost too-whimsical donkey, the dog who pauses to sniff a shrub, the group of men drinking by a ruined fountain.

If I try, I can hear the song they are singing, not a carol, something lustier.

My mouth moves, shaping the words, trying to sing with the infectious melody. One of the men is leaning to hand me his wineskin, his dark eyes glint with mirth and more. I reach . . .

A sharp sting breaks the sound of the singing. Bewildered, I find myself in the gallery beside the Christmas tree. Professor Isabella is shaking me, her face creased with worry; her cheeks flushed with embarrassment. A few of the other patrons are staring at me. A security guard has halted his step forward, seeing Professor Isabella has quieted me.

We walk outside. I am trembling with embarrassment and the lingering sensation that I have been torn from another world. Afraid to look at Professor Isabella, I shuffle along, my hands buried in my pockets, my eyes fixed on the grey pavement in front of my feet.

"Sarah?"

I do not answer.

"Sarah, are you all right?"

Daring to look, I see that her expression shows only concern. Biting my upper lip, I try for words. There are none— no eloquent apologies lurk in my memory waiting to be recycled by a sincere heart.

"How do you feel, Sarah?" Professor Isabella asks gently.

"I cannot sing the songs I sang long years ago," I try. "For heart and voice would fail me, and foolish tears would flow."

"Sad and foolish?" She smiles. "I've been there. It isn't fatal, my dear. Feeling foolish is like having a head cold: you don't die from it, you only wish you could."

I smile and suddenly hug her, not caring who sees. Then I link my arm through hers and we go this way back home.

Abalone is awake and greets us with a warm smile.

"Where you been?" she says around a bite from a sandwich.

"Sarah wanted out and we walked over to the museum."

"Flash. How'd it go? Did she like it?"

"I think so." Professor Isabella hangs up her coat. "She had one of her spells while we were looking at the Christmas tree. Started singing in Italian."

"Italian? Where'd she learn that? I thought that she didn't speak anything at all until you started teaching her."

"As far as I know, she didn't," Professor Isabella pauses, "but I think a common error we make with the mute is thinking that those who cannot talk also cannot hear."

I grin. "More safe I sing with mortal voice, unchang'd to hoarse or mute, though fall'n on evil days."

Professor Isabella groans and Abalone laughs, though I suspect more at my teacher's expression than at my joke.

Several days later, when I indicate that I want to go to the museum again, Professor Isabella is clearly reluctant, but when she learns that Abalone is planning on incorporating me into another vehicle heist, she is swayed by this, rather than by my borrowed eloquence.

"We'll go again," she agrees, wagging her finger at me, "but for my reasons and those alone. I'd better do what I can to get you at ease in a crowd. You are still too prone to your spells. And, if Abalone is going to make a thief of you, then I had better get in my lessons while I can."

I giggle. "Lay not up for yourselves treasures upon earth, where moth and rust doth corrupt, and where thieves break through and steal."

"Something like that," she replies. "Abalone will teach you well how to build up the treasure we all need to survive in this sorry world—and she'll do it far better than I ever could. But"—again the finger wags—"man does not live by bread alone. Sometimes, once those physical cravings are satisfied, the real hunger for 'why' rather than 'what' and 'how' awakens and that's a much harder hunger to satisfy."

We hurry across a Park to which cold has returned. Professor Isabella has a roll of charge slips ready in her pocket and whenever we pass a person sheltering under a roadway or in a door, she drops one. I can see the guilt on her face and know that she wonders why she, rather than one of them, is comfortable in an apartment with heat and plenty to eat.

Today, the Christmas tree and its soaring angels are gone and we concentrate on the medieval Christian art that is displayed in the gallery. Professor Isabella quietly tells me tales about saints, apostles, and martyrs.

I soak up the stories and look at the figures: Peter, well-meaning but humanly flawed; bald Paul, with the fanatic's light in his eyes; beloved John, younger than the rest; Mary Magdalene, the Tail Wolf who loved Jesus. The novelty of face and form given to figures I know from the vast amount of Biblical lore in my memory fascinates me. My delight is so great that I can nearly ignore the voices that whisper to me from the gilded statues and the flat faces in the large-eyed paintings.

Wisps of prayers come to my ears, offered by the devout to the god and saints they could not help but believe stood before them embodied in stone or painted wood. Processional statues mourn the loss of garlands and finery and the pomp that attended them on their special days. Censers breathe out memories of the pungent scents that once seeped in heavy white clouds from the red/white charcoal within them to perfume cathedrals and small wood and thatch churches alike.

I shake my head and grab Betwixt and Between, letting their spikes dent my hand, the dull pain helping to clear my head. I concentrate on the pictures of the four evangelists on the corners of an altarpiece. The words attributed to them are engraved in my memory and I love these men for giving me tongue. Each is shown as a symbol: ox, man, eagle, and lion.

Professor Isabella comes up beside me, slipping easily into her role as lecturer.

"These symbols are probably adapted from the Assyrians, an ancient people from one of the regions through which the Hebrews journeyed. Archaeologists, that is people who study a culture by trying to guess what it was like from the ruins, have found these same emblems in the Assyrian ruins. They have painfully pieced together what we believe they represented for the people who made them: gods, heroes, sacred guardians. If only the stone and clay could speak!"

I wrinkle my brow. "The very stones prate of my whereabouts?"

She misunderstands my question. "Yes, exactly—the archaeologists study the stones to make them 'prate' of the people who once built with them. Come along, Sarah, I'm tired, and a cup of tea would ready me for our walk home."

Still reflecting, I trail after her. As we sip tea and hot chocolate in the museum cafe, I am silent, busy making plans. I don't believe that Professor Isabella, tired as she is, even notices.

The museum gives faces and personality to many of the people whose words live in my brain. Portraits show me faces of people famous and not. Some of these are only remembered because they were the subject of a famous artist. These continually mutter indignantly of their lives: the rooms in which they hung, the history of those they glorify. Over the course of many trips, I am learning to listen without becoming lost in the chatter of the inanimate spirits.

Sometimes I come out of listening to what a painting or sculpture has been telling me and find Professor Isabella quizzically watching me. I wonder what she makes of the questions that I whisper sotto voce to the art treasures. Does she hear reason in them or are they hopeless ravings of one walking the borderline of insanity?

During many visits Professor Isabella teaches me, often reading to me both before and after a visit to a certain gallery to give me reference points.

Abalone begins to participate in these lessons, first sitting with her own work on the fringes of our discussion and listening covertly, later giving up even the pretense of not attending. Sometimes she comes along to the museum, but more often she continues to live the schedule ordained by the Jungle Law of dusk to dawn.

As I grow more confident in my strange ability, I notice that Betwixt and Between are very cautious with me. They still tease me, but there is a gentleness in their words. And, even when I ask directly, they refuse to tell me about the Ivy Green Institute.

This annoys me some, for Abalone is having trouble finding records of the place. When she has time away from forgery and code-breaking, she has been searching record-bank after record-bank for some mention of the place. Occasional references have convinced her that the place did once exist, but equally, she is certain that someone or someones wish it to be forgotten.

I do not argue with my dragons except when we are alone, for I have learned that these conversations—heated as they can become—trouble Professor Isabella and Abalone more quickly than anything else that I do.

"Those who cannot remember the past are condemned to repeat it," I am arguing for the hundredth time one afternoon.

"Let the dead past bury its dead," Betwixt stonewalls.

The door unlocking interrupts us as Professor Isabella returns from the grocery store. I go to help her and when we make dinner I consider with bad temper refusing to feed Betwixt and Between.

I give in to their pleading, though. First and foremost, we are friends, and I cannot believe that they refuse me from a desire to bring me harm.

My lessons are not only in arts and literature. Abalone has

succeeded, to her surprise as well as mine, in teaching me to recognize certain of the code symbols used in programming. The idea came to her when she realized that although reading words and numbers of more than two digits still defeats me, I can memorize the pictographs used for illiterates.

After teaching me those for simple traffic commands and warnings, she decided to try and teach me programming icons. Admittedly, the process freaked me out—I had years of resistance against looking at characters that swarmed on the page or screen like guppies in my eye sockets—but slowly I caught on.

In early February, Abalone is ready to take me on another theft.

Excited, I view myself in the bathroom mirror, unable to believe that the reflection does not show how I have changed. Eyes, hair, skin—all are the same. Perhaps brighter, shinier, rosier, but nothing shows of the knowledge of people and places, nothing shows, nothing at all, of the happier, more confident Sarah.

This time, we alter our appearances in a public rest room in a near-empty office complex. Abalone is neutral in dark blue coveralls and boots, her hair under a matching billed cap. Her computer is easy to hand in a tool kit. I am dressed as a junior executive—tailored trousers and blazer of grey-blue linen. Then we go our ways.

I am not certain when things begin to go wrong. My first hint is when I see behind me lights flashing gold and orange. From my lessons, I recall that these are police lights. Even if I did not, Betwixt and Between would have been enough to remind me.

"Cops, Sarah! Step on it!" Betwixt yells.

"No," Between counters. "Pull over, everything will be fine. Abalone's got it under control."

Ignoring the muttered "I hope" that follows this declaration, I steer the vehicle to the curb. Although there are few passersby, I realize that my first reaction isn't fear—it's embarrassment. Trying to calm my frantically beating heart, I open the window as the officer walks over.

"May I have your license and vehicle registration?" he asks with a faint Spanish accent. "Wait here."

He carries them back to his partner in the police car and while she runs them through the computer, he idly drums on the front bubble pane. When his partner says something, the drumming stops and his attitude becomes tense and listening. His partner gets out to assist him as he's already walking forward.

"Ma'am, please get out of the car, slowly, so that I can see you . . ."

He continues to direct me in wooden tones through a simple body search. Mechanically, I obey. Somehow, as he is patting me down, I realize that he is nearly as nervous as I am. This does not comfort me.

In a short time, I am arrested for vehicle theft. "My" car is taken in tow and I am stashed with my belongings in the back of the patrol car.

As the patrol car pulls away from the curb, the flashing orange-and-gold lights fall on Abalone standing in an alleyway, leaning against a wall. Her expression is neutral and indifferent.

The police station that officers Martinez and Chen take me to is quiet enough that my appearance makes a stir.

"We've got ourselves an MV thief," Martinez brags. "I think it's one of the ring that's been working this area."

In the brighter light I can see that his skin is dotted with acne. He's young, a rookie.

"Hush!" Chen reminds her partner. She's an Eurasian with grey streaks in her close-cropped hair and rank stripes on her uniform shoulders.

Martinez looks chastened for all of five seconds, but he listens when Chen directs him to take my shoulder bag and inventory the contents. Then he is told to run an ID check on me, first through police records and then farther.

"Is there a secretary available? I want to get a statement," Chen asks the desk officer.

"'A,' okay?" When she nods, he slides a code flimsy to her. "Here's the key."

Chen takes me into a small room with white stuccoed walls. In the center is an oval table surrounded by several chairs. She seats me in one.

"Put your hand on those grey outlines and look at the shield projected on the wall."

I do this, recognizing the devices as similar to ones recently installed at the Home. A light flashes and I am holographed and printed.

Chen's attention is for a screen set in the table surface as she calls up the correct program from the secretary's memory. Watching, I think that I am seeing afterimages from the retina printing, for over the data streaming by in a sickening stream a single pictograph superimposes itself: a line drawing of a face, fingers held to lips: the universal illiterate symbol for silence.

Pausing, her fingers on a tab, Chen asks, "Can you read?"

I shake my head "No."

"Okay, I've set this for audio, then. Listen carefully and answer all the questions. Be sure to follow the directions. I'll be back in a few minutes."

I can feel her desire for a hot cup of coffee as she leaves. Then I watch as the door slides and merges into the wall. We had rooms like this in the Home. No windows, no door once it was closed, nothing so crude as ventilation ducts. Escapeproof.

I tug at my hair and try to listen to the computer secretary's directions.

"First, be informed before you answer any questions that anything you say can and will be used against you in a court of law. Do you understand?"

Forgetting the pictograph's warning, I whisper, "Yes."

The computer begins its interrogation, starting with name and moving into the details of the arrest. This time, I remember to stay silent. Patiently, after each question that I refuse to answer, the computer asks "Are you invoking your right to remain silent?"

I do not even answer this and after a pause it states, "For the record, subject chooses to remain silent."

The neuter voice eventually falls dumb, and I study the room. I miss Betwixt and Between intensely and hope that they are being treated well. As I think of them, I become aware of a little voice. I listen carefully and soon I hear that it is reciting the same phrase over and over in a sing-song voice.

"I've got a secret! I've got a secret!"

Standing, I search and find that the voice seems to be coming from near where the police shield is projected on the wall. I touch, but find no pattern in the rough stucco. The voice continues even as I search, perhaps more gleefully. I do not believe that it knows I can hear it.

"I've got a secret! I've got a see-cret!"

Finally, my voice low, I say, "No one ever keeps a secret as well as a child."

The chant stops, startled, then begins again more hesitantly, "I've got . . . a secret. I've . . . got a secret."

"There are no secrets better kept than the secrets that everybody guesses," I taunt.

"My secret!" the voice insists. "I've got a secret!"

"He's a wonderful talker, who has the art of telling you nothing in a great harangue," I suggest.

"I've got a secret! I do! I do!"

I turn away, yawning. "The secret of being a bore is to tell everything."

"Believe me! I've got a secret! You'd love to have my secret. Would! I've got a secret!"

I do not turn from studying the ceiling, apparently enraptured by vague patterns in the stucco. The voice from the wall cannot bear my indifference.

"Here. I'll share," it teases. "Press the blue diamonds on the center of the shield."

I hasten over and press. The wall starts to slide.

"I told you. I've got a secret!" the smug voice says.

I pat the wall as I step through the revealed door and hear the voice resume happily, "I've got a secret!"

The corridor is comfortably wide and dimly lit, even after the door slides shut behind me, from recessed panels. I follow it until it ends in another door. Through a one-way panel, I see that I am at the edge of the reception area. An officer has just brought in a group of vandals.

Heart leaping, I recognize Abalone, Peep, and Chocolate. My Pack!

As I watch, Peep and Chocolate start an argument, shoving and pushing each other. A few officers move to break them apart and are drawn into the scuffle. Under the cover of the distraction, Abalone reaches and touches a few icons on a desktop computer. Bells begin to chime from various workstations. A few more taps and drawers begin to fly open and shut. Suddenly, it begins to rain.

As chaos reigns, Abalone begins to slip off down the corridor toward the secretaries. I choose that moment to step out in front of her.

Her face shows her astonishment, but she merely indicates a side exit. I run, stopping only to scoop up my dragons from a desktop. As my hand touches them, the lights go out and a horrid cackling surges from the speakers. The rain falls harder. We vanish into the kind streets.

When we have run far enough, we stop and change our appearances some. Then Abalone takes us to a computerized restaurant, where she thrills the little wolves by making the vending machines spit out food on command.

"Wizard!" Peep laughs around a pink coconut snowball. "Really flipping!"

Abalone bows with an ironic grin, but I can tell she is pleased. For her own reasons, she rarely displayed her talents before the Pack and this homage thrills her. After eating, we send them off to the Jungle with promises to meet again.

Happy as I am with Abalone's rescue, I am still puzzled as to what went wrong. My initial unworthy thought that she set me up is gone. Once they are well fed and we are on our way home, Betwixt and Between are able to offer me some answers.

"There we were, no shit," Betwixt says, "in the interrogation room, tossed on a ledge with the junk from your bag, a red tag hung around the base of our necks. They'd finished with the ID cards and the other stuff and Martinez lifted us in his heavy hands. 'Wonder why a pretty dish like that is hauling a bit of junk like this around?' says he."

"Betwixt!" Between exclaims. "You're overdoing it."

"He did say it, didn't he?" Betwixt challenges.

"Well, yeah, but he was a jerk."

"So, let me finish!" His red eyes gleaming, Betwixt continues, "The rookie tosses us a few times, 'Hollow body,' he muses, flipping open his switchblade, 'Drugs?' The point was right at our belly when Chen came in and told him in no uncertain words that he could be accused of tampering with evidence if he wasn't careful."

"When she left," Between cuts in, "Martinez decided to heal his ego by telling another cop who wandered in how we got caught. Seems Abalone accidentally used the VIN number from a car that had been stolen. I guess when she scanned for a likely number it was neither on file as in use or as stolen. When we went driving by, eager rookie Martinez ran our number as practice and nearly lost it when he hit the jackpot."

I giggle and Abalone looks at me. She clearly is feeling guilty at putting me in danger. I wish I could tell her what Betwixt and Between have told me, but the knowledge is walled in my throat.

I settle for hugging her. "True luck consists not in holding the best cards at the table: luckiest he who knows just when to rise and go home."

She smiles ruefully. "You think I pushed my luck, Sarah? Took that bucket to the well one too many times?"

I shrug, motioning to indicate that we are free. "The net of law is spread so wide, no sinner from its sweep may hide. Its meshes are so fine and strong, they take in every child of wrong. O wondrous web of mystery! Big fishes alone escape from thee!"

Abalone squeezes me. "You're right, Sarah. Don't worry about the rent. I've enough socked by for now. I'll let this scam die for now—it's a big city."

When we get home, Professor Isabella is nervously waiting. Abalone fills her in as we sit in the kitchen drinking thick, strong hot chocolate.

"I'm glad you got her out," Professor Isabella sighs. "Clever of you to reprogram the station's computer before going in so certain icons would trigger rather extraordinary results. You really are a wizard."

"The best part," Abalone admits, her good humor returning, "was that I'd reconfigured some of the standard commands I knew they use to try and stop what I'd done. So when they tried to turn off the sprinkler system, it poured harder and when they tried to override the lights, they triggered other stuff that made it even harder for them."

She sips her cocoa. "I think most of Sarah's records were wiped. She says she got my message and didn't tell the secretary anything. I made sure her photos and prints were wiped. We couldn't salvage the fake IDs but that'll be minimal help."

"If they even try and track her," Professor Isabella agrees. "The case is minor enough and they still can return the stolen goods. What I want to know is how Sarah got out of the secretary room."

"Yeah, those things are impossible unless you know the code. Maybe I accidentally tripped it by freaking out their computer system," Abalone sounds unconvinced.

I consider trying to explain and give up almost before I begin. "Walls have ears."

They look at me and then sigh. I smile and shrug, palms held upward, but when I go to bed that night, a happy little voice sings, "I got a secret."

EIGHT

❧

FEBRUARY IS ICY AND UGLY. OFTEN WHEN PROFESSOR IS-
abella and I go to a museum (I have learned that there are
more than one—I had believed that the one was vast
enough to hold everything), Abalone insists that we take a
cab or rent a car.

She confesses shamefaced that she is doing legit freelance
programming work. However, she hastens to add that all
her ID is forged and the names are tags. I am curious why
she is so secretive about her identity. Even Professor Isabella
and I only know her by an alias.

The help Peep and Chocolate gave us has reopened our
grapevine to the Jungle. They never meet us at our apartment,
nor do we go to the Jungle. I wonder if Abalone misses Head
Wolf as much as I do. She must, but she never shows it.

Sometimes we will cruise in a rented car with tinted windows by the corner where the little wolves strut in their
tights or second skin trousers. Under the watchful eyes of

the Four, we'll buy a night of the boys' time. Then the two Tail Wolves become little boys for a night.

"We can't do it too often," Abalone cautions one night when I start weeping after dropping the boys off. "We can't make them soft. They've got to stay fierce, keep their pride. Otherwise, when some horny old creep comes after them, they'll forget that they're doing this because they're of the Pack. Then they'll cry or forget to smile . . ."

She lets herself trail off. To mollify me, Professor Isabella suggests that we make certain that the boys meet Jerome and learn the location of When I Was Hungry. I agree, eager to see Jerome again.

Soon after this, Abalone comes home ashen-faced and shaking harder than the frigid day could account for. Without pausing to remove her wrap, she drops something into my lap, then into Professor Isabella's.

I look down wonderingly at the picture of a girl with cream-colored hair and jade green eyes. She is something like me, I think.

"Brighton Rock!" Professor Isabella reads. "'Spot our Girl and Win!' Why it's a candy ad! But what is Sarah doing on the advertisement? It can't be a coincidence!"

Abalone hangs up her cape and pours herself tea before plopping down on the floor.

"I don't believe in coincidence—not where Sarah's concerned." She turns a card over. "Listen: 'Creamy outside, tart lime inside.' That's just an excuse for using Sarah's face on these cards."

"I see." Professor Isabella carefully bookmarks the volume of *Don Quixote* that she's been reading to me. "Where did you get these?"

"I had work up near that police station where Sarah and I had our mishap. I don't know what made me pick the card out of the gutter, but when I did I recognized Sarah right off. I snooped around a bit then and discovered that they've been handed out since about a week after our scrape. Lots of people are hot on them—wait for new cards with clues and stuff. Heck, they're even buying the candy to get the cards."

"And if you spot the girl," Professor Isabella muses, shaking her head, "you get a prize. Why, they've turned the entire City into a means for finding Sarah."

"I'm sure of it," Abalone agrees. "I did some scouting. The places where these are being handed out most thickly are near our police station and around the Home and the Jungle, our hunting grounds."

"Not here," Professor Isabella asks worriedly.

"No. Apparently you two have been careful enough with your trips. Won't last. Someone at some museum will remember the weird, pretty girl with the dragon who stands muttering at walls. They'll assume that the fruitcake bit is meant to get attention."

I arch an eyebrow at her. "A little nonsense now and then is relished by the best of men."

"Sorry, Sarah." Abalone has the grace to blush. "I only mean how you seem to people who don't know how much sense you have under all that hair."

Mollified, I reply, "We be of one blood, ye and I."

Abalone presses her lips together. "That's what's so bad about this, Sarah. Not even the Master Words will protect you—even from your own Pack. Remember, Mowgli was nearly sold out by his own Pack members because they were just young and thought with their bellies and not with their hearts."

"Baloo," I say, pointing to her, then to Professor Isabella. "Akela."

"That's right, dear." Professor Isabella laughs. "Your teacher bear and your old, grey wolf. I wonder if Head Wolf . . ."

She stops as Abalone glowers at her. There is a sick silence. Then Abalone speaks, her words clipped and as cold as if to a stranger.

"Only the foolish turned against Mowgli."

"I'm sorry, Abalone. I forget myself."

"Don't."

Although Abalone and Professor Isabella would have been happiest keeping me inside the apartment full-time, they rapidly learn that this is impossible. Recordings, visual and audio alike, do not hold my attention unless someone else watches with me. I cannot read or write and sewing occupies me only so long.

Professor Isabella reads to me, but when she becomes weary and her attention wanders so does mine. Abalone gives me lessons, but after a certain point I am unable to concentrate on the little icons, no matter what pictures or sounds she programs as my reward.

I assign myself the task of keeping the apartment clean, but these chores rarely take more than two hours. In the end, Betwixt and Between watch out the window with me or I talk to the old stone walls of the building. They are somewhat more responsive than the wall in the police station, but often I must ask many questions to get a response. The furniture is impossible.

I find that talking to the walls or to Betwixt and Between for too long worries Professor Isabella. Soon, ashamed at myself, I feign emotionally charged conversations in order to get her to take me outside.

Abalone always disguises me. She has ruled out dyeing my hair, preferring the variety of her wig collection. My eyes are hidden by contact lenses or sunglasses, my features by cosmetics. Professor Isabella also has a few disguises and chuckles about playing "dress up" at her age.

The computer door guard doesn't care how we look as long as finger and retina prints match what is filed.

Meanwhile, Abalone is tracking down Ivy Green Institute. Often she is frustrated by dead end after dead end.

We persevere in this fashion for some time. Tracing the Brighton Rock candy campaign, we note that venders in the now ominous cream and jade are being posted at museums. Professor Isabella decides that we should avoid these even in disguise and takes me to concerts, plays, and zoos.

How well I follow concerts varies widely. Often I end up listening to the Hall rather than the music. Plays delight me, however, especially old friends like Shakespeare and Shaw, whose words, like the Bible's, I think of as my own.

Zoos are a problem. I have not been much around animals. They were forbidden in the Home and the pets of the Free People tended to stay near their handlers. However, my timidity is not an excuse; Professor Isabella is determined to educate me about animals in more than theory.

We go and look at the caged creatures and I finally see wolves, bears, panthers, and owls in the fur. Professor Isabella must explain that there are no dragons like Betwixt and Between in zoos, but she shows me lizards and snakes. My dragons amuse themselves by making snide comments at the expense of their unicameral kinfolk.

These visits continue until I lose some of my fear. Then she takes me to the Petting Zoo, where there are animals to touch. Visit after visit, I refuse to do more than quickly pat a silken nose or hastily feed food pellets to an eager goat or llama.

Finally, however, I consent to make friends with the guinea pigs, starting by feeding one or another from the far side of a carrot or string bean and proudly progressing to the day I actually hold a stout black-and-white boar with whorls like flowers in his fur.

We come home to tell Abalone, full of triumph.

"Sarah actually held a guinea pig today," Professor Isabella announces almost before we are in the door.

"If thine enemy hunger, feed him," I offer, thinking how less sharp the teeth looked when chewing on a carrot.

"You held a guinea pig and fed it?" Abalone asks.

I nod happily.

"Great," Abalone is clearly impressed. "Not bad at all. Oh, by the way, I located Ivy Green Institute today, even cracked some of the files."

. . . .

"Not bad." Professor Isabella smiles and winks at me.

I smile, but I am not certain that I am ready to learn more. What I have discovered has hardly made me happy. Still, even as I am trying to shape the protest, Abalone is beginning to pull files up from her tappety-tap's memory.

"Sarah. There's a birth date here and a description." She drums the table. "This next is what gets me—no parents are listed but there is a brother, Dylan, and a sister, Eleanora."

Dylan. Pale of hair. Eyes almost without color. Dylan. Brother.

I shudder. Betwixt and Between call for me from my bag. I grasp toward them, but the room is spinning, the floor coming to meet my head. My hands are too slow to catch me.

When I awake, I am on a sofa in the living room. Betwixt and Between are propped near me. Four ruby eyes are bright with tears.

I reach and brush away the tears. Funny how in all the time Betwixt and Between have been with me, I never learned until now that dragons purr.

I am scratching the dragons under their chins when Abalone comes in, a beer in one hand, her tappety-tap in the other. Seeing me awake, she crows with delight and slides to her knees by the sofa.

"How y'doing, Sarah? Feel better?"

"I was thirsty and you gave me drink," I hint.

Grinning, she hands me the beer can. It is almost full and I must sit up so as not to dribble on myself. Refreshed and feeling clearer-headed, I hand her back the can.

"Enough?"

"Drink deeply, but never too deep," I remind her.

"The Law—the Jungle—seems so far away," she muses. "Not real. Dozens of kids living strung up and strung out in a big tin can. Weird. I kind of miss it."

"Sarah's awake?" Professor Isabella comes from her room, a book in one hand. "I'm delighted. I suspect all the new things today have been enough to unsettle her."

"I'm not sure," Abalone says, sucking on her beer. "She took to the Jungle easy enough and you've been teaching her gently enough. No, she seemed to flip when I mentioned Dylan."

"Yes," Professor Isabella nods. "We've both been suspicious that our girl knows more than she can tell us. You may be triggering some painful memories."

"When to the sessions of sweet silent thought," I add, "I summon up remembrance of things past, I sigh the lack of many a thing I sought, and with old woes new wail my dear time's waste."

"Still," Abalone says, "whenever you're ready, Sarah, I think we need to review the rest of what I've found."

She picks up one of the "Brighton Rock" cards and turns it in her hands before speaking again.

"We know someone wants Sarah and, frankly, I don't understand all the psychobabble in her records. I can research, but it seems a waste of time with you two here."

Professor Isabella touches my forehead, softly, lightly. She pushes back my hair.

"There is no fever, Sarah. Are you strong enough to go on?"

"I am a brother to dragons, a companion to owls," I state defiantly, and my dragons thrum approvingly.

. . . .

"Okay, then." Abalone flips open the tappety-tap and Professor Isabella sits by my feet on the sofa.

Betwixt and Between are reassuringly strong, but I remember their tears. I will learn, but I will not go away from them as Dylan did.

Abalone looks at me and I nod.

"Here we go then." She strokes my past up from her memory. "Like I said before you decided to crash your hard drive, Sarah, these records list a brother, Dylan, and a sister, Eleanora. When I get a feel for the Institute's system, I'll try and learn more about what's with them."

"Wait," Professor Isabella asks. "You said the Institute's system. I'd assumed that it was defunct—no more."

"Me, too," Abalone says, "but I think 'gone underground' would be a more accurate description. The Ivy Green Institute is still out there and I suspect that it wants Sarah back."

I shudder, flashes of memory surfacing. Rolling hills, manicured lawns, all seen only through windows. I am small, but if I pull over a stool, I can see. Sometimes Dylan watches with me, his dragon close at hand.

"She's getting white again." I hear Professor Isabella's voice as from a distance. "Give me that!"

I taste cocoa so hot that it burns and the burning forces away the memories. Taking the mug, I smile as confidently as I can. A few more sips and Abalone continues.

"The coding here is screwy, but I've finally resolved it into a chart or graph. Thing is, I can't quite figure out what is being measured here."

Professor Isabella leans forward and looks. "There should be a key for those colors. Did you check for hypertext files?"

"Too obvious." Abalone swats herself and searches; in a few moments she has superimposed a block of orange on the pale blue screen. My head swims when I try to read the text, so I lean back and listen.

"The black line indicates something called 'magical thinking'; the red line is empathy; the purple is memory: lavender for short-term, violet for long-term," Abalone reads, shaping her mouth around unfamiliar jargon.

"What was that chart titled, Abalone?"

Abalone flips off the hypertext. "'Brain Scan Mapping.' Weird. I didn't know the brain could be mapped."

"Well, it's not completely, but my guess is that a place like Ivy Green Institute would be very skilled at such things. Look through your pirated files, my girl, and see if you find anything further on these terms."

Abalone taps a few codes in what I recognize now as a search sequence. Finally, she shakes her head.

"There is nothing I can find quickly, but there's a lot of garbage in here, programming I'm not set to read. Let me have a day to clean things up."

"Fine. I'll do some research. I know what empathy and memory are, but this magical thinking bears further investigation."

I prop myself up on the sofa. "They also serve who only stand and wait."

"Or take a long nap," Professor Isabella says, pushing me back and drawing the covers over me and my dragons.

By the next evening, Professor Isabella has finished her research and Abalone has brought the Ivy Green files into a readable form. I have spent the day nervously housecleaning and every surface glistens. The air is heavy with the scent of polish.

"Who wants to start?" Abalone asks, propping her computer on her knees and leaning comfortably against a wall.

"Let me," Professor Isabella requests. "I've been reading since yesterday and have come up with some rather interesting information."

"About this magical thinking?"

"Yes."

Drumming the floor with my heels, I suggest, "Make haste, the better foot before."

"Briefly, then," Professor Isabella says, "magical thinking is a concept referring to the irrational tendency of people to associate the qualities of the animate with the inanimate. In earlier days, this took the form of imagining that spirits dwelt in items or places. The practice is common. The Japanese Shinto is centered around spirits or 'kami,' for example. The ancient Greeks imagined natural spirits—naiads, sylphs, dryads, which inhabited water, air, and trees."

She pauses to check her notes. "The temptation to lecture further is overwhelming, but let me move closer to my point. Even though people no longer formally acknowledge their belief in spirits for the inanimate, the practice remains. Athletes are particularly conspicuous for their belief that a certain 'lucky' item—shoe, shirt, bat—affects their play. Children insist that a certain treasured toy is 'real'—not a thing of cloth or plastic. Even otherwise balanced, rational individuals will attribute traits of life to an unliving object."

I nod. This makes perfect sense to me—so much so that I wonder at the need for a lengthy explanation. Abalone looks skeptical.

"You mean, like superstition?"

"Yes, but more." Professor Isabella raises a finger. "Imagine if you can someone, an actual person if possible, whom you truly hate."

The expression that flickers across Abalone's face is so ugly and intense that there is no doubt that she has fastened on someone quite specific.

"Now think of someone you like and trust—Head Wolf, for example."

Abalone nods.

Professor Isabella smiles. "Now imagine I have two identical shirts here and I tell you that one was worn by Head Wolf and one by the other person. Which would you choose to wear?"

"Why, Head Wolf's!"

"Even if I told you that both shirts had been laundered several times since being worn?"

Abalone grins. "Yep, even if."

"And if I gave you the wrong shirt by accident and you learned that you were wearing this other shirt?"

Abalone shakes as if to rid herself of an uncomfortable feeling.

"I wouldn't like it very much—I'd feel sick."

"Magical thinking." Professor Isabella gestures, palms outward. "No reason to it, just a human quirk. Or is it?"

"Go on," Abalone prompts. "How does this tie into Sarah?"

"I suspect that she . . . Well, pull your files, dear. I don't just want to toss out guesses."

"Okay." Abalone works for a moment. "There's a series of these Brain Scan test charts. My guess from the dates is that they are the results of tests done at different times."

"Yes, that makes sense."

"Then there are these charts." Abalone angles the screen so that we can see. "They're comparing three sets of results. The colors stand for different people. Most often, Dylan, Sarah, and Eleanora. Sometimes other people."

"Hmm, other test subjects or possibly controls." Professor Isabella drums the table. "Any write-ups on Sarah?"

"Some, really jargon filled but, from what I get, the fact that she didn't talk made it tough for them to guess what she had. They knew she had something, not how much. Dylan seems to be the big favorite; Eleanora scored way up there on memory, but lower in empathy and nearly null in magical thinking. After a point, she isn't shown on as many charts, usually just an annual survey."

"Sarah's files end when?"

"About when she must have been transferred to the Home. I'll do some more hunting to see if either of the others have later records."

"Very good. However, what you have found thus far confirms some of my guesses." Professor Isabella steeples her gnarled fingers. "I believe that Sarah and her siblings were part of a project to cultivate magical thinking. Whether they were the result of breeding for the tendency or something else, I cannot guess at this point. What I can guess is that the experiment was most successful with Dylan. His charted abilities are higher than Sarah's in magical thinking and empathy. Sarah's memory is listed as better. Eleanora, although extraordinary in some ways, was apparently a washout from the experimenter's point of view. What do you think so far?"

I nod. This matches my awakening memories some, although Eleanora is but faintly remembered and those memories see her as near grown while I am quite small. I doubt that I saw her often.

"I pass with relief from the tossing sea of Cause and Theory," I comment, "to the ground of Result and Fact."

"Yeah," Abalone agrees, "but what I don't get is why anyone would want to create superstitious people."

"Ah," Professor Isabella smiles. "Not superstitious— magical thinkers—people who so believe in or perhaps sense the living spirits in the inanimate world that what is dead matter to you and me might somehow be able to communicate with them."

"Sharp old bird, ain't she," Betwixt comments.

"Sharper than most," Between cuts in. "Now, hush."

I scratch them both at the base of the necks and listen.

"Whoosh!" Abalone shakes her head so that the locks dance like candle flames. "That's a lot to believe: Sarah able to talk to 'things.' She can't even talk to people."

"I'm not certain that Sarah can talk to things any more easily than she can to us. I've noticed that even when she's muttering to herself she uses the same quote patterns as the rest of the time. What I am saying is that things may be able to talk to Sarah."

"What do you think, Sarah?" Abalone asks. "Has the professor hit on the truth?"

I hesitate. The professor's theories about Ivy Green and investigation into magical thinking are tantalizing. They fit many curious holes in my memory, holes that I am beginning to be suspicious about. I should remember more. I had been nearly an adolescent when I left there for the Home. And some memories—of Dylan especially—have been coming back so vividly.

I shake myself out of conjecture and try to honestly answer Abalone's question.

"'Tis strange, but true; for truth is always strange—Stranger than fiction," I finally say.

"Oh, wow!" Abalone's eyes get round. "If we could only be sure about this."

Professor Isabella smiles slyly. "I think we have proof already, Abalone. When I take Sarah to a museum, she often spends time muttering to a painting or sculpture. I started noticing that she was quoting things I had never read to her—but I dismissed this, thinking someone else must have taught her and she's simply remembering. You, however, have had a more definitive experience."

"What?" Abalone is clearly puzzled.

"What did Sarah say when you asked her how she got out of the secretary's cell at the police station?"

"She said something about the walls having ears," Abalone says slowly. "Oh, flip-it! You mean . . ."

"That's right. What if for Sarah the walls don't only have ears, but mouths as well? What if the wall told her how to get out?"

She looks quizzically at me. In memory I hear a happy voice chirping "I got a secret" and smile.

"Day unto day uttereth speech, and night unto night showeth knowledge," I reply, nodding.

"Let's test this out," Abalone says, leaping to her feet. "Sarah, can you hear anything talk?"

Again I am at a loss how to answer honestly. I am beginning to believe I might be able to hear anything speak if I try hard enough, but on the occasions I have—such as the terrible day in the Jungle when memory of Dylan opened my mind—the rush of voices has been more than I can handle without being overwhelmed.

I shake my head, reluctantly telling a half-truth.

"I am a brother to dragons, a companion to owls," I suggest, proffering Betwixt and Between.

"You're saying you can hear them?" Abalone confirms.

When I nod, she goes on, "What I have in mind is for Sarah to go into her room and close the door. Then we'll whisper something to Betwixt and Between and if she can really communicate with it, she'll be able to tell us what we said."

"I'll agree," Professor Isabella says, "if we use a quote from some work that Sarah knows. I've noticed that she can't parrot anything—she needs to attach importance to it. I suspect that this is a side result of her empathy."

"Flash with me," Abalone agrees. "Are you game, Sarah?"

"Yes." I nod solemnly.

"Us, too," Between says, "and thanks so much for asking while you're at it."

I go to my room and sit on my bed, contemplating the

oddness of this all. Around me, I can hear the comfortable grumbles of the building's brick walls as they twinge and settle in the chill and damp.

A rap on the door summons me. Abalone and Professor Isabella look expectant and Betwixt and Between sit in the middle of the rug, looking smug.

I pick them up and scratch Between's eye ridge and Betwixt's jawline coaxingly. The dragons sigh happily.

Between says, *"Merchant of Venice,* One, three. The bit about the devil and scripture."

I smile, aware that the dragons are salvaging their pride by being a bit difficult. Then I look at Abalone and Professor Isabella.

"The devil can cite Scripture for his purpose. An evil soul, producing holy witness, is like a villain with a smiling cheek, a goodly apple rotten at the heart: O, what a goodly outside falsehood hath!"

"She got it!" Abalone says excitedly.

"This is hardly a controlled experiment," Professor Isabella murmurs, "but, ruling out telepathy and other unlikely phenomena, I agree. She does seem to have it."

They are so excited that even Betwixt and Between willingly accede to further tests. When we have finished some hours later and are sipping tea with honey, Abalone suddenly looks apprehensive.

"If Sarah can talk to things, does that mean she can, like, well, learn stuff about people? Private stuff?"

Professor Isabella smiles softly. "Probably. But the question isn't really 'can she?' it is 'would she?' isn't it?"

"Yeah," Abalone says, scuffing her feet on the linoleum.

"Once I learned how to crack files, I got really interested in finding out what other people were hiding. I guess I'm wondering if Sarah is like that, too."

"Ask her," Professor Isabella suggests.

"Well, Sarah, I figure you know I've been kinda secretive about some stuff. Did you ever, like, check me out?"

I shake my head, patting her hand. "A secret's safe 'twixt you, me, and the gatepost."

"Does this make me the gatepost?" Professor Isabella chuckles. "Honey, you didn't even ask, did you?"

I shake my head. "Those friends thou hast and their adoption tried, grapple them to thy soul with hoops of steel."

Abalone squeezes me. "You're all right, Sarah. Y'know, weird as they make them, but all right."

Smile fading, Professor Isabella says, "I'm worried. If Ivy Green let Sarah go something like fifteen years ago, why do they—or someone—want her back now?"

"Now?" Abalone shakes her head. "I'm not sure, but I can think of lots of reasons for wanting someone who can do what she can do."

"We can keep asking questions," Professor Isabella says, "but you do realize what this means. We have to get Sarah out of here—this is no longer just keeping her from getting recommitted. This is keeping her from getting kidnapped."

Abalone considers this. "What do you have in mind?"

"I was thinking we could go out into the countryside, get Sarah to a place where she doesn't have to be walled in but where she can go out of the house without someone identifying her as the Brighton Rock girl."

"I'm not sure that she'll be any safer," Abalone objects, "and I'll find hiding my tracks harder away from a city. Here I can go to any of a thousand places to link my computer—anyone traces me and they find a rented room or a closed office. Out there . . ."

As Abalone trails off, Professor Isabella nods.

"Perhaps there is safety in numbers. We'll need to dye Sarah's hair and she'll need to wear contacts to recolor her eyes. We can't take risks with wigs now."

I strike a pose. "I dream of Jeanie with the light brown hair."

"I was thinking of red—a less-flamboyant shade than those that Abalone favors—it would go well with your coloring. Perhaps we can manage dark brown eyes."

I nod, well pleased with the image. I had been disappointed that they hadn't disguised me more thoroughly earlier—the romantic image of it enthralled me, but then I had heard Professor Isabella saying, "It broke my heart to have to hide her this way—at least at home she can be herself."

But two days later finds me with auburn hair and dark brown eyes and red corneas. The cosmetic contacts that Abalone has brought me burn somewhat. She promises me that she will bring me other sets.

And then we go on living. Professor Isabella takes me to museums and as February moves into March, the Brighton Rock ads are withdrawn from the market. The candy stays on, however. Apparently, the ad campaign had been useful for something.

One afternoon, I am changing myself into the brown-eyed stranger in the mirror when there is a banging in the direction of the living room window. One contact in, one contact out, I rush into the living room, bumping into Professor Isabella.

As we are jostling to get through the door, Abalone, still scrubbing sleep from her eyes, steps into the room.

"Damn!"

She runs forward and shoves the window open. Two small figures fall into the room. I recognize Chocolate's dreadlocks and hear Conejito Moreno cursing indignantly from the bottom of the pile.

"Peep! Chocolate!"

Forgetting that we are in hiding, I joyfully raise the boys to their feet, removing Conejito Moreno's ears from beneath Peep's foot and handing him to his friend.

Close to tears, the little Tail Wolf clings to me.

"Abalone! Sarah! We be of one blood, ye and I, and *Madre de Dios*, they have the Head Wolf!"

Her eyes widening and suspicion bordering her mouth, Abalone checks outside before shutting the window. Flicking the lock into place, she turns.

"Slow, Peep. Don't flip. How'd you find us?"

"We look for two days, Abalone," Chocolate says. "It not easy to find you, but we got lotta ears and eyes, but this no matters. What we here for is not friendly visit. They got Head Wolf."

"They?" Professor Isabella asks, simultaneously with Abalone.

"Yeah," Peep is shaking too hard to continue, so Chocolate fills in.

"They, the Home from where Sarah come. Two days ago. Come and get him with the police and all when he go to do some fix-up on the tromp the eye painting over the east Jungle entrance. Take him so fast that not even the Four can help. We come here 'cause Sarah know that Home, maybe she know why they want Head Wolf."

"Shit!" Abalone has hooked up her tappety-tap and is fingering icons and pulling files. "Let me tap into the Home."

Professor Isabella leads the frightened boys to the sofa and I go for coffee with lots of sugar and cream. As I pour and mix, I listen.

"What is the Pack doing about this?" Professor Isabella asks.

"Not much good," Peep says. "Most of the *lupos* were sleeping when Head Wolf got taken—y'know the Law."

"Why was Head Wolf out in the daytime?" Professor Isabella asks. "He's usually fairly strict about keeping his own rules."

"Some gang come and slash and spray," Chocolate says. "The canvas need quick fix now and then Head Wolf was checking how much work he need to do."

"Then the police come," Peep says. "We saw it all, 'cause we had stayed out for breakfast at Jerome's place."

"Too damn little," Chocolate mutters angrily. "We too damn little and too damn scared and by the time we get some of the Four it too late. But we run after fast and check that what we hear is true. They take Head Wolf to the nuthouse."

My pulse is beating too fast. This is too much to be coincidence. My hands start trembling so hard that I slosh the hot, sweet coffee onto the rug. No one but the rug notices.

"Got it!" Abalone growls through bared teeth. "The boys are cool. Head Wolf is in the Home. By the Opened Door that freed me! They have a record on him, an old one."

"Really old or fabricated, Abalone?" Professor Isabella asks.

Abalone taps and new characters and colors overlay the ones already on the screen. She studies for a moment.

"Really old, I think. Some of these programming commands are outdated. Only a truly paranoid forger"—she grins briefly—"would bother to write a new file in an obscure older mode—especially if all they needed was a reason to grab him."

"Do you know where they got him?" Peep asks.

"Pretty good idea," Abalone says, "and I can narrow it down."

"Good! Then we go, we get the man out of there," Chocolate says, already on his feet.

"Not yet," Professor Isabella countermands, pressing him back to his seat. "We need to think on this."

Abalone raises cold eyes, her hand rests on her shirt, touching the hidden tattoo. The Tail Wolves look guardedly at the older woman. Even I am aware of feeling a sudden flash of hostility.

"We aren't leaving him there," Abalone states.

"No, I didn't expect you would," Professor Isabella looks stern. "And neither do 'They'—Brighton Rock failed. Now they're asking us to bring Sarah to them. Head Wolf is just bait, an engraved invitation."

Abalone nods impatiently. "I guessed, but we don't need

to bring Sarah. Me, the Four, the boys—we can bust him out. Sarah'll be safe."

I squeak indignantly. Professor Isabella smiles coldly.

"Why have they taken him to the Home? Because only Sarah knows it well—even my information, if they even know of me, is dated. My guess is that the only way we will get in is if Sarah is with us."

"Us?"

"I may be of one blood with no Wolf," Professor Isabella says with another cold smile, "but even Kaa fought with the Seonee Wolves when his friend was in danger. I'll help as I can."

Professor Isabella insists that the Tail Wolves sleep. Agreeing, Abalone arranges for a message to be sent to the Jungle. Later, she will slip out to meet with the Four. Meantime, she calls up files on the Home, on Head Wolf.

"My oh My oh My oh My," Abalone murmurs. "Shoulda known. Shoulda known this is how they'd see him."

Her hand covers the picture between her breasts, a picture I suddenly realize was drawn by needle and pain and dye by Head Wolf himself with the same art through which he makes stone into wood and metal into paper. A twinge of envy touches me as I sense an intimacy beyond mere sex between this wild forger and her chosen lawgiver.

Professor Isabella leans over to look at the screen. Her tongue touches her dry lips as she reads the data.

"Ah, yes," Professor Isabella agrees. "I suspected as much: paranoid with delusions, homicidal. Chemical equalizers unsuccessful. Quite a record here."

Her musing trails off and she gestures with sudden urgency for Abalone to scroll the data upward.

"Did you see this?" she includes me with a glance. "He was once within the Mental Rehab system, a resident of the Home like both of us. But he was never released; he escaped."

"Escaped?" Abalone scrolls the data. "Why would he have stayed so close? That's crazy!"

"Precisely," Professor Isabella chuckles dryly.

I blush as I recall a monologue, half-forgotten in the drowsy indolence following lovemaking.

"To pull the very whiskers of death," I say.

Abalone looks at me, "Head Wolf said that to you?"

I nod.

"He got a kick out of it then," she says, "out of knowing he was hidden right under their eyes and that they couldn't touch him."

"Couldn't?" Professor Isabella tilts her head. "Or didn't care to? Still, Abalone, I recognize this code. It means they have him scheduled for transfer within twenty-four hours. They may have decided that we weren't going to respond and wanted him out of the way."

"If it were done when 'tis done, then 'twere well it were done quickly," I say.

"*Macbeth*, Act One, scene seven," Abalone replies, reaching for her night cloak.

"Lines one and two," Professor Isabella adds, her words punctuated by the sharp, closing snap of the door as Abalone heads out into the night.

NINE

THE NEXT NIGHT COMES COLD AND DARK, DARK, THAT IS, IN
the shadows and alleyways through which we make our approach on the Home. In the skies above, where we might
seek omens of favor, the ambient city lights have washed
out the stars as too much milk washes the taste from coffee.

We rattle through the subway tunnels to a rendezvous
point where Abalone says we will be met by the Four.

"They've abandoned the Jungle," she had told us when
she returned the night before. "The place isn't safe any
longer. Even the social workers are daring to come there
now—got a couple of the Cubs. Gray Brother told me that
he and Head Wolf had anticipated such possibilities and
that there are other hideouts. None so good as the Jungle,
but they'll do for now."

When we skulk our way to the rendezvous point, we are
met almost immediately by a slight figure, white and grey in
the shadows: Edelweiss. Murmuring the Master Words for

greeting, she slips a hood over her icy hair and beckons for us to follow.

We do. Me, once again cream-haired and jade-eyed, though the former is mostly concealed by a cap and the latter behind tinted shades. Betwixt and Between ride in a daypack that leaves my hands free. Professor Isabella is next, incongruous in her tidy tweed slacks and matching jacket. Her soft-soled pumps click slightly against the sidewalk as she walks, her breath coming a little fast. Abalone is once again blue-lipped and fire-topped, her wolf tattoo shows through a cutaway in her charcoal skintights, her tappety-tap hanging from a broad belt around her waist.

I nearly do not recognize where we have come until Edelweiss is pushing the door open. Then the scent of stale coffee and cream of mushroom soup wafts from the humid interior and I know.

Professor Isabella whispers, "When I Was Hungry."

I can hear puzzlement in her voice.

We walk down an L-shaped hallway, through the darkened kitchen, toward the rumble of voices. I recognize several and realize that my heart is quickening in anticipation of rejoining the Pack.

Anticipation flips into dismay as Edelweiss leads the way into the pale fluorescent light of the main cafeteria. The long plastic tables have been shoved into a rough U and the Pack members lounge on tabletops, chairs, and floor. In the center of the group, sitting stiffly on a garish orange chair, is Jerome.

No bonds restrain him, yet he sits as if tied. Only his eyes move, watching the young men and women with fear and betrayal. I wonder to how many he has given food and shelter.

Although Edelweiss means to keep us in the L, I circle right and run forward, skidding on the linoleum floor and ending up on my knees by Jerome's chair.

He puts out a hand to steady me and though his grip is strong, I feel an almost imperceptible trembling.

"You know these people, Sarah?"

I nod. "I was a stranger and ye took me in."

"So that's where you went. In all your visits, you never told me." Jerome's hand does not leave my arm, but his attention shifts outward. "What do all of you want here?"

Grey Brother, the leader of the Four, runs his finger along the wide scar beneath his right eye. The scar is genuine, his lime green hair and orange eyes are not. He caresses the howling wolf tattooed on his left forearm before speaking.

"We're gonna free Head Wolf," he says, "and you're going to get us in to him. We know you work in the nuthouse."

"The nuthouse—the Home, y'mean?" Jerome asks, and at Grey Brother's nod continues. "Sure, I work there, but in the cafeteria. I never go much beyond the kitchen areas. I don't know where your friend is."

"No?" Grey Brother weighs and dismisses this. "So, you gotta have a pass. Open the door for us and draw us a map. We'll go from there."

"Pass? Sure, but it's only good if the security computer clears it and at this hour they won't clear me without some personnel checking." Jerome chuckles without humor.

"They're always worried about the staff stealing from the place."

The gathered Pack members mutter angrily, nervously.

"Shit!" Grey Brother says, flipping open his knife. "You're no good to us."

I stand and spread my arms, interposing myself between Jerome and the angry youth. Words are not necessary and I stare, willing him to remember me as one of Head Wolf's favorites.

Whether he does or not, he steps back and the knife vanishes up his sleeve.

"Sarah, I won't hurt him—now—but what are we going to do about getting to Head Wolf?"

I meet the orange eyes. "The next way home's the farthest way about."

He studies me. The room becomes so quiet that I can hear Abalone and Professor Isabella coming in past Edelweiss. I don't look to them—this must be my victory or Grey Brother will never treat me as an equal.

After what seems too long, the leader says, "You're offering to get us in there? Do you really remember the place?"

I laugh. "The very remembrance of my former misfortune proves a new one to me."

"I'll take that as 'yes,'" Grey Brother decides. "Abalone, you're with us on this?"

"If you promise not to harm Jerome," she says. "I can get you through the security, better than he could."

Grey Brother stares at her. "He's seen us."

"Doesn't matter. If we get Head Wolf away, they'll never

find us. If we don't, what he knows can't hurt us any worse."

Again he nods. "He can wait the night here and go free in the morning."

"Let me call my wife!" Jerome cuts in. "She'll worry herself sick."

Something melts the hard lines of Grey Brother's face. "She will? Then we'll get you home. Bumblebee, Tapestry, when we've been away an hour, escort the man home."

Jerome's eyes widen with surprise. "I'll keep quiet, brother. I don't want to get involved with this. Some of those doctors ask questions in ways I don't want to try. Just let me go home."

He whispers softly, so only I can hear, "Take care, Sarah. I don't know who scares me more—your friends or your enemies."

An hour or so later, we are ready to go. Abalone has learned that Head Wolf is being held in a maximum security area on the tenth floor. The plan she and Grey Brother evolve involves various feints to draw attention away from our goal.

"They must be tightly timed," Abalone cautions, "or we'll be dealing with the police, too. I will reroute what backup calls I can, but I may miss some."

Grey Brother briefs his various teams, then turns away without another glance for them. He has insisted on heading the group that will break into Head Wolf's cell. He has insisted equally strongly that Abalone remain outside.

"You don't need to be inside," he states flatly. "What

you're doing is too important to let you get flipped off by some stray shot. Sorry, Shellfish, you're out."

Abalone stares at him with such pure anger I fear that he will melt. Then she nods stiffly.

"Professor Isabella goes. She may be slow, but she knows the Home and she understands Sarah's talk. You'll need that, Grey Brother. Trust me."

He agrees and so I find myself preparing to reenter the Home through an infrequently used fire port on the eighth floor. Our group is small: Grey Brother, Professor Isabella, me, and a member of the Four tagged Midline. Peep operates the hovercat, wafting us silently to the iris in the wall.

On cue, the iris cycles open when we pause. Faintly, we hear shouts and know that the first diversion has begun. Without a word, we move.

Midline goes first, a slender Oriental with unnaturally golden skin. He steadies himself with a lean, muscled arm, then he is gone into the corridor. When there is no alarm, we follow, Grey Brother courteously assisting Professor Isabella.

The familiar scents of antiseptic not quite concealing urine and illness make me shudder. From my pack, Betwixt and Between warble, in duet, "Mid pleasures and palaces though we may roam, be it ever so humble, there's no place like home."

I shush them, for though I know that none of the other three can hear them, I need my ears. Concentrating tentatively, I hear whispers from wall, door, carpeting.

Midline trots a few steps ahead, Grey Brother covers the rear. We make no effort to hide from the security cameras.

If Abalone is doing as promised, they will record nothing but empty corridor, white walls, and light green carpet.

Our goal is a service crawlway that will take us up between floors without triggering the alarms in either stairwell or elevator. I listen for it and find it, locating its slight complaint over an aching hinge.

I tap Grey Brother, pointing to where I can hear the door. Squinting, he looks up, nods. Midline braces him and he opens the hatch, hanging the portable ladder he has carried wrapped around his waist. When this is done, Midline climbs up. We ascend after.

All of this is done without sound, so I hear clearly. The hatch sighs on opening, the ceiling moans when the ladder grapples dig in, the metal rungs in the access tunnel gasp in anticipation of our feet, wheeze as we pass.

For the first time, I wonder at the humanness of these sounds. Why should something with neither lungs nor nerves express pain or displeasure as a human might? Some filter vibrates loose behind my eyes as I contemplate this; my senses tremble. I fight back a strong urge to retch.

No. I cannot lose control. Suspecting that to hear and see as the inanimate do would drive me madder than I am, I push away the thoughts. The power to perceive so is there— but the symbols my mind chooses are safer.

Only Betwixt and Between notice my lapse. They rumble reassurance as we continue to climb.

On the tenth floor, we emerge into a small bathroom, tiled in pale blue. A coatrack near the door bears two heavy coats and a hat.

"Nurses?" Midline whispers.

"Guards," Grey Brother replies with a quick shake of his head. "Abalone says that they have a roving patrol of the floor. We'll need to watch for them."

Their conversation does not keep me from listening for what the tenth floor can tell me. Already, I am learning to filter out the inconsequential—a different skill than the simple defensive blocking that made me nearly deaf to all but those close to me like Betwixt and Between. With gratifying speed, I find what I am hunting for; even before Midline eases the door to the corridor open, I know the direction we must go.

I wait until we come to a cross corridor and Midline hesitates. Then I tap him and gesture right. My guidance is accepted without question and I feel a surge of power. I am almost disappointed when he takes his next lead from something stenciled in black on a wall.

But soon such pettiness is washed back by a tingle of warning. I know we are nearing Head Wolf's room, but this is more. I strain to hear over the complaints of the carpet as we step, over the chortle of the lights as we make shadows on the white walls. For a moment, it seems that there is too much, that I will not be able to sort out the strain that troubles me. Then I hear it.

Joy. Pure, malicious joy.

My dragons hiss as they too sense what I do. I cast about seeking to localize the source. When I do, it is too late.

Midline has reached the door that ends the corridor. His cautious approach melts into boyish enthusiasm as he sees the letters on the card in the door. Only his impulsive dash forward saves him from the tranquilizer sliver that lances into the corridor from what had appeared to be a flat wall.

Too late, we all realize that a white-projected hologram has concealed the open doorways to each side of the dead-end corridor, one to each right and left, before and behind. Now that we know they are there we can detect a faint shimmer from their presence, like a mirage without heat.

Head Wolf's black door waits, solid, closed, and locked at the corridor's end.

Midline rolls flat beside the left side door nearest to him. Here he is safe from the man who had fired at him, who stands inside, dart gun in hand. The angle is bad from the other doors, so Midline is marginally safe, but pinned.

I also roll toward the wall, startled when Grey Brother jumps up, punching a drop ceiling panel aside and pulling himself upward into the recess. With the litheness of the Jungle, he vanishes.

Only Professor Isabella does not move quickly enough; the dart fired at her comes at an angle and buries itself in the thick tweed of her winter coat.

From where I am squashed against the wall, wishing myself as small as my dragons, I can see the anonymous halos of our four attackers, white ghosts, outlined by an unreal wall that still chuckles over the deception it has wrought.

Overhead, Grey Brother's voice is muttering intently. I cannot make out the words, but suddenly the holographs vanish. The figures of our attackers are clearly visible for a brief moment, then everything vanishes as the lights go out.

But before darkness shrouds us, I recognize one of the

people waiting in the doorway. Her smile glints from perfect teeth: Dr. Haas.

Darkness favors those of us from the streets. I force myself to remember this as I crawl rapidly toward the glow of the small, red safety light on Head Wolf's door. My allies must remember this too, because no one activates the small light sticks we each carry.

Our enemies are less certain of themselves. Their deception had necessitated turning off the self-powered lights over each cell door; the only remaining light is from the bars over the distant stairwell and over Head Wolf's door.

One by one, hand flashes come on: three clear targets revealed. I think I know who the holdout is, but she must wait. Head Wolf needs me. On hands and knees, I move to his door.

Before the lights went out, I had seen the keypad to the left of the door. Abalone had reported that each lock was a self-contained unit so she could not open the door, even when she got into the Home's computer system. Grey Brother carried some materials to force the door, but he would need light to use them. My way was no longer just an option—it was the only hope left to us.

Closing my ears to the sounds of struggle behind me, I open my hearing to the door in front of me. For a frightened moment, I think I will be unable to hear. Then, faintly, I hear the door, drowsing solid. Next to it, like a whistle of electronic fire, is the snap and babble of the lockpad.

Reaching tentatively in the ruddy darkness, I find the rectangle set nearly flush with the doorframe. Brushing a fingernail across, I feel that the numbers are raised—intended no doubt as a convenience for a nurse or orderly who might need to feel out the code while dealing with a struggling patient. As my hand touches them, I hear the hiss and babble increase in frequency.

When I concentrate, the noise resolves itself into yaps and purrs of sound—no real words, but something I can understand.

I move my hand to the long sigil in the upper left corner. The purrs vanish, but when I move my finger down the purring begins, hesitates when I pass the second row and thrums loudly when I rest on the center figure. I press.

I follow the purrs down to the right, up to the top center, over one, then across to the far corner. The purring grows loud here and so I press twice. Beside me there is a click and a soft swish as the door opens.

Opening the lock has activated a self-powered light inside the cell. This one is yellow and slightly brighter. Thus, as I step into the doorway, I see Head Wolf.

He is sprawled on a foam cot that is a raised piece of the padded floor. The glossy black hair is tangled and matted with sweat; his eyes move vacantly, independent of each other. A steady stream of saliva has coursed from the corner of his mouth to pool in the hollow of one shoulder. Although he wears paper coveralls, he seems indecent, stripped of his dignity.

With a low moan of anger, I am moving to help him when Betwixt and Between yell.

"Sarah! Drop and left!"

I do and the dart sails over me and bounces limply into the padded walls. Coming up from my roll, I look up and see Dr. Haas aiming at me again. Already, though, I have learned something about these little guns, so instead of rolling to the side, a motion that she could track, I roll towards her. My velocity is limited, but I connect soundly with her shapely legs and then start to my feet.

"Goddamn you!" she swears, adjusting her arm.

I look past her and smile. "Thou shalt not take the name of the Lord thy God in vain."

"Bitch!" she says and then crumples as Professor Isabella hits her solidly below one shell-like ear.

Now that I have time to look, I see that the battle is over. The three security guards who had attended Professor Haas are all down. One bleeds heavily, his jaw at an odd angle. All, however, appear to be breathing.

Midline has gone into Head Wolf's cell and, swearing softly, is preparing him for our escape. Grey Brother watches down the corridor, a palm computer in one hand. Suddenly, I understand how the power went off at such an ideal moment.

"When the dart hit me," Professor Isabella is telling me, her voice still adrenaline charged, "I realized that my best bet was to let them believe that I had been at least somewhat affected—otherwise I'd get another dart for sure. So I went down and helped as I could without giving my cover by tripping a few people. But when I saw her go for you . . ."

I hug her with one arm, then move to help Midline. He scowls protectively, but lets me take Head Wolf's legs. I hang one over each arm and trundle forward; Midline manages the heavier upper body.

Climbing through the access ways is out with our unconscious leader, so Grey Brother contacts Abalone.

"We've got 'im, but no way we getting out where we come in. What you think, girl?"

Her voice comes back, tiny but reassuring. "Go to the stairwell back the way you came on your right. Go up two flights. There's a ladder to the roof. I'll have pickup there for you."

"Good." Grey Brother motions with his head and we trot after.

Abalone has let the lights come on again. When at one point they flicker, Midline chuckles and even Grey Brother relaxes.

"The Four are with us," he explains to Professor Isabella. "They just blew a minor power link. It'll distract from our pickup."

We make our way to the roof and as Grey Brother is undoing the manual hatch, Abalone's voice comes from the palm computer.

"Caught something on the vid," she says. "The blonde is up and has made some call. I only tapped into the end, but she's got people heading for the Jungle."

Grey Brother snaps the catch and starts to climb onto the roof. He halts midway. His head is outside, but by stretching my ears I can hear him.

"Abalone, some of the Free People may still be living down there. I cleared those I could, but . . ."

He trails off, but I don't need to hear the finished sentence. The Law permits the Wolves to lair where they will within reason. If some of the Pack chose not to take Grey Brother's suggestion, they could be there still.

Professor Isabella has also heard. "Grey Brother, those kids are in trouble. That woman is dangerous and she won't hesitate to grab other hostages now that we have the Head Wolf."

Grey Brother vanishes upward. A moment later his arms descend to help Midline raise Head Wolf. I can hear the faint whoosh and drone of the hovercat's power plant. Midline waits to assist Professor Isabella upward. As I climb the ladder, I hear her.

"You don't seem surprised that I think we may have further problems with the blond woman."

"No."

I can almost hear Midline shake his head.

"It's her. Sarah," he goes on. "She's what they want. Why would they stop when they don't have her?"

Professor Isabella's face as she emerges from the trapdoor wears a musing expression. She extends a blue-veined hand to help Midline up. He accepts, although he hardly needs it. We hurry to the hovercat and crowd in.

His mien serious, Peep sits behind the controls. Grey Brother is already in the back, with Head Wolf leaned up against him. I slide in beside, supporting Head Wolf, and Professor Isabella squashes beside me, letting Midline have the other front seat. As Peep eases the vehicle off the roof and spirals us away, I think that Abalone would find him a more-talented apprentice than I am.

We are descending into a dark alleyway when Grey Brother shakes himself.

"Peep, pick up Chocolate and Bumblebee—no, she's

gone—Chocolate, then, and the two of you take Head Wolf to the Cold Lairs. Edelweiss is there. She'll know what to do for Head Wolf."

"Okay," the boy nods. "You're not coming?"

"No." Grey Brother shakes his head. "Me an' Midline are going to make sure the Jungle's clear."

I struggle for words; fortunately, Grey Brother sees my expression.

"Wanna come, Sarah?"

I nod, smiling.

"Count me in, too," Professor Isabella says.

A grin quirks Grey Brother's face. "Might be kinder if you went with Peep. Edelweiss and the rest will want to know what's been going on and Peep can't tell them. Y'know?"

"I know."

The hovercat comes down and Professor Isabella leans back so I can climb over her and out. She puts an arm around Head Wolf's still limp body.

"Closer than this scoundrel would let me get if he were awake," she chuckles. "May as well enjoy it. Mind Sarah, now."

"We be of one blood, she and us," Grey Brother answers, swatting Chocolate as the boy takes the seat Midline has abandoned. "We'll mind her, best as one can in a war."

"War?" Professor Isabella looks down as the hovercat begins to rise. "What do you know?"

"All I need to," Grey Brother waves. "Someone wants one of ours and they will hurt any of us to get her. That's war as I see it."

TEN

THE GRAVEL ROLLS UNDER MY FEET AS I RUN BESIDE GREY Brother, a familiar gritty grind of asphalt and granite from forgotten roadways and footpaths. Around us the tanks loom, mesas within the canyon of empty buildings. Once this canyon had been a home. Tonight it is an alien landscape of dark steel and darker shadows.

I pick out the tank that had held the Jungle off to the edge of the canyon. There are a dozen ways that could have brought us in closer, but Grey Brother chose this one after speaking with one of the Four.

Even Abalone does not argue with him, but lopes alongside, her tappety-tap thumping against her hip. Occasionally she reaches and adjusts the padded nylon case and then smiles at me.

I think she means to reassure me, but I am chilled by the feral glimmer in her eyes. So long she has been my Baloo, little thief, little hacker, I had forgotten the bare-chested child of the streets who had rescued me.

We draw nearer to the Jungle without seeing anyone. This is not good. Grey Brother had sent some of the Four in with Midline from another angle. We should have rendezvoused by now. I feel a metallic bite of fear. Midline would have sent someone if he could not have come himself—a Tail Wolf, a Cub, someone. This is bad.

Grey Brother has apparently reached the same conclusion. He leads us until we come to a smaller tank that faces the Jungle. The side is corroded, making a cave of sorts. He stoops and enters, hunkering invisible in the shadows.

We creep in next to him. Together we listen for any sound, look for any sign from the direction of the Jungle. For a long time there is nothing, then a flicker of light, bright only because of the surrounding murky darkness.

It is gone before we can pinpoint it, but my mind fills in the details. Something—someone—has disturbed one of the heavy curtains that cover the entries into the Jungle. At least some of the lights are on within.

Abalone mutters something angry.

Grey Brother whispers back, "Yes, they in there. They got the Four I sent on and more maybe. But how we get them out? They see us when we go in, even if we go by one of the Lesser Trails."

"Lesser Trails?" Abalone asks.

"Yes," Grey Brother laughs softly. "Secret ways that Head Wolf makes. Only some of us know. He not want us to be trapped by cops or gangs. Always someone there who knew the Trails and is sworn to bring the rest out if trouble comes."

"Does Midline know?"

"No." I can hear him shake his head. "Only me an' Bumblebee an' Chocolate an' Head Wolf, of course."

"Damn."

There is a long pause, then she whispers again.

"I thought he might be able to get them away if we could distract the Bander-Log"—she tries to laugh at her tag for our enemies and fails—"and maybe turn out the lights."

"Monkey folk?" Grey Brother does laugh. "I wish, Abalone, but these is meaner than the Bander-Log. You think you can kill the lights?"

"Know it. From the bit we saw, they gotta be using Head Wolf's lines and I always helped him pay the power bills. But what good will it do? Without a look inside, we can't see where our Pack members are or even in what shape they're in. And without that . . ."

She shrugs hopelessly but I feel a rush of excitement and sick terror. I remember the day that Betwixt and Between told Conejito Moreno about Dylan and how all the Jungle had seemed to speak.

Now . . . I don't know if I can do it, but again, I must.

I tug Abalone's cape. "I am a brother to dragons, a companion to owls."

She starts to hush me, then stops. "You are, aren't you, Sarah. But can you do it?"

"The walls have ears," I nod, gesturing toward the looming steel shell.

"What's she mean?" Grey Brother asks.

"Sarah thinks that she can find out what's going on in there, without us having to go in," Abalone explains.

I hear a sharp intake of breath.

"I'm not asking. Head Wolf make her one of us and I never thought it was just 'cause she was a cute piece of ass. If she can do it—good—but how will she tell us what she learns? We don't have time for her riddles."

I have been wrestling with the same problem. Now I etch the pebbles with my fingertip, forgetting Abalone and Grey Brother cannot see what I am doing because of the darkness.

"When we mean to build," I whisper, "we first survey the plot, then draw the model; And when we see the figure of the house, then we must rate the cost of erection."

"No time for that . . ." Grey Brother begins indignantly, but Abalone interrupts him with a smothered laugh.

"No, Grey Brother, she doesn't mean that kind of erection. She's saying that she thinks that she can draw us a plan of what she sees—like a house builder would—and then when we see what's there we can make our plans."

I nod happily as Betwixt and Between snigger.

"I can't understand her when she talks that way," Grey Brother complains, but I can tell that he is hopeful. "You stay close so I can figure what she's telling. Can she do her hoodoo from here or do we need to get closer?"

Closing my eyes, I stretch for contact with the Jungle, but the noises will not resolve themselves into anything I can follow.

"He seems so near and yet so far," I admit, regretfully shaking my head.

"Then we'll sneak in closer," Grey Brother says. "Do you need to be near an opening or just near the Jungle?"

I open and shut my mouth like a cartoon clam, unable to find an answer. Abalone recognizes my dilemma and rephrases the question.

"Sarah, is getting nearer to the Jungle wall enough?"

Relieved, I nod.

"Good," Grey Brother growls, "then we'll go over by one of the Lesser Trail doors. Abalone, while she's sketching, can you check out what it'll take to kill the lights and then hustle back to rejoin us?"

"Done. Where do I meet you?"

Grey Brother hesitates, as if reluctant even now to share the secret Head Wolf entrusted him with.

"Over behind the south face—near the sign that says 'mical Stor' in orange paint."

"I know the place." Abalone nods and with a light pat for me she is gone.

Grey Brother motions for me to follow him and I do, matching step for step as Abalone taught me long ago. I wonder again if Grey Brother hates me for the disruption I have brought his home, his people. I am glad that I do not have the words to ask.

When we reach the metal wall, I huddle against it, gripping the barely perceptible curve of the surface with my flat palms. The metal is cold and slightly pitted although it looks quite smooth. In the faint ambient city light, I can see Grey

Brother watching me with just the faintest hint of superstitious respect on his impassive features.

Wanting a friend, I pull Betwixt and Between from their perch and set them between my knees. There is a patch of dirt next to me and I experiment with marking it with my fingertip. I can draw fairly easily, rearranging the lumpy dust into patterns.

Closing my eyes, I stop procrastinating and begin to listen.

Nothing but Grey Brother's breathing and my own heartbeat. Then nothing but the heartbeat. Then nothing.

Nothing. Or. Yes.

The metal is tired. It has held liquid that burned. Then the liquid was gone and the sides of the cylinder had collapsed the smallest amount inward in response to the missing internal pressure.

Wind. Rain. Outside. In? In. Weakest spots had given way or had been broken by vandals. Through these had come the refugees.

Rats. Bats. Cats. Dogs. A hawk that roosted in the upper rim. Mice. Small birds who nested on ladder rungs. Finally, people. One. Two. Many.

Pinpricks of pain as the ropes are hung, platforms and curtains suspended. An eerie sense of fullness and satisfaction at being full again after so long empty.

This all washes through me as the lines and scars on a man's face tell you his life: that he loved the wind, never wore sunglasses, broke his nose in a brawl and was too proud to fix it. So the old tank that became the Jungle tells its tale to me.

I listen more closely and can hear individual reactions. The upper reaches are dark and empty. The ropes and hammocks weave a vacant web. The floor. Yes. That speaks. I draw a ragged breath, damp my ears to the myriad voices that seek to claim me, and focus.

The entire babble, even of this relatively limited area, is still too great. I make my way to an edge. This is better. I will inscribe the ring of the Jungle base first, then move in.

Now I lower my hand to the dirt and, with an improvised stylus made from a piece of wire, I draw what I hear.

First, the edges. My circle is wobbly but recognizable. I carefully mark the openings, their painted canvas screams Head Wolf's mad vision of freedom while pulling the very whiskers of those who would lock him away.

Circling in, I find one of the Lesser Trails, a drainage pipe, its trapdoor hidden beneath a slab of metal. I mark it and continue on. Head Wolf's lair, a crumpled mass of fabric calls to me, begging for repair and return. For a moment, I smell musk and man sweat and feel the stroke of his hands as I lean back against a mound of pillows.

I wrench myself away from the spot, for the memories are strong here and the place is alive with powerful passions—mine, his, others. I could grow lost in the clamor of memory.

Circle inward. Another Lesser Trail, this a weak spot in a wall, one that could be opened easily with a good heave of one of the hunks of stone piled with apparent carelessness nearby. The thin metal weeps of its aching sides to me. Fatigue will take it in a decade if not sooner.

Inward. Cookstove. Fire Circle. Song notes. A life

choked out in a brief flash of violent sound. I mark the physical landmarks. The intangible I hurry past.

Then. Yes! This section nearly shrieks with recent noise: Children's tears pool in the rough cracks in the metal floor; blood, still warm, congeals beside. The floor speaks of weight, heat. Burns where a bullet has gouged it.

Have they given up the dart guns then?

Feverishly, I mark what I can. The clump that I think is our people, scattered figures that may be guards. Only one is high up. Apparently, they do not trust the Web.

Almost by accident, I find another of the Lesser Trails, not far from the center of the Jungle. This one, I sense, is the one we wait near. It connects to a similar drainage system as the first.

Struggling for more detail, I am at last overwhelmed by the competing noises, stories, sounds, complaints, secrets. I fall away from the wall, obliterating an edge of my drawing. The important part remains, however.

For a few breaths, I hide my face in my hands. Then I look at Grey Brother, noticing that Abalone has returned.

"The rest is silence," I say.

"She's given us a map," Grey Brother says, pointing at my dust scrawls. "Our people are here an' here. Guards there and over there."

He looks at me to check his interpretation. I nod, still so tired that I feel close to sobbing. I can't let Grey Brother or Abalone know or they will insist that I stay out and this I cannot bear. I must go in and help—these people are in trouble because of me.

I ease myself back against the Jungle wall and try not to let my friends see how heavily I am leaning.

"One of the Lesser Trails comes up there," Grey Brother says, mostly to Abalone. "I could go in and you could kill the lights."

"We go in," Abalone says with a scowl that does not accept argument. "I've rigged the lights so that I can kill them remote. Besides, you'll need the extra hands."

Grey Brother does not contradict and together they lay out their plans. I am too tired to make much sense of what they are saying and after learning that I am to come up last and cut any prisoners free who need help and then lead the way to an upper port—the same, I realize idly, that Abalone first brought me through—I let myself drift.

My next clear memory is soft Spanish curses and Grey Brother struggling to lever up a rusty access port. After Abalone jumps on the lever a few times, the lid lifts and a damp, caustic smell rises. I wrinkle my nose as I tuck Betwixt and Between into my pack.

"Some water down there," Grey Brother explains unnecessarily as he climbs down. "Smells crappy, but won't hurt you none."

Abalone doesn't say anything but ties a bandanna over her lower face before starting after him. I shrug and follow, listening to my dragons bicker about how best to describe the putrid odor that wafts up.

At least they don't have to wade in the stuff, I think as I slog along behind Abalone. The water is cold and glows faintly in the pale light of the green chem stick Grey Brother holds in one hand. A strange, glittering sludge sticks to my jeans where they cut through the water.

After a half dozen steps, my wet skin begins to burn.

Grey Brother and Abalone do not comment, so I follow without complaint. Finally, we stop before another short series of rungs set into the wall. Grey Brother wedges the chem stick into a crevice and climbs.

Abalone comes after, one hand on the ladder, one unbuttoning the flap on the tappety-tap's case. I wait at the ladder's base.

Grey Brother looks down, his eyes dark pits with burning embers smoldering at the bottom.

"Ready," he hisses, his hand holding the hasp that will open the trapdoor.

"Light's out." Abalone nods, touching an icon. "Now!"

Grey Brother opens the trap so quickly that the first cries of astonishment come clearly to me. Unbelievably, he pauses, halting his first leap out. Then he twists and apparently reorients himself.

"Fuck! Map's backward!" he yells before launching himself out.

Abalone repositions herself without question and as she clambers up and out, I follow. Through shouts of "Cover the door!" and "Where the hell did they come from!" I hear the glad howls of the Pack.

I am just out of the tunnel when Abalone touches another of the icons on her computer. The lights come on again. And then cut off. And on. Off. Somehow she has reprogrammed the lights so that the effect is similar to that of a strobe.

Around me, I can see a baker's dozen of people dressed in midnight blue jumpsuits moving jerkily about. Near the room's center are seven or eight Pack members, Midline among them.

Then the lights go out again, but I have my bearings. I cut Midline's bonds first and he tumbles back, unable to catch himself on numbed hands. But I do not waste my time apologizing. In the dark, it is difficult to cut the bonds. I must feel first to find the rope by touch and saw at that rather than the hands that it binds.

By the time everyone is freed, Midline has regained his feet, but he is the least of my concerns. Grey Brother and Abalone have been quite busy. As well as varying the lights between strobe and darkness, Abalone is forcing her tappety-tap to emit squeals and wails that echo and reverberate from the metal walls, making verbal communication difficult.

Grey Brother is more direct. In one lightning flash, I see him fell a blue-suited man with a fist to the groin. Upon regaining his feet, Midline moves to join his friend.

The way to the upper port is clear and I lead most of the Pack members that way. Some break off to help Grey Brother and Midline. I anchor the rope that snakes to the platform, listening for either Dr. Haas or the person I had sensed on high-guard earlier. I find the high-guard first.

She is working her way hand over hand through some of the ropes remaining in the Reaches. During a bright flash, I see that her eyes are tight shut, that she is guiding herself by touch alone.

This gives me an idea.

I scramble upward until I am in the lines most nearly parallel to her, where a rough swing remains. Tossing a stray length of rope weighted by a buckle from my belt, I loop a line over hers, bringing the stray end back to me so that her guideline is within the V of my rope. Next, I gently tug the taut line from which she hangs, testing the tension. This established, I begin to shake her line.

Some of the Free People love this game—called it spaghetti snakes—but all but the best played it with a safety net or at least a catcher below. She has neither.

When she opens her eyes. I ease up on all but the lightest vibration. I see her spot me, check her situation. Realize. If she doesn't retreat, I can shake her down. There is no way she can touch me, crouched as I am out of reach, our only connection the tension in the line I control.

She moves forward, testing. I start shaking the snag-rope. She stops. So do I. The lights go out, but I can feel her motion and start pulling again. She stops.

I wait, expecting her to retreat, but when the lights come on again, the erratic flashes reveal that she has somehow gotten to her gun and is aiming at me. Even as the Law warns me against killing, my hands pull again on the snag-rope. Hard. The motion sets me swinging and my next jerk is harder.

Her shot goes wild.

I haul again, roughly, violently. She falls. The lights go out, but not before I see her hit in a staccato splatter of bright blood.

Looking up, I see most of the erstwhile prisoners have

left the Jungle. All that remains is for me to follow. I make my way to the ladder and scramble upward, my sneaker toes bouncing against the metal wall in my haste.

From below, I hear a shout. The voice is commanding, female, familiar.

"Forget these! The one we want is getting away!"

I climb faster and hear a pair of dearer, closer voices.

"Hey, Sarah! You're shaking us loose!" yells Betwixt.

"My claws are slipping!" screams Between.

I stop and leaning precariously from the ladder, jam the rubber dragon deeper into my pack.

"Ouch! Not so hard!" Betwixt grunts, his protest muffled by the nylon bag.

I grin and keep climbing, but the pause has enabled my closest pursuers to catch up with me. There are two: a man and a woman in the same blue jumpsuit uniform as the woman I killed. The man's left eye is swollen shut; the woman's sleeve is ripped. Both look grimly angry. Dr. Haas follows a distant third.

Ducking through the no longer concealed doorway into the abandoned building, I concentrate on remembering the steps into the maze I must run. Some light shines through the broken windows and gaping roof and as I set my foot to the trail it begins to call out to me.

I run as quickly as the uneven surface will permit, rejoicing that my Pack members have escaped and that in a few moments I, too, will be free.

The maze's song guides me until suddenly it is broken by the dissonant wheeze of a dart gun firing.

On reflex, I flatten myself against a post and then resume running, unable to dodge much beyond the erratic demands of the maze.

"Cut her off!" the man's voice yells.

His answer is the dusty Sheetrock giving way beneath his feet and his partner's cry as she also begins to fall.

"Shit! The floor's bad," the woman calls.

Glancing back, I see her pulling herself up.

"No shit!" her partner agrees. "And I'm wedged here. Get me a rope—if I wriggle, I'll fall."

I keep going. Only a few yards more.

"Fools!" a cool calm voice cuts the darkness. "She's getting away."

I hear a click, a wheeze. There is no way for me to dodge as the tranq sliver solidly hits my shoulder, knocking me off-balance and crashing down through the floor. I concentrate on falling, slowing my descent when I can by grabbing at protrusions. One hand is badly skinned when I thump down into a foot of stagnant water.

The stuff in the sliver is screwing up my head, but not so much that I can't hear a voice from my back wailing, "God! We're hit!"

Dragging myself to my feet, I assess my position. From the distance I've fallen, I'm probably in the basement of the abandoned building.

The sliver pierced through my pack and apparently through some portion of Betwixt and Between before hitting me. I guess that this is why I haven't been knocked out yet. Still, I am feeling woozy. I can tell the direction of the

Jungle and slog that way. Above me I hear shouting, but the words are indistinct.

I crawl out of the pit, breaking the fragments of a rotted wooden door. While I am crouched in the doorway, two figures in navy jumpsuits run by. "She can't have gone far. . . ."

They're out of my erratic hearing before I can find what they are going to do. I stagger out, my course a jagged line. I'm not sure where I'm going, but the vague idea comes that if I can find the Lesser Trail we used to enter the Jungle, I can hole up there and surely Grey Brother or Abalone will find me.

I hide again when two figures appear, but I am too dizzy to pull my feet in from a patch of light. As I stare stupidly at them sticking out, wondering if they might be mistaken for soggy shadows, a hand touches my shoulder.

I look up and see Abalone's blue lips curl in a smile, a smile that fades as I try to speak and only manage to faint.

ELEVEN

TWO DAYS LATER, I AM FINALLY WELL ENOUGH TO GET UP
and move around. It seems that Dr. Haas—or one of her
cadre—managed to hit me twice. One dart spent most of its
drug piercing through Betwixt and Between's foot before
hitting me. The other hit squarely. The force of the combined impacts was enough to make me fall and though Professor Isabella mutters about the damage I did myself
wading to get out of the basement, she admits that I was
lucky.

"Not only did you survive the fall but the doubled dosage
could have killed you," she tells me as she winds fresh gauze
around my hand.

Head Wolf has not been so fortunate. Although he no
longer drools or stares vacantly into space, he has fallen into
a coma from which he does not awaken. Members of the
Pack take shifts at his side, patting water onto his chapped
lips, checking the IV Bumblebee has hooked up.

We are currently holed up in a most peculiar cave: the Cold Lairs. Midline had discovered it when he was still a Cub and it had become a secret between himself and Head Wolf.

"Paid my dues for a month or so with the information," Midline recalls when telling me about it.

The cave is a pocket beneath a freeway. Apparently, once there had been a tunnel, perhaps a water main here, but when the freeway was restructured and magnetized, the tunnel was no longer needed. Instead of filling it in, the contractors had sealed it over, no doubt padding their pockets with the money not spent on the job.

The weather shifted the asphalt and concrete used to seal the place, breaking a crevice to the underworld. After Midline reported his find to Head Wolf, the Pack leader arranged to have the freeway's power grid tapped, another entrance made, and then both openings concealed behind thick curtains of kudzu.

This retreat is not as comfortable as the Jungle, but it serves to keep most of our Pack together.

Professor Isabella has drawn medical supplies for Head Wolf on her ElderAid card and now the Pack views her as one of their own. I am pleased, if slightly jealous, to see the littler Wolves crowding to her, begging her for stories or asking questions.

The first night when I am well enough to walk about unassisted, Abalone waits until the bulk of the hunters have left and then invites me and Professor Isabella for a walk.

She has completely abandoned her young executive guise and returned to the paints and street struts she favors. As we walk to an automatic diner, she tells me how she and Grey Brother created a false trail that would have eventually led Dr. Haas and her people to the apartment. Once there, they would have found signs of a hasty departure.

"If they looked hard enough," Abalone brags, "they would have found enough evidence to convince them that the three of us fled up the Shattered Coast and into the East Megalop. I bought us tickets on a shuttle and then rented a hovervan. They'll figure one is a decoy and one the real route, but they won't know which. While they chase down dead ends, they'll never be sure that we didn't find some third route. Meanwhile, we'll be here—the last place they'll look."

"That will give us time," Professor Isabella says, holding the autodiner's door for us.

I look first to confirm that the place is empty. Then I shake my head in query—unable to frame the question.

"What do we need time for?" Professor Isabella guesses.

I nod, accepting the soup and sandwich Abalone hands me.

"Because, my dear, we are done with running away. This time we are going to find these people and strike back."

I choke on my sandwich and, as Abalone thumps my back, she explains.

"We got to, Sarah. They're getting mean now, not just clever. They've hurt Head Wolf and any of the Pack could be next, especially if they do it in a fashion that would make national news."

"Say a gaudy murder or a poisoning—'Brighton Rock' candy would certainly get our attention," Professor Isabella notes with a dry smile. "You've already proved that you won't let anyone else be hurt without rising to the bait, so they're sure to hit where you're vulnerable."

"A man may be in as just possession of truth as of a city," I suggest, "and yet be forced to surrender."

Abalone shakes her head vigorously. "No way, Sarah. We don't know why they want you, but I doubt it's to hand you your inheritance check and send you on your way."

"Besides," Professor Isabella adds with a sip from her coffee, "these people probably have your brother and sister. We may be able to help them if they need help or, at least, learn more about your heritage."

"Curiosity killed the cat," I remind her.

"Ah, but your forte is dragons"—she smiles—"and owls. Think our proposal over and then Abalone wants to show you an interesting toy she's found."

With this as incentive, I bolt my meal, only to be teased by the others, who linger over their vended meals as if in a high-class restaurant. Getting into the game, I saunter over and punch myself a dish of ice cream. We are all in cheerful spirits when we depart.

Abalone leads us to a small park that is nearly deserted at this hour. She sits on a stone bench and motions for us to join her. We sit breathing in the honeysuckle-heavy air.

"Nice, isn't it," Abalone comments. "Might get rain later though, but not for a while."

I nod, aware from a dozen nonverbal signals that she is about to spring her surprise.

"T'Whoo!"

The noise makes me jump. Abalone giggles, but Professor Isabella is calmly brushing her skirts into place.

. . . .

170

"T'Whoo!"

A piece of silver-grey moonlight detaches itself from the trees above us and comes soaring down on outspread wings. The owl's flight is liquid, soundless, utterly natural, but I don't need to watch for breathing to confirm that the little bird that glides in to roost on the bench across from me is not a bird at all, but a cleverly crafted machine a mere five inches tall.

Feeling more happy and alive than I have since the Brighton Rock scam drove us into hiding, I get up and kneel before the owl. Betwixt and Between forget to be jealous and hiss their delight at this cleverly made newcomer.

I stroke the curved back, giggling when the amber eyes cross as the owl tries to keep watch on my finger.

Abalone asks anxiously, "Do you like it, Sarah?"

I nod vigorously. "Yes!"

"It's a nearly perfect replica of a saw-whet owl, one of the smaller North American owls. This little critter can go anywhere an owl might and since saw-whet sometimes hunt in the daytime, that's just about anywhere. It has a small camera built in, though the resolution isn't very clear. Otherwise, it's just a nifty little robot. We were wondering . . ."

Uncharacteristically, she trails off and Professor Isabella continues for her.

"Sarah, we accept that somehow you are able to do this 'magical thinking.' We don't have a very clear idea of how you do it. We were wondering if you could somehow talk to this, as you seem to with Betwixt and Between."

I look at the little machine, already feeling a creeping fondness for it, but its spirit is not yet awake. It does not have the experiences of the old buildings or the smugness of the lockpads. Certainly, it does not have the personality of Betwixt and Between, who speak with me like a person would.

I narrow my eyes speculatively. "I look upon every day to be lost, in which I do not make a new acquaintance."

"You can do it?" Abalone asks.

Stroking the bird, I nod again. "To be swift is less than to be wise. 'Tis more by art, than force of num'rous strokes."

"You can do it, but not quickly," Abalone clarifies.

I nod, wondering if the delay is a bad thing.

Professor Isabella cuts in, "Sarah, we told you we want to go after the Institute. Abalone has narrowed down where they are located. The place is quite isolated, which is good, because it means no nosy neighbors, but it is really secure. They use no outside programming so she can't hack in as she did into the Home's data bank. Anything more complex than this owlet is likely to have its signals scrambled by their jamming field. Hell, I don't understand all of this technical stuff, but what it boils down to is that we can get in but we need to be very careful."

Abalone hands me a control pad no thicker than a credit slip and neatly concealed inside a wide bracelet.

"I made certain to get one that uses shapes and colors rather than numbers or letters to identify the icons." She grins wickedly. "You mix things up when they're written, don't you?"

I flush and she squeezes my hand.

"Don't let it bug you too much. I thought that Grey Brother was gonna strangle you when we came out of the

Lesser Trail all backward. We figured out later that your map was perfect but reversed. Even that wouldn't have queered us except that somehow one of the edges had gotten rubbed out and we didn't catch that the doors were in the wrong places."

Hiding my embarrassment, I study the control pad: a red X in the center with geometric figures set like the spots on the "5" face of a die. Each is a different, bright color, and I guess that they are pressure rather than heat sensitive since each is perceptibly raised.

Abalone explains the pad to me and when I prove that I have the basics down, she takes us to an open field where I can practice. Setting Betwixt and Between between my feet, I work with the tiny owl until I can easily make it rise and fall, soar and fly, glide and perch.

Only when the damp has soaked through my shoes and Professor Isabella is making noises about hot coffee do I stop. I am reluctant to tuck the owl away; already it seems a pity to put such a wild thing in a box or bag, but I yield to reason.

As we walk, I reflect on Abalone and Professor Isabella's determination to go after my enemies. The Institute. I, too, am curious. Perhaps more than either of my friends realize. Yes, I decide, I am very curious.

That night, I dream of a place that is almost familiar. A young man, who I somehow know is Dylan, is lying in a narrow bed. The sheets are white and folded in boxlike corners at the base of the mattress.

Moving only his pale green eyes, he looks across the room at a closed door. He moved his lips and although no sound comes, I understand that Eleanora, our sister, is behind that door. I am starting forward to open the door when Dylan slides his hands from under the counterpane. Unfolding the sheet, he draws it over his face. His hands move beneath the sheet to rest on his chest and the doorknob begins to turn.

I am just beginning to understand when I wake up and, of course, nothing makes sense anymore.

I try to diminish the dream, but something of its mood remains with me when Abalone again takes me to a park to practice with the owl.

During our break for a late-night snack, Abalone is troubled by how I toy with my food.

"Hey, eat up, Sarah. That's good stuff there—full of preservatives and artificial flavors. It's your favorite."

I manage a weak, unconvincing grin.

"Something hurting, Sarah?" Professor Isabella asks. "Your period?"

She laughs at my confused expression.

"I forgot, that's a thing of the past. You all get implants now. I remember that when I left the Home they decided I was too old to waste one on. So, let me change my question. Is your stomach hurting?"

I am tempted to nod, but instead I try and explain. "I dreamt that I dwelt in marble halls, with vassals and serfs at my side."

"That sounds like a nice dream," Professor Isabella says. "Why are you so troubled? Want to go back?"

A sudden shaking seizes me, so violent that I spill my

juice on the floor. Abalone leaps up but instead of wiping up the juice, she flings her arms around me.

"It's okay, Sarah. It was just a dream."

I hug her back, wishing I could explain the fear I suddenly felt. Terror of returning to the Institute, where surely I had seen Dylan. Fear of learning what I may.

My smile is crooked. "To sleep: perchance to dream; ay there's the rub; for in that sleep of death what dreams may come?"

I pause and Abalone finishes the lines.

"When we have shuffled off this mortal coil/ Must give us pause; there's the respect that makes calamity of so long life," she recites.

"You know *Hamlet* very well," Professor Isabella says conversationally, with a sidelong glance to where I am trying to gather my composure.

I feel Abalone tense, but she picks up a napkin and begins to mop the floor. Perhaps sensing that I am still shaken, she decides to answer the implied question.

"Yeah, I did it in high school. I was the youngest member of the cast. Did lots of little stand-in roles so I was onstage a lot. Heard the play over and over and knew it better than the leads, I think."

In the pause that follows, I hold my breath, knowing with certainty what Professor Isabella will say, dreading Abalone's response.

"That's quite an achievement—*Hamlet* at fourteen. Your parents must have been very impressed."

"Twelve," Abalone bursts out. "I was just twelve. If they

were pleased, they were sure funny how they showed it. They wanted me to get Ophelia, y'see, and never quite let me forget that a grown-up got it."

"Grown-up?" Professor Isabella lifts an eyebrow. "This was an adult's production? I thought it was your school's."

"School's?" Abalone laughs bitterly. "I never had a school—not for long anyhow. I started doing commercials before I was out of diapers. Except for a year when I was seven, I was never in school more than a semester. The other kids hated me for getting what they figured were vacations.

"Hah! That's how I got good with this." She taps her computer. "I did all of my classes on it."

"So your parents kept you educated," Professor Isabella asks carefully, peering over her coffee cup's rim.

Abalone stands up, ignoring that the napkin in her hand is dripping orange juice down her pant leg. For a moment, I think she is not going to answer.

"Educated?"

Again that bitter, barking laugh.

"Oh, I got educated. Mom and Dad read tapes to me when I wasn't even born yet—'prenatal' tutoring, y'see. It got more intense when I was around to work with. They had me talking eight months early, walking six months early, and reading when I was three. The theater and film stuff was just a sideline to pay the rent."

She finally notices the juice and stops to stare at her soaked pant leg.

"So?" Professor Isabella probes.

"So? I did it all. I was going to be the girl genius, darling of the media. Brilliant, talented, and lovely. Funny thing happened, though."

She stops and the look that crosses her face is so ugly that I must force myself not to look away.

"There was this big shot, the type who makes or breaks dreams like my folks had for me. One day I was told that I had an interview with him. Just me. No Mom. No Dad. They dolled me up, took me to this golden glass tower, escorted me to the right floor, and left me on my own. I wasn't all that scared. When you're—young—one big shot is pretty much the same as the others. Parents are what really matters.

"I walked into that office and a slim, baby-faced man ushered me right into the Presence. I went in, took the chair I was offered, and parroted the proper responses to familiar questions. Mr. Big seemed kind, if sorta gross: fat and over-dressed.

"At one point, he asked me to stand up and read a script for him. I did and while I was, he got up and walked around me. I was used to being looked at, but something about the way he did it, staring and circling closer and closer, gave me the creeps. Then he came up behind me, slid his arms around me, and grabbed my breasts—what I had. I flipped out, dropped the script and everything. I think I made some excuse about needing the bathroom, because Mr. Big pointed to a door.

"I got through there and sure enough, there was a fancy little bathroom. My Mom was there, too, and I was so scared that I didn't even wonder how she got in there. I started to blab everything to her, but she hushed me and said, 'I know you were startled, but he's a very important man. I want you to think about that.'"

Abalone's eyes have grown very wide, but not one tear mars their brightness.

"I thought. Then I went back in there and let that bastard fuck me, knowing Mom was hearing every bit—hell, she might have been filming it for all I know. When I left there, Mom and Dad took me to a fancy restaurant, showing me the contract that Mr. Big had signed.

"That night, I left. All I took was the computer and I started stealing right off, replaced my old board and . . ."

She shrugs.

I reach out and squeeze her. "One fire burns out another's burning; one pain is lessen'd by another's anguish."

"Your dream stop bugging you?" Her smile is almost genuine. "That's good. Anyhow, I'd kinda wanted you to know all that, but it's not easy to talk about and I really don't want anyone else to know. I think if my folks find me, they still have legal right to me."

"Your secret is safe with me, Abalone," Professor Isabella promises, her face drawn and tight.

I hug Abalone again. "The rest is silence."

She hugs me back. "I trust you, Prof, and Sarah, you'd be impossible to get anything from, even if you would tell. I'm safe with you. Now we have to make you safe from them."

TWELVE

~

A WEEK GOES BY BEFORE THE OWL BEGINS TO COMMUNICATE
with me. At first, all there is are sighs and vague feelings,
similar to those I had gotten from the apartment house.
Within two weeks, it was calling to me in little chirps and
hoots.

Professor Isabella had been reading to me about saw-
whet owls, so I knew what to expect. Betwixt and Between
reassure me that words will come in time.

"We didn't talk People at first," Betwixt confides when
Between is napping. "At least I don't think so."

He pauses as if puzzled. "I don't know what we were
talking; all I know is that Dylan started understanding us
better and we did him."

This raises something I have been wondering about, but I
must search for words and even when I find some I know
they are not quite what I want.

"Speech is civilization itself," I say. "The word, even the

most contradictory word, preserves contact—it is silence which isolates."

Hearing me, Between wakes up, catching only the tail end of my borrowings.

"Wha' she say?" He yawns.

"I was telling her not to worry too much about the owl talking and telling her about Dylan and us. Then she asked something about speech."

"What did you say?" Between asks.

I repeat myself.

"Are you worrying about the owl still?"

I shake my head. "Am I my brother's keeper?"

"Oh, you want to know if Dylan could talk," Betwixt says. "Yes, he could, maybe had to think over things, but he spoke. So did Eleanora, I think, but I don't remember her too well."

"Me, either," adds Between, "and how about lunch?"

We are finishing our lunch—a night meal for we have returned to the time schedule set by the Law—when Abalone comes bounding up, her tappety-tap bouncing on one hip. She slides to a seat on the floor beside us.

"News," she says, "big time. Where's Professor Isabella? I'd rather go through this just once."

I shrug, but Chocolate, who has just come in, says, "She's up by the stove—reading class!"

He grabs a notebook from under his pallet and pelts toward a small circle clustered around one of the camp stoves.

"I guess we'll tell her later. Up for a walk?"

I nod, scooping up Betwixt and Between and placing Athena, as Abalone has named my owl, on my shoulder.

Abalone leads us to a grass island with a small grove of trees nestled within one of the loops of the highway's cloverleaf. At this hour, traffic is minimal and we dart across the dark pavement easily.

We seat ourselves where we are least visible from the road and Abalone pulls a couple of beers from a cooler cached beneath a rock. After sipping for a moment in silence, she puts the bottle down and wraps her arms around her knees.

"I think that the Institute is relocating, Sarah."

I sit up from where I have been lounging on the grass, surprised to find that I feel both dismayed and relieved. My hands flutter as I seek words to express my emotion; Abalone misinterprets my gesture as curiosity.

"How'd I find out? I'd been tracking what commercial traffic went in and out, thinking we might get in that way with the least fuss. Started noticing that there were a fair number of midsize moving vans, nothing flashy or likely to catch the eye of the neighbors—if they were looking—but enough to cue me."

In the flash of a passing headlight, I see her blue lips twist almost cruelly. She sips a bit more from her beer and goes on.

"The vans weren't marked, but I checked license and registration and traced them to a moving rental company. The Institute may not link out, but this jobber did and I was able to hack in and learn that the big move is scheduled for two nights from this one."

Although fear has set my heart to pounding so that I can barely speak, I manage some familiar lines. "If it were done when 'tis done, then 'twere well it were done quickly."

"Yes." Abalone leaps to her feet. "That's why I want to talk with Professor Isabella; we'll need to move tomorrow night. We may even be too late already if the people went out in the early vans. I'm hoping not, but if this is a dead end, we'll track them down all over again."

We take our time walking back, stopping to bring some beer to a couple of late-working Tail Wolves. When we get back, it is nearly dawn and Professor Isabella is drowsing over a book. She wakes quickly, though, when Abalone tells her the news.

"Are we ready?" she asks. "Maybe we should let them go, then find where they've gone and go in when we're better prepared."

"There's no time like the present," Abalone urges. "Their security must be lower to allow for the traffic. We've got to jump while we can."

Professor Isabella sighs, but nods agreement. "I presume you can get transportation for us? Or am I silly to even ask?"

"Transport and driver," Abalone promises, "and a bit of extra muscle. Midline is coming along. Won't hear 'no.'"

"Then don't tell him," Professor Isabella smiles. "He's talented and knows what we're up against; I'll feel better for having him."

"I'll have Peep and the vehicle ready at dusk tomorrow."

Even with the soothing hum of the highway overhead, I have trouble falling asleep. There's just too much to worry about. The owl chortles disapprovingly at my diurnal restlessness and Betwixt and Between sing lullabies in duet.

Near midmorning, Abalone hands me a beer. I suspect that she must have put something into it, because the last thing I remember after setting the bottle down is Betwixt and Between harmonizing on nearly infinite verses of "Rock-a-Bye-Baby."

Abalone wakes me just before dusk, giving me only enough time to wash and dress. She hands me a black pullover and slacks. I notice that she is wearing something similar, a scarf tied over her bright hair; her lips are still painted blue.

By the time I have dressed, Peep has driven a blue panel van into a cul-de-sac near the Cold Lairs. Abalone takes the seat next to him. Midline stretches out to sleep between the seats and almost before we are on the road, he is snoring softly.

"I envy him," Professor Isabella says, tugging at a pullover which rides up until she tucks it into her waistband. "I'm too old for this."

"You can stay with Peep," Abalone calls back. "He'll be waiting with the van and I'm going to signal him when we're ready to leave. Apparently, most of the jamming stuff has been moved out."

"No," Professor Isabella replies. "You may need me."

Abalone periodically drills Peep on some contingency plan, but otherwise we talk little for the rest of the ride. Some hours into full darkness, Abalone directs Peep to pull the van into a field and shut off the power.

When we open the back hatch and step into the dark, I am amazed at the velvety fullness of the darkness. Here there is no ambient glow from buildings and vehicles, only the half-moon and fainter stars give any light.

My owl seems to approve, but I am still intimidated. My

only comfort is that Peep and Midline appear to share my discomfort. Professor Isabella is studying the sky with apparent pleasure and Abalone sees nothing but her computer screen.

"You can't see the Institute's buildings from here," she says, "because there is a ten-foot-high stone wall around the compound. Most of the wall is impossible to cross—topped with electric wire. I found a place where a fallen tree grows near the wall on the outside. None of the branches cross—their grounds keepers were careful—but there is a tree of about the same height on the other side. I figured we could anchor a line, like in the Jungle, and get over that way."

"If the pictures you showed me are any good, I can set our line," Midline says. "Even found a pulley Professor Isabella can slide with since she don't climb like we do."

Professor Isabella bobs a self-mocking curtsy. "Midline, can the rope be removed? What if the Institute patrols see it?"

"Peep'll reel it back from higher up—there's some chance of it brushing the line, but it shouldn't alert them. There must be a margin for natural things like leaves or birds." Midline shrugs. "An' I'll pull out my arrow. The rest is up to chance and who knows what."

"Once we're over the wall," Abalone says, sketching a small map on her screen, "we should be able to see a cluster of buildings across a park from us. We want to make for the small, low one to the right. From what little I've got, it's used for residences. We stand to find Dylan and Eleanora there."

I look at the detailed map, fighting disorientation as severe as if I was looking at print. Uneasily, I look away and my stomach calms. As I regain my composure, Midline leads the way toward a darker shape that must be the tree. I follow, realizing that I have missed the rest of Abalone's instructions. I don't get a chance to ask, because Abalone asks me to send Athena up and make sure that the way is clear.

The wall crossing goes without a hitch and I drop lightly to the ground at the base of a gnarled oak. Shutting out the others, I study the illuminated cluster of buildings across the manicured park. Memory strikes me solidly and I know that I have been here before.

As planned, Abalone starts toward the small cottage. I hustle forward and stop her, grabbing her arm. When she turns to face me, the moon reveals her perplexed expression.

At a loss for words, I can only point to the cottage, shaking my head vehemently. Then I point toward the largest building, a flattopped three-story thing, intermittently lit.

"Wisely and slow; they stumble that run fast," I whisper.

"Huh? Sarah, what's wrong?"

I gesture toward the larger building. "The play's the thing, wherein I'll catch the conscience of the King."

"King?" she starts to ask, then nods. "You think that we'll find them in that building? Why?"

I smile bitterly. "I remember, I remember the house where I was born, the little windows where the sun came peeping in the morn."

The other two are stirring, restless and curious at the reason for our delay. Abalone beckons them forward and explains.

"Shouldn't we let Sarah lead?" Midline suggests. "She

may remember something else, an' the owl can scout for her."

Abalone agrees, promising to be as close as my shadow, and now I lead the way across the park. The well-tended lawn springs beneath my soft-soled shoes and the night wind whispers through the new leaves on the trees. From the bag slung across my shoulder like a bandolier, I can hear Betwixt and Between muttering to each other, but I do not shift my focus to listen.

Ahead is the building and my memory fills in details that the darkness does not reveal. It is stone, rough and red, grainy to the touch, though not crumbly like sandstone.

The lower floor will not interest us. It is mostly offices and entertainment areas: a ballroom, a conference center, a lounge. The second floor is labs and test areas, some recreational facilities, but these are for the patients, not for the guests: treadmills to measure heart and respiration, rooms with walls of one-way glass, an Olympic swimming pool.

The third floor is our goal. Rooms for the resident patients. Dylan. Me. A kitchen and dining area. A playroom. Somehow it does not occur to me to wonder if this will have changed with the passing years. Maybe the place itself tells me. Change of that sort is not important to its purpose.

Purpose.

Something touches a buried memory, but eludes me like the moth Athena futilely snaps at as she soars just ahead of us. Then we have arrived in the building's shadow and the others are waiting for me to tell them what to do.

The building's flat roof makes an entry directly into the third floor seem possible, especially if we target one of the empty rooms. Holding a finger to my lips, I motion for the others to take cover behind some azaleas thickly covered with red flowers that smell faintly sour. Then I send Athena to look in each window, charging her to remember what was within each.

After a few moments, she returns. Her report does not take the form of anything as simple as words, but I manage to learn that most of the rooms are empty of all but dust and darkness. One or two show signs of human inhabitants, but none of these are a man with white hair and pale green eyes. More than this is beyond my limited ability to understand.

I reassure myself that both the second- and third-story windows above us are dark and the rooms untenanted before I turn to the others, who are waiting with nervous tension.

I gesture upward, motioning as if swinging a grapple.

Professor Isabella looks sharply at me. "You think we should climb up?"

I nod and Midline purses his lips, surveying the height involved.

"We can do that," he says, pulling gear from his belt.

"Okay," Abalone whispers. "Anchor a line to the roof and I'll go first. I want to check if the upper windows are wired. The lower ones are."

Midline steps just outside of the azaleas' shelter and I fight the impulse to huddle small. If anyone sees him, we are all in equal danger. But the night remains quiet and the stretch of park is uninterrupted by guards or other hazards.

A nearly inaudible clunk announces that the grapple has

found purchase and Abalone climbs upward with the primate grace of one of the Free People. She stops outside of the third-story window and wrestles out her tappety-tap.

Something troubles her. She hangs there, studying a reading. Then from a pouch at her waist she removes tiny tools, visible only as points of light in the shadows. After working for a moment, she presses up against the window frame.

I hear Professor Isabella intake her breath in apprehension, but no alarms go off and Abalone vanishes within. Midline gestures for me to go next and I scramble up, certain that I will be spotted. Yet, I dive safely into the room, rolling past Abalone, who motions for me to go and listen at the door and warn her if anyone is coming.

Obeying, I feel a soft breeze as Midline enters and hear soft grunts as Professor Isabella is helped in. There is the sound of metal on stone as Midline retrieves his grapple and then a cessation of outside noises as the window is slid shut. Abalone comes to crouch beside me, chortling nearly inaudibly when she finds a computer jack on the wall. Relieved some from guard duty, I turn to study the room.

Staring in pure disbelief, I realize that I know this room. The brass bedstead in one corner looks smaller than it did when Dylan and I played pirates on it and the ivory dresser is thick with dust, but this is my room. Unbelieving, I study the rainbow of dancing teddy bears that borders the room, remembering how when I couldn't sleep they would sing to me.

The faint sound of those chiming voices reaches me, but I push it back. More important is remembering where various rooms were in relation to this one. Adult perspective threatens to scatter my memories like sparrows before a cat—then I sink back and let memory rise.

Yes. Dylan's room is across the hall and to the right. Eleanora's is beyond his, but it has been empty . . . Past, present, and future threaten to rise and flood me with their contradictions. Can Dylan be here at all?

Meanwhile, Abalone and Professor Isabella have been reviewing the data that is scrolling rapidly across Abalone's screen. Midline stands out of sight of window or door, ready to take any who might have seen our entry and come looking. A sheathed knife waits below his hand, ready as its owner, but I know he will prefer empty hands to weapons.

Quietly, I rise, and inspect the room's other door. If memory matches reality, this opens into a bathroom. Tension has made me suddenly desperate to pee and without word to the others, I gently turn the doorknob, remembering the struggle the task was for my smaller self.

Midline's arm pulls me back.

"No exploring," he growls in my ear.

I blush, realizing how stupid I nearly was, yet aware of the *sotto voce* clamor of past experience luring me to act like a child rather than an adult.

Sitting heavily on the floor, I pull Betwixt and Between from their bag and cradle them, inhaling their strawberry fragrance in slow, deep breaths.

They, in turn, appreciate being let out.

"Gee, it's awfully dark in here," Betwixt says.

"Dusty, too," Between sneezes.

I start to hush them and then remember that only I can hear them. Instead, I whisper, "Am I my brother's keeper?"

"You?" Betwixt seems confused for a moment. "No, but I see what you're getting at. This is definitely the place."

"I wonder if Dylan has the same room?" Between says, his voice rising with excitement. "That would mean he's just down the hall! Do you think he'll remember us?"

"Of course, he will," Betwixt replies, but I can hear the nervous edge to his voice. "Weren't we his best friend?"

Their colloquy is interrupted by a whisper from Abalone. I crawl over to join her and Professor Isabella by the door. Midline inches closer, but keeps his watchful station.

"We've dumped loads of data," Abalone says, "too much and too fast to read now and my memory is at capacity. There were no maps or room assignments in what I skimmed, so we'll have to do a quick physical search. Sarah, do you have any ideas?"

I nod. In the shielded beam of a light, I sketch what I remember of the corridor using the pile of the carpet for a canvas. Across from my room, just to the left, is a door to a stairwell. To the left the corridor jogs and there are several rooms. To the right, there is the large sunroom and one other: Dylan's. Finishing my map, I place an X where Dylan should be.

Abalone studies my map. "Good detail, but things may have changed since you lived here."

Midline coughs what I realize is a laugh. "And she may have flipped directions, like by the Jungle. What say we split? Me and the Professor go left, an' you and Sarah, right. We won't be so far apart for us not to holler for help."

Professor Isabella raises a startled eyebrow at Midline's choice of partner, but nods agreement. "Remember, though, Dylan and Eleanora may not wish to be 'rescued'— this place may be all they know."

Abalone stands, reaching for the door handle, before I can adjust to the shocking thought. I hadn't wanted to leave the Home, had I? Would they feel any different about the Institute?

"I've unlocked the electronics on this level," Abalone whispers. "Ignore any telltale that reads 'Locked' and go through."

Then she presses down the handle and pulls the doors open. Quietly, I follow her into the hallway and to the right.

Walking after her down a hallway that seems nearly unchanged since I was a resident here, I am escorted by a shadow of my smaller self. Up and down this grey, nubby carpet, I would run, chasing Dylan and, more distantly I recall, Eleanora. I loved active games like these, because even then I couldn't talk.

Dylan was less active than I. I think his head often hurt him, for my memories of him frequently show him with head in hands in a darkened room, speaking only in a husky whisper.

The click of the door latch startles me from my reverie and I walk after Abalone from the pearl and grey of the hallway into a man's bedroom. It is empty, but even as I register that, I am recovering from the expectation that, like so much else, this room would be unchanged.

A faint scent of shaving lotion tints the air, but there is something besides its sharp spice—a mustiness that tells me even before Abalone turns on a low beam light and I see the dust on the dresser tops, the barren closet, its door ajar— that no one lives in this room any longer.

Dylan, apparently, has moved on and my dragons hiss my disappointment. Abalone has arrived at the same conclusion.

"They've moved him," she whispers. "Let's see if the others have had better luck."

They haven't. When I step into the hallway again, Abalone hard on my heels, someone grabs my shoulder and pulls me to the side. Someone else grabs Abalone. I feel myself quickly and efficiently patted down. The bag with Betwixt and Between is taken from me and Athena is removed from my shoulder.

I hear Abalone cursing a long and brilliant line of profanities that sear my ears. When I am allowed to turn, I see that they have taken her tappety-tap and that a large man in the same dark blue as those who attacked the Jungle is twisting her arm.

Professor Isabella and Midline are standing with guards behind them. The trickle of blood from one man's lip reveals that Midline did not subdue easily. Too late, I remember the floor's uniform soundproofing—a source of both amusement and annoyance to me and my sibs.

But memories are unimportant now, faced as we are with a half dozen guards and Dr. Lea Haas. If she is hoping to intimidate the Free People, she must be disappointed, for Professor Isabella's words are calm.

"We were coming to meet you when these people leapt

out from the stairwell. I am afraid that we were a bit over-matched, despite Midline's valor."

Midline shuffles his feet as if embarrassed, gaining a suspicious look from his bruised guard.

"Get them below," Dr. Haas says coldly. "Accidents can be arranged, especially for dregs like these. Sarah, though, she can stay here—in her old room. There's something in that."

Her words give me an idea which is no sooner thought of then enacted. I slide my fingers to Athena's control bracelet and touch a series of moves. Immediately, there is a loud, pained cry and a flurry of silver-grey wings.

"The bastard bit me!" is all the guard has time for before the Pack sprints for freedom.

Professor Isabella opens the door to my room, dodging inside. Midline chooses not to follow, preferring to deck the guard nearest to him. The other, the one with the bloody lip, is fumbling for a tranq gun.

I think I hear him mutter, "Not even for union rates," but I am too busy to be sure.

With Professor Isabella and Midline freed up, I dive Athena at the guard nearest to Abalone. When he raises his hands to shield his face, Abalone throws her full body weight into a punch between his legs. He shrieks, doubles, retches, and she seizes her computer before it can hit the floor.

A touch of night air tells me that Professor Isabella has the window open in my room. Two guards down and a third occupied with her injured comrade. Midline distracts a fourth, using the doorframe as a shield from the tranq slivers. A pair remain by Dr. Haas, trying to get a clear line to one of us without hitting one of their allies.

I decide to continue equaling the odds. The owl swirls up and around, diving at the man firing at Midline. Automatically, the man raises his gun, shooting at the darting, dodging blur on wings.

"Don't fire at the bird," Dr. Haas shouts. "It's the blond girl who's doing it! Get her!"

Actually, she is not completely correct. Athena's own circuitry is handling her immediate activity, but if they get my wristband . . . In my moment of revelation, I completely forget the guard behind me. She turns from helping the man Abalone had hit and grabs me.

My arm is pinned behind me with expert pressure and minimal force, yet moving brings sudden, sharp pain. I freeze in place.

Dr. Haas tosses her white lab coat over Athena and the owl sinks, still beating her wings until a safety override shuts off the motion and she crumples. I wonder if only I hear the chirped anger.

Abalone and Midline are poised to spring, but I call out desperately, "There's such divinity doth hedge a king . . ."

Abalone completes the line, sliding the door shut, "that treason can but 'peep' to what it would."

I barely hear Midline's whispered, "We be of one blood, ye and I" before the door clicks shut.

Suddenly brave, Dr. Haas's two goons leap forward and to the door. Dr. Haas walks to an intercom.

"They won't get away," she says to me as she flips it on and begins to rapid-fire instructions.

But when the guards burst open the jammed door of my bedroom, the room is empty. The grounds are searched, but no one is found, nor does security report any unauthorized vehicles crossing the Institute's airspace.

No one even tries to question me and even if they did, I had been so distracted when Abalone reviewed her escape plans that I could not have told them how it was managed. But I do remember that Peep has been Abalone's pupil and suspect that alone is enough to guarantee a quick and easy escape.

But this is small comfort; larger is the knowledge that the Institute will not trouble them further. Now that I am returned, they will have no reason.

I hope.

THIRTEEN

NOT EVEN AN HOUR AFTER MY SURRENDER, I AM TAKEN TO A panel van and from there to a small airfield. At some point, I must have been sedated, because I remember very little of the ensuing journey.

When I come to myself, I am in a room that smells hospital but proclaims prison. The windows are sealed and the door has no latch on the inside. Yet, I had expected something like this. What I had not expected was to find Betwixt and Between and Athena waiting for me on a small round table. Athena's control band sits beside her.

I leap up from the narrow bed, slowing as my head swims.

"Careful, Sarah," Betwixt cautions. "I think this room is monitored. Watch what you say."

"I have drunken deep of joy," I promise, "and I will taste no other wine tonight."

"That's careful enough," Between mutters. "I can barely understand her."

I hug them, ignoring the hardness of their rubbery spikes. Then, more gently, I stroke Athena's wings, checking for damage from her fall.

"Oh, dear girls, we are in a pickle," Betwixt says. "I watched as they brought us in and this place is about as accessible as a hibernating mud crab. I am not sure that even Abalone's magic can find us. We may be stuck."

Picking them up and setting Athena on my shoulder, I go to the window. The prospect is not promising. A green tangle surrounds us above and below. I remember Sherlock Holmes's horror of the countryside and wonder what he would make of a tropical jungle which not only isolates, but conceals and destroys as well.

Next, I inspect my quarters. The room I awoke in contains a foam extrusion bed, the round table, which is of only slightly firmer stuff, and some cushionlike chairs. A sliding door reveals a comfortable bathroom, equally designed with the resident's safety in mind. There are no sharp edges, no hard surfaces; there is not even a deep sink and certainly no tub.

The decorating scheme in both rooms is uniformly done in shades of tan and beige, lighter for the walls and floor, darker for the furnishings.

Tour completed, I sit on the bed. After the activity of the last several weeks, the abrupt stillness galls. The green curtain of foliage gives me no sense of time and I have nothing with which to amuse myself.

Idly, I stretch my hearing to find what the room might

say, but it only reeks of newness. All I learn are the locations of the concealed monitors. Betwixt and Between are correct; anything done in these rooms will be monitored.

Unwilling to talk, I activate Athena and lose myself in the owl's pleasure in flight. Gradually, I slip out of my concerns and into a simple world, dodging after dust motes in the sparkle of the sunshine.

They leave me alone for several days; two, I think, but it might be three. Meals arrive on some irregular schedule and though Betwixt and Between complain about the blandness of the fare, I do not care what I eat.

The thin paper receptacles the food arrives in crumple into brown dust after a few hours, but until then I can fold origami figures, remembering Bumblebee teaching me and Chocolate how to make them one night when it was too wet for even the Tail Wolves to go out and do business.

I eat and sleep and play, but refuse to speak, and after some time, they come to me. More specifically, she does: Dr. Haas.

She comes into my cell, white, golden, emerald. My eyes are hungry for color after the dull, tan room, the unremitting green without. She is some relief and as such I study her.

Seating herself on one of my spongy chairs, she flashes her white shark's smile at me.

"You know, I don't believe we've ever been introduced— even though we've met several times. I'm Lea Haas and I'll be working with you here at the Institute."

I refuse to play her pretty game and sit mute. Betwixt and Between hiss "Bitch" and Athena hoots soft agreement. Allowing a faint smile to curl my lips, I study her. Was that the faintest blush on the alabaster skin?

Before I can decide, she has shifted, crossing one leg over the other. "Sarah, you are due some explanation. Since you cannot—or will not—converse with me, I am forced to lecture."

I say nothing and she sighs. "Being difficult will not help you, Sarah. It may even hurt."

Again pause. Again I stay silent. Again the sigh.

"As you may remember, Sarah, you were born in the Institute's original complex. What you may or may not know is that you were part of an attempt to breed for some very specific and very improbable talents. Enhanced memory and empathy were the lesser qualities; the goal of the project was to maximize what has been dubbed 'magical thinking,' the ability to obtain impressions from what are commonly termed inanimate objects."

I must have given some signal that I understood, for she stops her lecture and looks at me.

"I see. You know something of this. Interesting."

Inwardly, I growl, unwilling to show any more. Dr. Haas studies me for a moment more and then continues.

"There were various attempts, but finally success, or something close, was achieved with three children. Even with these three, the results were less than ideal. The eldest, a girl named Eleanora, did show potential, but her main talents were in memory. The youngest—you, Sarah—showed incredible potential, but was unable to communicate. The middle, a boy named Dylan, was highly talented, but so sensitive that he was prone to collapses. Still, the project intended to develop all three.

"Then came a budget cut that severely crippled the Institute. Eleanora was dropped from the project. Sometime later, after another cut, Sarah was also dropped. Since she was nonfunctional, she was institutionalized. Independent funding was found and work on Dylan was continued. Eventually, he gained control of his abilities and proved invaluable."

She stops and I am suddenly aware that I am leaning forward, waiting for her next words. I gesture impatiently, tired of the farce, tired of being strung along.

"What next?" she interprets, smiling thin-lipped. "Dylan was working for the Institute on a sensitive project when he suddenly died."

I cry out, an inarticulate thing that is pure pain.

"Yes, your brother is dead. But the Institute needs to finish his project and only someone with similar—or greater—talents can do his work. That's you, Sarah."

Squaring my shoulders, trying to ignore my dragons' weeping, I sit up straight, proud for once to be locked away from such people by my insanity. For once, by saying nothing I truly speak as fully as I wish.

"Oh." Dr. Haas almost laughs. "You wonder how we're going to manage anything because of your 'autism.' There have been many advances in the years since you left us, Sarah, and some of them are going to take us right inside your head. You'll be able to say all you want, just as freely and fluently as you—or as we—wish. Think about it. Won't it be wonderful? And while you're thinking, I'll be setting things up for your first session."

She leaves and I fall back, trembling, on the bed.

"She wasn't telling the whole truth," Between says.

"I agree," Betwixt adds. "She's hiding something."

"But I couldn't catch what," Between says. "I tried, but she's too good. One thing she was lying about was Dylan's death—at least she didn't tell the whole story."

"He is dead, though," Betwixt replies sadly. "I'm sure."

I roll over and bury my face in the beige bedding, my own instincts agreeing with what the dragons are saying. Yet, I don't have any answers or even any free will. I suspect that if I do not at least go through the motions of cooperating, they will have ways prepared to force me.

So when two of the navy-uniformed guards arrive, I jump to my feet and smile. They do not stop me from taking Betwixt and Between and only hesitate slightly when I set Athena on my shoulder. That they do not refuse me my petty arsenal confirms what I have deduced. Even if I were to win my freedom, there is nowhere for me to go.

Our first stop is a room tiled white on walls and floor. The only furnishings are a chair with padded arms and headrest and a long table covered with various pieces of unfamiliar gear. Another of the blue uniforms, a stocky, brown-haired woman, is waiting.

"Now," she says, her voice hardened with some nasal accent, "I know you don't talk, but I hear y'do hear, so listen up. The word is that you are to have your hair shaved clean off. There are two ways we can do this. One is you can sit down pretty and pretend you're at the beauty parlor going for a flipping avant-garde look. The other is me and my buddies sit you down, strap you in, and you lose the hair just the same."

I walk and sit, clutching Betwixt and Between and wondering if there is some reason for this process or is it only a bit of malice intended to humiliate me. The machine in the woman's hand buzzes merrily and my hair drops off in heavy, cream-colored chunks.

As she works, the barber and the guards discuss some ongoing poker game, without a single word to me beyond "tilt your head" and "raise your chin."

I had nearly forgotten how the sane treat the insane during my time with the Pack, but I fall into the role of malleable dummy easily enough. When she finishes, she holds up a hand mirror. The jade eyes that stare out at me are all the rounder within a face unframed by hair. I lift a hand and rub the naked, smooth surface. It feels strange, and softer than it looks.

"Pretty, eh?" the woman grunts. "Now, next you go over into that corner shower and wash off any hair. When you're done, put on the wrap you'll find in there and bring all your old stuff here."

Obediently, I go over and am relieved to find that there is a curtain I can draw, providing at least an illusion of privacy. After washing, I towel off and find the "wrap." This proves to be a knee-length robe and a pair of loose drawstring trousers made of soft, grey cotton.

Once dressed, I bring my denims and shirt, which whisper to me of the Jungle, out to the woman.

Wrinkling her nose, she accepts them, "Right. March her

up to Comp-C. Dr. Haas and Dr. Aldrich are waiting for her."

As we walk, I try and recall if I remember a Dr. Aldrich and decide that I do. Vague memories of a very tall man with a soft, deep voice come back. He must have been very important for me to recall him so immediately upon hearing his name.

Although the complex is able to house many people, we pass relatively few, making me believe at least some of Dr. Haas's tale of economic hardship. Comp-C turns out to be an antiseptic upper floor filled with the subliminal hum of electricity and large machines. Almost everything that is not white is painted a brilliant neon orange that shrieks at my eyes.

My guards escort me to a door that opens in anticipation of our approach. I step in alone. Dr. Haas, in her familiar lab coat and predatory smile, awaits, but I dismiss her to study the other.

He is not so tall as in my memory, but still he towers over me. Like many very tall people, he stoops forward and the stoop has been permanently frozen into his bones, nearly concealing the incongruous potbelly that juts from his skinny frame.

"Sarah," he says, holding out a hand. "Welcome. I am Dr. Aldrich—you may remember me from years ago."

I do and only with the greatest self-control can I offer my hand in return. He beams, seeming unaware of my discomfort.

"I see you've had your hair done. Very good. For the next several weeks, we are going to do numerous—painless—

brain scans on you. All that thick, lovely hair would have gotten in the way. Once we know what we need, you should be able to grow it all back."

He is lying. I can tell this so easily that I am amazed that he even bothers. Dr. Haas only smiles.

The next hours are a blur to me. I am lightly strapped into a chair and various things are attached to my shaved scalp. Some hurt, most do not. Some of the tests seem remotely familiar, but the rest mean nothing. I think that I am doped because when I begin to focus again, the light from the one high window is gone. Dr. Aldrich is musing aloud to Dr. Haas.

"So, the language block is genuine, not an act. It's a wonder she has as much control as she does."

"We will be using the direct link then."

"No choice, I'm afraid. Should be fascinating. Wonder how she'll take it?"

"Wonderfully, I'd guess." Dr. Haas chuckles. "My guess is that she'll find it quite addictive."

"Yes." Dr. Aldrich sounds bemused. "Dylan did, didn't he."

Hours spin into days as I am shuttled from test to test. I come to recognize the staff regulars and guards. Only three are really important: Dr. Aldrich, Dr. Haas, and Jersey.

Jersey must have another name, but I never learn it. He is a chunky man, overweight, with watery grey eyes—he also is as bald as I am. Jersey is the operator and, I think, designer of the machine by which Dr. Aldrich plans to circumvent my inability to speak as other people do.

Despite his sloppiness and the fact that he smells like rotting potatoes, I like Jersey. Perhaps because, as with Head Wolf, I recognize that he is utterly insane.

"We're not going to bother to explain what we're doing, Sarey," he says one morning, "because you wouldn't understand it. What's going to happen—now, that's important, so tune in and listen carefully."

I fold my hands around Betwixt and Between and sit very straight in my chair so he will know that I'm listening.

"Now, in a bit, we're going to link you up with my computer here. Dr. Haas'll give you some stuff to make you drifty and mind that you take it, otherwise the probes don't feel so good. I know, I've done it both ways. You'll feel like you're going to sleep and then do you know what will appear?"

"A miniature sleigh and eight tiny reindeer?" I suggest.

He grins. "Nope. Better. We'll be in a nice, comfortable room and you'll know it right off because it'll have a picture like this one on the wall behind my chair."

Taking a card from his pocket, he slides it across to me, "Know it?"

I shake my head.

"That's Van Gogh's *Olive Orchard*," he says with a sigh, "one of my favorites, and I've got it—there at least. When you see it, let it be a sign to you that you are able to talk and we'll have a chat. Got it?"

I nod slowly, still confused.

"Don't worry," he smiles. "It'll be flipping great. In fact, why should we wait and let you get nervous? C'mon!"

He goes to the intercom and pages the doctors. There is

some brief discussion, then argument, but when he comes back to me, he is smiling again.

"We'll be ready in an hour. I'm to either send you to your room or keep you distracted. Your choice."

I study him, reaching, sense no threat or hidden motive. Wanting a friend in this place, I smile.

"God Almighty first planted a garden," I offer. "And, indeed, it is the purest of all human pleasures."

"You want to garden?" Jersey asks incredulously.

"I am tired of four walls and a ceiling," I explain, feeling a pang as I recall Professor Isabella using the same words. "I have need of the grass."

"Okay," he says, "but only the roof garden. I'm no jungle beast."

I smile and if he wonders at my amusement, he does not say.

The roof garden is hot and humid, the air heavy with a thousand scents. Betwixt and Between puff their approval from where I carry them. We walk around on the gravel paths, looking at orchids pale and bright that evoke images of prom dresses and weddings. This continues for nearly a half hour, until Jersey is streaming with sour sweat.

I return indoors without protest, knowing cooperation is essential. Once we are in, I struggle for words to try and thank Jersey.

"Don't worry, Sarey," he says, smiling mysteriously. "Don't fight for it. You'll be talking easy in just a bit. Now, sit quiet and I'll go and rinse off and be back."

After parking me in his office and pouring me some iced

tea, he leaves. When he returns with Dr. Haas and Dr. Aldrich in tow, he has not only showered, he has changed into loose pants and a top similar to those that I am wearing. Patting the back of my hand as he walks by, he grabs a handful of wires and other gizmos and then motions us all through another door.

The annex is twice the size of his office and whereas the one is cluttered with gadgets and related debris, this room is nearly spotless. The walls are painted a restful shade of blue that in no way competes with the array of computer equipment that borders the four walls. The only other furnishings are four strangely sinuous chairs and a startlingly prosaic table.

I am given no time to frame questions or grow concerned. Dr. Aldrich motions me into one of the chairs, his impatience a blunt, musky thing.

Gingerly, I lower myself onto the weird stretch of ebony plastic and gasp when it conforms to me so perfectly that I tap the surface to confirm that I am indeed sitting on something.

Jersey glances from where he is arranging wires and electrodes on the table and chortles at my expression.

"Flip you, did it?" he asks. "Won't bug you with the details, Sarey, but that thing is so sensitive to posture and other comfort signals that it'll react to a fart."

Dr. Aldrich makes a disapproving noise.

"Hey, that's scientifically accurate and necessary," Jersey grins. "When a human is interfacing with the computer, minimal distractions are best. These chairs guarantee that there will be no physical discomfort and the other senses will be dealt with during the hookup. Now, I want you to set me up first so Sarey can see what will happen to her."

Dr. Haas makes as if to protest, but Jersey waves her down. "No, I'm the expert here. If you'd listened to me more in the first place, maybe Dylan wouldn't have . . ."

He trails off, suddenly at a loss. I look blank, as if I hadn't heard the last exchange.

Hurriedly, Dr. Aldrich steps into the gap. "Fine. You first. Then Sarah. Let's just get onto it."

Although I listen as Jersey narrates the placement of various electrodes about his head and body, I only catch that they will capture some things and monitor others. I am more concerned about why—or how—Dylan died.

When my turn comes, I sit very still, refusing to jump, even though the cream they smear on my scalp is cold. Finally, as Jersey promised, we are each given something to drink.

Almost immediately, I feel a drifting sensation, similar to when I am falling asleep and believe that I am awake only to discover that I have been dreaming all along. The sensation is not unpleasant, and I let myself slip into dreams, coasting away from the annex of Jersey's office into the familiar, sleepy, swirling darkness behind my eyes.

When colors appear in the darkness, I focus on them with idle curiosity. Green-grey and grey-blue drift above a field of brown-gold. As I concentrate, they begin to resolve themselves into twisted trees against a stormy sky growing from a dry field. Nearly as quickly as I recognize Van Gogh's *Olive Orchard*, I realize that the picture is hanging on a wall painted a tasteful antique ivory. Beside the picture, a faintly proprietary expression on his face, is Jersey.

But this is and is not the Jersey I know. The omnipresent stench of sour sweat is gone. He is more attractive, flab turned into muscle. His bald head glistens as if polished.

"Welcome, Sarey," he says, "to this cooperative hallucination. You look lovely—but you wouldn't know, would you? Look here."

He turns and for the first time I notice that there is a full-length mirror with a silver gilt frame hanging on the wall. When I see my reflection, I gasp with surprise.

"I have my hair!" I say and then clasp my throat in wonder, for the words are shaped just as I had thought them.

Jersey laughs. "Yes. Guess you didn't like losing it, for all so quiet you were about it."

I continue studying my reflection. My hair is not the only thing to have reappeared. When I reach to touch the heavy cream strands and reassure myself of their reality, I feel something tickle below my ear. Pushing back my hair, I see that my ivory wolf dangles in its usual place—it had been taken from me when I first awoke after my surrender and I had believed it forever lost. My clothing is unremarkable, jeans and shirt of the style that Abalone had given me.

Yet, although fully dressed, I feel as if I am naked. Casting around to fill the loss, I see Betwixt and Between sitting on one of the comfortable-looking easy chairs. Athena perches on the back.

Seeing me, Betwixt winks. "Can't do without us, now, can you?"

"You know it," I say and then am instantly tongue-tied.

I cover for this by picking up the dragons and perching

Athena on my shoulder. She swivels her head to look at me and then begins to preen her feathers, chortling softly.

Jersey is gaping at me. "You brought them through! This is unprecedented! I didn't . . ."

He trails off and looks so uncomfortable that I reach over and pat his arm.

"I am a brother to dragons, a companion to owls," I state simply. Then, afraid that the words will suddenly fail, "Where are we? What kind of place is this?"

Jersey regains some of his composure and saunters over to one of the chairs. Leaning back in it and picking up a daiquiri from what I had believed was an empty table, he sips and sighs happily.

"This place is in our minds, Sarey. Ours and the computer's. Mine, mostly, since I did the set programming, but yours, too, which is why you look like you want to, and, I guess, why your friends are with you." He shakes his head. "Does that help?"

"Not much," I admit. "How come I can . . . talk?"

"Because you can think in a coherent fashion and because you want to," Jersey says simply. "It was pretty obvious that you weren't just mimicking or reciting quotes at random, so it was a fair bet that if you were given a chance to say what you were thinking, you would be fine, and so here we are, chatting in a nice room."

"Why?" I ask, marveling that I can shape the simple monosyllable.

Jersey puts his glass down. "Two words: Magical Thinking. Your ability is extraordinary, but you can't talk to tell the doctors what you hear. So, I provide the bridge and over you walk."

"Why?" Between asks, stretching his neck toward a nice succulent plant growing next to my chair.

Jersey pulls at his ear. "Did you say something?"

"No, Between did," I answer, puzzled that he cannot tell—the little dragon's voice is definitely masculine.

"Between?"

"Between"—I point—"Betwixt. They're quite different people—from the neck up, that is."

"Oh, boy." Jersey grabs for his glass. "Sarey, I won't say if you don't, but I've got bad feelings about this."

"Say?" I laugh. "To whom? And what? Are Dr. Haas and Dr. Aldrich watching us?"

"No." Jersey relaxes some. "No way unless they link up with us and they don't do that too often. There are potential . . . side effects."

I ignore his discomfort, enjoying this new freedom. Noticing a bowl of fruit on the table, I set Betwixt and Between down and they trundle forward and start decimating Bartlett pears. Athena seems content to sit on my shoulder for now.

"We aren't seeing exactly the same thing, are we?" I hazard.

"Probably not, not on minor details, but part of what the computer is doing is picking up what is most—important— to you and to me and creating a consensus reality from them. Self-image is really important, so that holds, same with what we're talking about, but the color of the walls or the style of furnishings wouldn't be shared unless it was important that it was—like with the Van Gogh or that mirror."

"I understand," I say, restraining myself from trying to make it important for him to see Betwixt and Between gobbling fresh fruit on his coffee table. "Somehow, I doubt all of this is to let me have a try at the spoken word. You started to explain before—it has something to do with magical thinking."

"Right." Jersey looks unhappy for a moment. "You got the basics from Dr. Haas, I know. What you didn't get is that the Institute has been supporting its 'research' through controlled use of magical thinking. It is almost too-potent stuff. I didn't know Dylan until—after—but he was something else even then."

"After." I lean forward. "After what?"

"Dylan had an . . . accident." Jersey flushes. "Damn, Sarey, I can't tell you. Don't ask me about him—ask anything else."

I am shocked; for a brief instant his image had flickered and he had become the overweight madman I knew. By the time he has control again, he also has my pity.

"Okay," I promise, "I won't ask, but don't forget that I want to know. He was my brother and I loved him even if I was a kid when we were separated."

"Family isn't all it's made out to be, Sarey," Jersey answers. "Let's get off this. You asked about why the Institute wanted you so bad. Simple. Magical thinking seems to break the rules most of us live by. Things talk to you—right?"

"Right. Yes." I smile. "You bet. Ten-four, good buddy."

Jersey chuckles. "Okay. Now, most of this world is based around the simple concept that things don't talk. Security systems assume that codes and ciphers are safely hidden between our ears. Conferences assume that the places they are held can be made secure. There's an old story about how a guy told a secret he couldn't bear to keep to a hole in the ground and it would have been safe except that the reeds growing there picked up the words and whispered them to the world. You get the picture?"

"Yes." I nod, remembering a code pad happily chanting, I got a secret! "I understand. They're using us to steal secrets."

"Yeah." Jersey smiles sadly. "You catch on fast. Street-smarts, but what can I expect with what you've been doing?"

I almost think he is going to say more, but he picks up his drink and sips the frosty thing. The level of ice never drops.

"So, Sarey, Dr. Aldrich had taken money to learn some things for some—powerful—people. Hell, dangerous people. And then Dylan—died—and he was up a creek without a paddle. Then Aldrich remembered you and when he sent for you, you had been discharged. There was sixteen kinds of bitchiness until you were found. Now I've got to get you acclimated and they'll pay off their debts and all."

"And I stay here?" I ask bluntly. "Forever."

"Yeah," he nods. "I can't see how they'd let you go."

FOURTEEN

⁓

OUR NEXT SESSION IS MUCH LIKE THE FIRST. WHEN BEING brought in for the third, my guard is reaching to ring for admittance when suddenly he stops. I am about to try and ask why when I hear the faintest sound of voices raised in argument. Stretching my hearing, I am able to make out the words.

". . . endangering her!" The voice is Jersey's.

"No, I am saving her and us." Dr. Haas is cool. "If she doesn't adapt to the interface quickly, our creditors will be very unhappy and if they get unhappy . . . Do I need to spell it out?"

"No." I can almost hear Jersey shake his head. "But . . ."

The guard steers me away before I can hear more. When we come back five minutes later, Jersey is hooking himself up, his anger only subdued. Dr. Haas smiles her unfriendly smile and, with a few bright comments about the weather (which never changes in our climate-controlled building), hooks me up.

Jersey is waiting across the white mist in the now-familiar room and barely gives me time to set down my dragons before speaking.

"Okay, Sarey, today we start work. This is something of a test. I'm going to show you a variety of items and you are going to tell me what they say to you. Got it?"

"You bet, boss." I smile. "But how can I hear what not-real things are saying? Isn't this place all in the mind?"

"Yes, but Dr. Haas will be handing you the 'real' object at the same time. It should work. It has in the past."

I don't need to ask: with Dylan. Instead, I nod.

"Ready when you are, Jersey."

The first thing he hands to me is a book. The cover and spine are blank, but this hardly matters. We'd already learned that I cannot read here any better than I can outside of the interface. Apparently, skills cannot be merely wished for.

Holding the book, I listen; the voice is soft at first, then easily understood, then even familiar. Tears spring to my eyes and I clasp the battered text to my breast.

"Oh, Jersey! It's *Mary Poppins*—the one my nurse read to me when I was small. I kept the book in my room and would listen even when she was gone. I thought it was lost!"

Jersey makes a note on a computer keyboard identical to one I had seen in the annex.

"Very good, Sarey. How about this?"

He hands me a small cedar block made of varitoned

shades of wood, polished to a high finish. I caress its smooth sides and admire its red-gold color. As I do so, I hear a soft giggle.

Betwixt and Between are busy eating a bowl of ice cream. Athena is chasing a moth by the ceiling.

The giggle comes again and I focus on the cedar block.

"Puzzle," it giggles, "puzzle puzzle puzzle puzzle puzzle."

I giggle, too, for its delight is infectious.

"It's a puzzle box," I tell Jersey. "Let's see. To solve it . . ."

Listening to the happy noise and the occasional groan, I press on the wood strips and in moments have revealed a small cavity large enough for a ring or a small deck of cards.

Jersey applauds and writes down some more notes.

"Tired, Sarey? Or can you do some more?"

"I'm a little tired. Let me have a small rest and then I'll try another. Am I doing okay?"

"Just great." Jersey leans back and reaches for a milkshake.

"Jersey, what were you and Dr. Haas arguing about this morning?"

He sputters into his shake. "How did you know?"

"The guard brought me by when you were—I heard."

"But those rooms are soundproof. The guard looked in through the window on the door. I waved him off. You . . ."

I shrug. "I am brother to dragons, a companion to owls. Tell me why you were arguing. You said I could ask about anything except Dylan."

"Well, that's not exactly what I said." He pauses. "Think

about it. However, Dr. Haas has been mixing the drug that eases interface. I found she was going a bit heavy on some components in yours. We got into a fight and she reminded me of my place."

"Which is?"

"Sarey, hon, you've lived in a fairly protected world. I don't know all the details, but you've always had people looking out for you. Not so for me—my computer work is my world and yet I've had funding troubles all along."

Remembering his madness, I understand.

"The Institute came when I was down. They said essentially: 'Hey, you can get in people's minds. We don't care about how or anything. We just want in.'"

"Wait, Jersey, you told me that the Institute had lost funding. How did they pay you? This couldn't be cheap."

"Sarey, the 'Institute' you're talking about is just one part of a much larger organization. I was working for them—research—and eventually they linked me up with Dr. Aldrich after Dylan's accident . . ."

He stops, aware that he's said too much.

"Accident?" I ask.

"No, Sarey, don't distract me. Now, what working with Aldrich was a chance at was legit research, y'know, with a big 'L.' I only learned too late all the crap that was going down and by then I would have had to give it all up and I couldn't. Can't."

He finishes and takes a long suck on his milkshake until the straw rattles against the bottom of the glass.

"Rested?" he says. "Let's try another."

We work for a while more. Some of the items are easy—others more difficult. One says nothing at all.

When we come back from the interface, I am praised by doctors Aldrich and Haas. My score is perfect—even the no-reading had been right—a brand-new item with minimal associations.

Despite my pride, I feel very drained and let them take me back to my room in a wheelchair. There I fall asleep almost at once and dream cryptic dreams.

Upon awakening, I do not immediately get up, but instead roll onto my back, reviewing the past day's events. My concern about what happened to Dylan had been muted by the excitement of learning to interface, discovering speech, making friends with Jersey. Now it comes back in full.

What had Jersey said? I struggle to remember his exact word, "Don't ask me about him—ask anything else."

I whisper the words, too softly for the monitors to catch.

Between hears and yawns. "What did you say, Sarah?"

I repeat myself, "Don't ask me about him—ask anything else."

"Jersey said that, didn't he," Between says. "Funny way to put it."

"It's a puzzle," Betwixt cuts in excitedly. "Must be or he wouldn't have told her to remember it exactly."

"Don't ask me," Between repeats slowly, stressing every syllable, "ask any-thing else."

I sit up suddenly and the motion detectors turn on the room lights. Blinking at the light, I run a hand through my nonexistent hair and wish for speech. Unable to explain myself, I hug Betwixt and Between and head for the shower.

My guards, I have learned, are not precisely the Institute's. Instead, they belong to the anonymous employer. Now that I have proven myself a cooperative patient, I am permitted to go around the building—although always with a guard in tow.

Now, I ignore the blue uniform stalking discontentedly behind me and pace the corridors, linger in the common rooms. Finally, in the dripping heat of the roof garden, I find what I have been seeking. In an ornamental pool by a stone fountain shaped like a leaping carp, I find Dylan.

Not Dylan, really, but a place where he went and where something of him still lingers just as my nurse remains in a favorite book or an artist in a painting.

The guard draws back to the shelter of a doorway within the climate control zone. Instantly, I understand why Dylan liked this place. He effectively could be alone.

Sitting on the edge of the fountain basin, I relax and let the random impressions form. The sweat beads under my wrap and rolls under my breasts, but I do not move. Slowly, less substantial than my reflection in the rippling waters, something is taking form. I reach out to it, confused by its silence.

There are no words, but I do find something: pain. The man who sat here was fighting pain of body and spirit that intertwined like the vines in the jungle around us. Fearing what I will find, I reach deeper.

My throat burns and I cup water from the fountain to cool it. The basin remembers another who did this, sputtering and choking each time with force enough to still the insects in the shrubs from their strident clamor.

Pain. A throat burned speechless? Yes.

The thing has told me all it can, but now I have some information to work from.

When I return inside, I study the guard. Surely he knows the information I want to learn just as Jersey does, but will be equally bound not to tell. The very walls must have answers, but they will not have noticed, not unless Dylan put his mark on them.

I carry my frustration with me, through my meal in my cell, through restless pacing and tossing and turning. No answer comes and when I finally sleep, I dream of the Jungle and its web of lines and hammocks.

I awaken with a contradiction screaming at me. Maddeningly, I see neither Jersey nor either of the doctors, so there is no one to whom I can talk. Feeling truly mute for the first time in my life, I circle the complex restlessly, prompting a comment from my usually taciturn guard about her not being paid by the mile.

The only thing I learn from my wanderings is a confirmation that certain areas, among them what I suspect were Dylan's rooms, are off-limits to me.

When I am finally taken to Jersey's computer annex, I can barely keep from urging them to hook me in. Jersey seems concerned at this, but Dr. Haas is pleased.

Dr. Aldrich enters just as the hookup is completed.

"Sarah," he says, just before Dr. Haas hands me my beaker, "you must get this precisely right. A great deal depends on it."

. . . .

I nod.

He shakes his index finger at me. "Precisely right."

Slurping down the liquid, I have only time to notice that the taste is somehow wrong. Then, without the comfortable sensation of drifting off to sleep, I feel myself being sucked out of my body. I am shifted and strained through something cold and impersonal, reduced to a strand of numbers, each screaming loudly for the others. When I see the grey-greens of Jersey's Van Gogh, I grab for them like a Cub grasping for a guideline.

My self begins to re-form, numbers becoming pulse and bone, skin, hair, eyes. Eyes that I open to find myself sprawled whole and gasping on the carpet of Jersey's sitting room.

He reaches down and helps me into a chair, offers me coffee.

I drink gratefully, notice that Betwixt and Between, staggering despite their four stocky legs, are nudging Athena to her feet. I pour them a pool of coffee to lap, not caring what it does to the table's finish. From under a lampshade, I find a moth that I feed to Athena.

Jersey watches curiously. "Feels like shit, don't it, Sarey? But I wouldn't bitch to Dr. Haas even so. Y'see, I did it."

"You? What?" Words, I am learning, are not always a help.

"Babe, I've decided to come down on the side of the angels." He winks. "That's you. Look, the whole trick to this interface of mine—well, not the whole trick, but one of the big ones—is in that potion you slug down. Does funny things to brain waves that let a properly set up bit of equipment read 'em. In a sense, Sarey, this ain't a virtual reality; it's real reality 'cause you know it is, right down where you are. Get me?"

"Sort of." I rub my head. "You did that to me?"

"Yeah." Jersey looks shamed, but only for a moment. "You see, the problem with my 'potion' is that it really hurts to be broken down that way, even if you know you'll get built up again. Do it too much and it can drive you crazy. So I played around with some other things until I found a mixture that eased the transition without ruining the effectiveness of the first drug. One problem."

"What?"

"It screws up the internal organs and is addictive as hell. Honey"—he looks me in the eyes—"when I perfected the telepathic interface, I really looked like you see me here. What you see out there is a result of the stuff I've been taking. Dr. Haas has been upping your dose—today, when she was distracted, I switched it for a more neutral one, but I didn't get the buffer quite right."

In the pain and confusion, I had almost forgotten my earlier suspicions. "She hates me. Why, Jersey?"

"Hates you?" Jersey looks puzzled. "I think she just wants the project to go down fine. I don't think she hates you."

"No," I flounder. "Things fall apart, the center cannot hold. I mean, things just don't fit."

"Hey, relax, Sarey. What doesn't fit?"

"You told me that after Dylan died, the Institute tried to find me, only to learn that I'd been discharged from the Home."

"Yeah, that's right. I remember Dr. Aldrich's cursing and

swearing when he heard. For a while there, he thought we'd have to use the third sibling. I got the impression that he knew where to find her, but that she wasn't as good."

"Fine. But, Jersey, the doctor who insisted on discharging me from the Home was Dr. Haas."

"You sure?"

"Could I make a mistake on something like that?"

Jersey shakes his head. "No, I guess not."

An odd look comes over his face. "Time to work, Sarey."

He reached into a chest by his chair and pulls out a small rectangular box of black plastic.

"This is a key box," he says, handing it to me. "We have the box, but not the key. We want you to tell us what it is."

Accepting the key box, I feel it carefully, finding that the four corners each depress slightly; one bears an almost imperceptible dimple.

A faint sigh of anticipation comes to me as I touch the corners. Glancing up at Jersey, I see his expression has not changed. The sigh then . . . I focus again on the black plastic box.

"There is an order in which these need to be pressed," I say, more to myself than to Jersey. "If I get it wrong . . ."

I stretch my senses; the feeling from the box is glee? And sorrow? Odd. Making as if I am about to press a sequence, I clearly mark the emotions, find them shaping into words.

"This is the end . . ." the box hums.

I remember Abalone and the safeguards on her tappety-tap.

"This thing destroys itself if the sequence is done wrong!"

"Yeah," Jersey says. "That's why we need to be kinda careful—it won't take any conventional tampering and the gal who knew the code series isn't exactly in a position to tell."

"Oh." I don't like the image that flickers into my mind. "Let me see if I can get it to tell me. There's one problem."

"What?"

"I think it kinda wants to blow up."

"A kamikaze key box? Give it up, Sarey."

"No, Jersey, things *are*, but I read them in part because of their associations. That's why some things are null to me."

"So if the person who associated with this didn't give a shit about dying, then this might not either?"

"Yeah." I bite my lip. "I never thought that much about it before, but that feels right."

"Do what you can"—he leans back—"and be careful."

Again, I concentrate, shutting out Jersey, the room, everything except the key box. This I hold in my left hand, positioned so that the dimple is in the upper left-hand corner. When I feel again the presence of the humming, I lower a finger toward the upper left corner. The humming does not change, even when I abort the move at the last second.

Disgruntled, I sit back. If it doesn't care, how can I fool it into telling me? Most inanimates do have an ego of sorts; this, though, doesn't seem to. Or does it? When I first tried, it did seem to react; therefore, this behavior now must be a feint.

Tossing it onto the coffee table, I grin at Jersey.

"Got it?" he asks excitedly.

"Nope"—I smile, trying to radiate indifference—"and I don't even care to try and find out."

Is it my imagination or do I hear a faint squeal of indignation from the box? Betwixt and Between tilt their heads, hearing it also. With an effort, I ignore the box, putting all my energy into projecting my view of our consensus universe, trying to force Jersey to see things the way I do.

When he rubs his eyes and stares up at where Athena is chasing a moth around a ceiling light fixture, I know I have won.

"What the hell . . ." he mutters, then, "You're doing this, aren't you, Sarey? Why? Why aren't you working on deciphering the box?"

"I have my reasons." I smile. "Who cares about a silly code anyhow? Jersey, we can have anything here. Why are we sitting snacking in a living room?"

Jersey looks shocked and even Betwixt and Between look from the bowl of corn chips they are decimating. But the whine from the box is so clear that even Jersey hears it.

"You may have something," he says a bit stiffly, noticing apparently for the first time that the stocky blue dragon on the table is no longer inanimate rubber. "What do you want?"

"I want to go home," I reply, the longing in my voice stronger than I'd intended. "Look!"

I point dramatically overhead where a miracle has taken place. Gone is the ceiling, gone the light. Athena is sweeping up into the rope-webbed spaces within curving grey metal walls. A rope ladder drops and swings slightly, alluringly, in front of us.

"It's the Jungle, Jersey," I say, "the best place I've ever lived. The Free People are away, I see, so it must be night.

C'mon, let's go. If we anchor the ladder, the climb won't be so bad."

Jersey hesitates and I sense him trying to overcome my re-ordering of our reality, but he has no power over my home-sick and guilt-torn heart. What had started as a ploy is becoming only too real and I can barely keep from climbing away.

I pick Betwixt and Between up, brushing chip crumbs from my shirt, feeling their claws anchoring them firmly to my side. Athena swoops and circles to my left shoulder. Jersey seems insubstantial, the Jungle more and more real by the moment.

"Coming?" I say, my foot on the ladder's first rung.

"Sarey, I . . ." Jersey is saying when a shrill voice from the table screams, "Up left! Down right! Again! Again! Again! Up right! Down left! Again! End."

I quickly repeat the code. Jersey grabs his computer pad and hammers in the instructions.

Then suddenly the world is torn away from me and I slump in the annex, crying wildly, my hands still curled to grasp the ladder and climb away.

FIFTEEN

～

DR. HAAS TRIES TO KILL ME THE NEXT MORNING. I GO OUT TO
the fountain to sit with Dylan's too-silent presence as has
become my custom. I am sitting there, trying yet again to
make sense of why all I get from this spot is a sensation of
pain, when I notice something sparkling among the pebbles
on the fountain bottom.

Idly, I dip my fingers into the water to fish it out.

A strong, humming jolt comes from the water. My arm
bones quiver as if suddenly the bone has been stripped away
and only the marrow remains. Leaping back, I stumble,
crashing into my guard, who has rushed from her customary place in the cooler doorway.

"Sarah, what's wrong!" she cries, catching me before I
fall.

"He hath loosed the fateful lightning of his terrible swift
sword," I reply, cursing inwardly that I cannot be more precise.

"What?" she says, setting me on my feet and going to look at the water. "Something cut you? Hey, what's that?"

"No!" I grab her arm back from the water's edge and she stares at me as if recalling that I am mad.

"Easy, Sarah, take it easy. I just wanted to see what was shining down there in the water, that bright silver thing."

I continue shaking my head, refusing to release her arm. "I do not see the hanged man, fear death by water."

She wrinkles her brows. "You're saying the water's dangerous, *amiga*? Not something in it?"

I nod. She is close enough to the truth and won't just dip her hand in. Still, I try to clarify.

"The fateful lightning," I repeat.

"Lightning?"

I nod eagerly and she puzzles for a moment.

"Lightning's in the water?"

"Bingo!" I cheer, trying to applaud, but finding my right hand still trembles deep within.

"*Jesu Domine!* You could have gotten electrocuted!" she exclaims, realization spreading across her square, dark features. "Me, too. Come on, *amiga*. I'll make a call, then take you to see the infirmary and check that hand."

Dr. Aldrich himself tends me. Miraculously, there is no serious damage, but he decides that I should not go on the interchange that day.

"Take her to her room and make certain that she rests." He hands Margarita a paper envelope. "If she won't—or can't—give her these. Oh, and she'd better keep clear of that fountain. We don't want any other accidents."

Margarita nods and escorts me back to my cell. While she

is helping me to change, a report comes over her radio. Much of the technical babble is meaningless to me, but I follow enough to understand that my "accident" is being explained as a result of corroded insulation on a power cable to the pump.

No mention is made of the sparkling lure, and Margarita has apparently forgotten it, her attention galvanized by her narrow escape from death and my part as her savior.

"You had no reason to do that, *amiga*," she says, tucking Betwixt and Between in next to me. "I've not said a friendly word to you since you come here. I don't break my contract, but I'll keep a good eye on you now."

Later, when I wake from a deep, dreamless sleep, I find a bowl of cut flowers brightening my colorless room. I don't need to read the note to know who has brought them.

I am certain that Dr. Haas arranged my accident, but I have no proof beyond my growing knowledge of her duplicity and awareness of her malice. I decide to not even mention my latest suspicion to Jersey. I prefer that he continue to see me as an "angel" he wants to help.

The rest of the day passes uneventfully. The shock has worn me out and I sleep much of the time.

When evening comes, I have a visit from Jersey. He has showered and is wearing a brightly colored shirt and cotton trousers. From somewhere he has even dredged up a tie.

"Hey, Sarey, I heard you had an accident today."

I smile demurely, choosing to emphasize my condition by not replying. I see the effect instantly. Jersey has grown accustomed to the chatterbox of the interchange. My silence hurts.

"Smile for me, honey"—he looks anxious—"big now."

I valiantly bare my teeth and Jersey's lip trembles just slightly. He leans to awkwardly pat my leg.

"Aw, really scared you, did it, baby?" He looks pensive. "Dr. Aldrich says no up-time today, but we'll go tomorrow. I'll let you show me that Jungle again."

I smile, too touched by his concern to refuse him the gratification of cheering me up. He stays for nearly two hours, playing chess. We are well-matched—his knowledge of strategy is excellent, but my memory is good and once I see a play I can use it for my own.

Oddly, I find myself comparing him to Abalone. An idea comes to me then, but under the dual impediments of language and the watchful videocams I restrain myself.

I am too exhausted not to sleep well, but I awaken early. As I am stripping to dress, my cell's door bursts open and Margarita races in. She tosses my robe to me.

"Wait, *amiga*, just a minute. You not know, but those horny bastards in the vid room, they get up early jus' to watch you shower."

She stands on one of my oversoft chairs, bouncing slightly as she neatly duct tapes over the front lens. She does the same in the bathroom.

Jumping down, she says, "There. Now, I do my job and stay here while you shower and dress. You don't gotta be a skin flick star."

I hug her and, seizing Betwixt and Between, head into the bathroom. My shower, even with the door open so that Margarita can make certain I don't do anything drastic, is the most privacy I've had since I've come to the Institute and I enjoy it immensely.

"You like the flowers?" she asks while I'm dressing.

"The flowers, they were radiant with glory and shed such perfume on the air," I answer, nodding.

"Good, I'm thinking, maybe I bring you a fish tank—a little one, since the big doctor says you not to go outside anymore." She grins. "Yeah, I think I do that."

Quotations for thanks seem insincere and so I hug her again. She escorts me to Comp-C and waves a cheery good-bye.

Fortified, I go in and don't even flinch when Dr. Haas hands me my beaker. A faint wink from Jersey warns me to be ready for the mule's kick but I find being spread out across a universe no easier despite his warning. Again, I come to myself sprawled on the floor of Jersey's sitting room.

"I'm not sure that whatever overdose she could concoct for me wouldn't be better than that, Jersey," I say, struggling up, finally accepting his hand.

"You're just saying that, Sarey," he assures me. "You like being in control of yourself. I can tell."

"Control?" I meet his eyes. "I wonder if I have ever been in control of my own life?"

"Not of your life, Sarey." Jersey doesn't smile. "Of you."

"Hmm." I am reluctant to admit that I see his point.

"Sarey, you never pressed for exactly why Dylan needed the 'services' of my machines, but you must remember that he wasn't . . . ." Jersey blushes, aware that he's on a delicate topic.

"Crazy? Or at least autistic?"

I see that Betwixt and Between have found a bag of French fries and concentrate on helping Jersey to see my addition to our consensus reality.

"Yeah, that. You know he could talk normally."

"Yes, I seem to remember that." I look at him and shrug. "I was pretty small when I left the Institute and they blocked my memories or something because I didn't remember him or them until I heard Betwixt and Between telling Conejito Moreno about Dylan."

"Conejito Moreno?" Jersey shakes himself. "Sarey, Dylan's 'accident' was probably pretty deliberate. You see, he drank some corrosive; I think it was a cleaner. It made a mess of his throat when he started throwing it up. He didn't die, but he couldn't talk."

I wince, wrapping a hand around my throat, understanding the silence and pain whenever I found Dylan's memories in the inanimate. Betwixt and Between have stopped eating and large tears are rolling from their bright ruby eyes.

"Dylan killed himself?" I ask, gathering my dragons close.

Athena lands near, cooing and hooting softly. Jersey seems to see, but does not allow himself to become distracted.

"Yeah"—he pauses—"He did. I don't know exactly why he did it when he did, but he hung himself. They didn't have cameras in his room like in yours."

Much makes sense now. I fight back my grief for the pale-eyed boy, for the man I would never know and soothe my wildly sobbing dragons. I wonder if he was permitted any other inanimate friends and if they weep for him in

. . . .
234

some dark closet or if they were tossed along with the rest of the trash.

Jersey's face goes blank and slack for a handful of heartbeats; I know he is getting some message from outside of the interchange. Then he refocuses, notices for the first time that a rope ladder again leads into the strung reaches.

"They want to know if we're ready," he says. "Shall I give the go-ahead?"

I nod and he fingers his screen. When he reaches into the chest this time, he extracts two plastic slips, much like cred slips except one is pink and the other a painful chartreuse.

"These," he explains, "are access cards for an account—more accurately, one is the access card and the other is a dummy. Your job is to figure which is which—only the man who carried them knew for sure and . . ."

"He's in no position to tell," I complete. "I get the picture. This shouldn't be too hard."

"Make it hard," Jersey suggests. "I mean, when you know don't tell right off. I'll signal that you're working and we can talk without making them suspicious."

"Okay."

I reach out with my inner hearing and almost instantly can tell. One card is dull and mute. The other chuckles steadily. A moment more confirms that the silence is indeed inertia and not a layer of concealment. The pink card is effectively "dead"; the chartreuse is our target.

Without telling Jersey my discovery, I put the cards on the table. "Want to see the Jungle? I'll show you my hammock and tell you all about my Pack."

As his answer, Jersey stands and grasps the ladder. I go up

in front to show him the ropes. He follows more slowly. When we get up to a Cub's platform in the lower reaches, I look down.

The sitting room is gone and Head Wolf's tent is pitched in its customary spot. Only the emptiness is atypical of the Jungle I knew, for even at the busiest parts of the night there would be someone around: sleeping, eating, screwing, singing softly.

I sigh with longing and spin tales for Jersey—carefully mentioning only those of the Pack the Institute already knew. He listens with fascination.

"Sounds like a primitive paradise," he says when I pause, "a simple—if brutal—Law, a patriarch, survival of the fittest."

"We weren't primitive!" I object indignantly. "We had lights and running water and even computers."

"Computers." Jersey's interest banishes his doubt. "How odd!"

"Not really." I smile, remembering the soft, happy murmur of Abalone's tappety-tap under her fingers. "One of my friends was so good that she could find anything on the datanet—anything at all."

My words are a challenge and I know that Jersey hears it, but I let it sink without pursuit. This complex is a sealed world, just like the first place, and neither Abalone nor anyone else will be able to see in unless someone opens a window. I've let Jersey know that someone might hear if he called—what he will do is up to him.

Finally, we climb down and relay the information about the cards. Then we are drawn back. When I come to myself in Jersey's annex, I realize that I am still quite weak from the accident. Still, I have enough energy left to be touched that Margarita has somehow managed to trade duty shifts and is there to take me back to my cell.

Warning me to leave the lights off when I undress, she locks the door behind me.

Although I am bleary-eyed with exhaustion as I stumble into the cell, I do notice the small hexagonal aquarium on the table. A lovely silvery fish with a luxurious fantail is swimming lazily above gently shifting sapphire glass pebbles. She darts shyly into a green crystal castle when I put Betwixt and Between on the table, but peers coquettishly out almost before the trail of bubbles from her retreat has dispersed.

Betwixt gives a low wolf whistle and Between growls appreciatively. Chuckling sleepily, I settle the disgruntled owl on the headboard and go to sleep.

Morning comes and the chunky, brown-haired woman I remember from the day my head was shaved buzzes my door to wake me up.

"Hey. I'm Holly. Margarita asked me to guard in here so we can do without taping your shower."

She looks vaguely embarrassed.

I smile and go off cheerfully. Holly doesn't get chatty, but I am still touched that Margarita was able to get her help—probably at some cost. Dylan must have made friends at the Institute, too. I wonder where they are.

Comp-C is empty when I arrive, but both Dr. Haas and Dr. Aldrich come in almost immediately. They are tight-lipped and dismiss Holly without a word.

Voluntarily, I take my place on the fluid plastic chair, even bending to assist Dr. Aldrich with the hookup. Conversation has become a pleasure that I anticipate and realize that I would miss if I left this place.

In my peripheral vision, I see motion from by Jersey's chair. Something troubles me, though, and I have just realized what it is when Dr. Aldrich stands back, giving me a clear line of sight.

Jersey is nowhere to be seen; Dr. Haas is linking herself into the computer interchange in his place. I want to ask, but can only gape. Dr. Haas appears to understand.

"Wondering where Jersey is?" she says with a sweet smile. "He won't be joining us—he was caught breaking one of the rules and isn't allowed out of his room."

Dr. Aldrich dismisses Jersey with a grunt. "No matter, we understand how this works. He isn't necessary."

The beaker is extended to me and I know that I do not dare to refuse to drink.

The mist curtain that envelopes me is a musky blue—layers of twilight sky that reach out and wrap me. I struggle through this, flailing my arms as if I am swimming. After floundering aimlessly, I let myself start to sink—although I am uncertain which way is up or down; nothing exists to give me a reference.

Then I see something white, framed in red. Eagerly, I direct myself toward it. Somehow I feel as if I am gaining velocity—a sensation like sliding down an icy sidewalk. The white resolves itself into separate blocks that at first I think are marble or ice. Then I realize that they are teeth and that the red that frames them is lips.

Too late to retreat or find a way to slow myself, I tumble out of the navy darkness into a golden void almost completely filled by the gigantic face of Dr. Haas.

She is already smiling, but the smile broadens when she sees me, slowly spinning as if weightless in the air before her.

"Hello, Sarah."

I stretch out my arms and legs in a vain attempt to orient myself in an up and down now defined by Dr. Haas's face. Glancing down, I see that she extends, neatly garbed in her usual white lab coat over a tailored teal suit. My only comfort is that from what I can feel of myself, I am much as usual in the consensus reality—my hair is back, my clothes my usual, and my owl and dragon are perched one on each shoulder.

"I said 'Hello, Sarah,'" Dr. Haas says in a voice that contains the rumble of distant thunder. "Don't you like talking?"

Still spinning, although more slowly now, I manage an angry, "Sure."

"Sure? That's it?"

She's enjoying my discomfort so much I can hardly bear it. Betwixt and Between hiss softly in one ear; Athena churrs and tightens her claw grip on my shoulder. Then, suddenly, I remember a single word.

Consensus.

She can't do this without my permission. My anger shifts from her to myself. It seems that I have been running from her, letting her order my life, since her first appearance at the Home.

. . . .

"Yeah," I finally reply. "That's it and so's this."

I concentrate, just as I did with Jersey and as easily as wiping steam vapor from a bathroom mirror, the setting changes to the familiar rope-strung cylinder of the Jungle. There is almost no resistance. I wonder at this until I realize that if I could make my presence known to Jersey, who created the interchange, surely I have the advantage over Dr. Haas.

Dr. Haas and I are on the same scale and I sit at ease on the edge of my hammock. She is gripping the edges of one of the cubwalks.

Athena launches from my shoulder and her departure sets me swinging. The vibration must be felt on the cubwalk as well, for Dr. Haas's hands tighten on the guide ropes. Her smile fades.

"What is it you want me to check for you?" I ask, feeding a French fry to Betwixt, deftly dodging Between's snaps at my fingers.

"Check out?" Dr. Haas says, nervously edging towards a ladder.

"Yes, isn't that the reason for these visits? I check out something and then tell you about it."

"Yeah."

Dr. Haas stops and I feel her concentrating, see for a moment solid flooring and aluminum side rails transform the cubwalk into a sturdy bridge. I remember the Jungle as it was, my own fumbling first attempts at the Reaches, the joy of graduating from cubwalks to the lines. Her feeble reordering vanishes before my reality.

When she looks up at me, she is angry, her emerald eyes

sparkling and hard. Maybe anger makes her say what she does next, maybe fear. Maybe just a desire to show me that she still has power over me.

"You're a bitch, Sarah. You always were, even when you were a little, sniveling, snot-nosed brat who couldn't even learn to finger sign."

Her hands are shaking so hard that the cubwalk trembles, but she doesn't seem to notice. Betwixt stops eating the French fry and Between doesn't even dive for it, transfixed as I by the next words of the tirade.

"I was important. I was the first! Then Dylan came along and he looked like he was going to be even better. But when you were tested, I hated you because even baby tests said you were good, that you just might be the best of all! How I laughed when they learned you were crazy—that you couldn't talk, couldn't read or write or spell. Now they'd have to come back to me, back to poor little Eleanora."

Now it is my time to shake. How had I not seen it before. Like me, blond hair, green eyes, but in her the colors were richer. We even had similar features, but the similarity was slight. Like stylized masks, our faces had been etched by our lives and hers had made her into a predator, a shark, lovely, graceful, and blood-hungry.

"Eleanora?" I push away disbelief. "Yes. But why have you treated me like this? We're sisters. We're alike."

Eleanora Haas sneers, but there is something pathetic in her disdain. "Alike? Oh, no. In what matters, I am your poor copy."

She starts inching toward the ladder again. "Dylan was good but he was naive. They'd kept him in a box, you see.

No current events or news, no idea of how the information he was providing was being used. They did give him carefully edited old-time stuff: fairy tales, science fiction, romances. He had a cute idea of right and wrong and he was definitely on the side of RIGHT—all in capitals, if you get what I mean."

Reaching the ladder, she begins to ascend, aiming for a platform that's more stable. I shift slightly so that I can see her. I say nothing, wanting only to hear the rest of her story.

"I showed him, though, news clips, photos, other stuff. Dr. Aldrich left me alone with him a lot because he was my brother—something nobody else knew. Dr. Aldrich liked keeping who his *Wunderkind* were a secret. Gave him an edge, you see, Sis.

"Essentially, Dylan caught on that he wasn't the sorcerer for noble houses, but the blackest of necromancers for the vilest of merchant princes. I take some pride in this—I mean the boy was so naive that he thought that sex was the weekly jerking off he did for the sperm bank. Try and get someone like that to understand what makes war or rape or robbery terrible."

Gripping Betwixt and Between so tightly that their back spines cut my hand, I lean forward to see her face.

"Why? Why did you want to do this to him?"

"I wanted him to kill himself, of course," she says, coming to sit on the platform edge. "He didn't though—not right off. He loved living too much. But he thought he found a way to live and yet stop serving evil. Like me he grew up with stories of little Sarah who wasn't good enough 'cause she was crazy as a bedbug and couldn't talk."

"Yeah, don't try and rub it in, Dr. Haas," I answer curtly. "Jersey told me that Dylan messed up his throat and couldn't talk and all the rest. What I still don't understand is why you wanted Dylan dead!"

"You don't, do you?"

Her emerald eyes study the Reaches with fixed, unseeing intensity. "I wanted Dr. Aldrich to train me, to bring out my abilities. And he would have if Dylan hadn't forced the Institute to get linked up with Jersey. Then, well, then you became an option again, and when Dylan hung himself, plans were made to recover you. Bring you from the Home to home."

She giggles and her hands pluck restlessly at one of the Web cables nearest to her. From my gently swinging hammock I can feel the dull thrum of her motion; it vibrates through me like her pulse in my body. After a few smothered giggles, she continues.

"I nearly stopped them, though, getting you discharged from the Home. Figured you'd die out there, nameless, voiceless, but when Dr. Aldrich started checking, he learned that you'd been sighted. Eventually, when the street people didn't turn you in—seemed to protect you even—we went after them."

She stops. "Why am I bothering to tell you this?"

"Bragging," I offer. "Couldn't tell anyone else and I can't rat on you unless someone comes here, so you're showing off."

"Maybe," she says conversationally, "because you're a safer confidante than even you may have thought."

She brings her hand up and then down hard and I see the flashing silver edge of the cutting tool she's had concealed in her hand. Quick as thought, I understand and, worse yet, I believe what she has been doing while she talked.

With her handsaw, she had been sawing away at one of the cables that supported the part of the Web from which I swing. With the anchor rope sawed through, the ropes holding me sag. I lose my balance and fall, tumbling toward the hard metal and dirt floor, recalling too vividly the mutilated body of the Institute guard who had died just this way.

In a futile gesture, I roll myself into a ball, protecting my extremities as even the newest Cubs are taught and praying that I will land on something to break my fall. Jolting off still-strung lines, I resist trying for one to break my fall, knowing that it would more likely break me and that the damage—or death—would be as real as I believed it to be.

I am bracing against death even as my body hits, bounces, and lands. My breath is knocked from me but I am basically unharmed enough to realize that I lie among the ruins of Head Wolf's tent.

Sprawled amid the rugs and cushions, snapped tent poles and painted canvas around me, I laugh and laugh. My face is buried in pillows, muffling the noise. Still, there is a maniac note to my glee that brings Athena to perch by my head and churr softly in concern. I stroke her soft chest plumage with a gentle forefinger and find, as I expect, Betwixt and Between nearby, squarely centered on a red fur cushion.

Moving slightly so that I can see the upper Jungle, I catch sight of Eleanora, her back to us, clambering down.

Softly, I warn my companions, "Don't move. She may think me unconscious or dead."

We wait, a frozen tableau, but the pose is for nothing.

"I know you're conscious, baby sister," Dr. Haas purrs. "So don't bother with the possum thing—or is it the ostrich one—not playing dead, but hiding your head?"

I hear echoes of forgotten nursery rhymes in her words, but let them slip away as I roll to face her.

"That's good enough," she commands as I start to get up. "Stay where you are. I rather like the picture, you languishing among the pillows."

As I shove myself into a sitting position, bruises scream at me for abusing them. Eleanora doesn't try to stop me.

"So, here we end it," she says, walking towards me. "I can't trick you like I did Dylan, but you're still in my way."

She seems different as she approaches, her walk stiff, her lithe grace missing. And something is wrong with her face— a network of lines seams her exposed flesh: hands, face, throat, legs. I shake my head and look closer, but the lines are still there.

Ignoring her warning, I shove myself to my feet. I feel as Athena flutters to my shoulder, landing with a faint tug on my hair. Betwixt and Between march from their pillow to stand between my feet.

Muscle aches fade instantly as I ignore them to focus on the woman stiffly lurching toward me—her image more menacing, more distorted than I know her to be. She smiles crookedly and, reaching into her bag, withdraws a tranq gun similar to those which had armed the Institute guards.

"Believe me, the slivers aren't sleepy dope; they're crystalline poison. Instantly dead—unfortunately painless. Believe me, I'd have it another way if I could."

Believe.

The word resonates in my mind. Of course. I look at Eleanora and see that the lines on her face and hands are seams, stitched there by an awkward hand. I remember Professor Isabella reading to me the story of a man who made a son from spare parts, but wasn't willing to accept the monster he had made. The monster, however, never stopped wanting the love and appreciation of the people who had rejected it.

Somehow, Eleanora—brilliant, pretty woman that she was—had never stopped wanting to be the chosen one, had never forgiven Dr. Aldrich for making her feel like the unwanted monster.

All of this flashes into my mind in the same instant that I am scooping up a large chintz pillow and hurling it at Eleanora. She dodges stiffly and fires her gun, but her movement ruins her aim. I cannot spare the energy to doubt that the slivers will kill me, just as she promises—our minds are too intimately intertwined at this point.

Unlike Grey Brother or Midline, I have no idea how to disarm her, but a strange idea comes to me as I scoop up an oval sofa cushion and fling it into her face. Dropping low, I reach and snag her ankle, pulling her off-balance to come thudding heavily to the floor.

She drops the tranq gun to catch herself and as she scrabbles to regain it, I reach out and grab her ankle. There, as I had expected, is a lumpy seam. Somehow, I find the loose end and, grasping it firmly, I begin to pull, feeling the familiar sensation of stitches coming loose, the faint popping and tugging gaining velocity as the thick surgical thread accumulates in a fluffy pile around Betwixt and Between.

Athena sees what I am doing and grasps a thread end from Eleanora's face and flaps upward.

"What are you doing?" Eleanora screams, forgetting her gun, clawing at herself.

And as she sees, she begins to come apart. Literally. Ankle drops from calf, calf from knee, a growing heap of body parts. There is no blood as they separate and the pile looks less like a dismembered corpse than a bunch of spare mannequin parts.

From where Athena pulls, the lovely head is falling apart in sections. Golden hair cascades like a wig to the floor; the face drops in sculpted panels, a bit of eye in each. The teeth ripple and fall like dominoes.

Except for the one cry of disbelief, Eleanora is silent and when Athena and I pull the last taut length of thread free to stretch between us, a single note like a plucked guitar string echoes in the empty Jungle.

Then I look down at my sister's wreck and weep.

SIXTEEN

~

WHEN MINUTES? HOURS? LATER I COME TO MYSELF IN THE Comp-C, Dr. Aldrich is nowhere to be seen. The door to the corridor is slightly open and I hear shouting. Immediately, I set about unbuckling and unwiring myself from the chair.

I've never done this myself before without help and soon I am in a frustrated tangle. I finally work myself free at the expense of some skin and a twisted left pinkie.

I am scooping up Betwixt and Between and heading for the door when I notice that Eleanora is still in her chair. Hesitantly, I tiptoe over and almost choke at what I see.

That she is dead there is no doubt, but what horrifies me are the vivid red lines that trace in a bloody network about her limp body. They look like the scores of a wire whip, fresh and angry evidence of her mind struggling to dismember a body it believed was ripping apart.

I back away from her corpse, out the door, and would have fled if I had known where to go. Instead, I stand foolishly in the middle of the corridor, at a loss without a guard or nurse to direct me.

A repetition of the shouting gives me a sense of direction and, sending Athena ahead to scout, I sneak toward the sounds. Arriving at a bend in the corridor, I bring Athena back to me.

Her once vague noises are beginning to take the form of words—perhaps because of enforced intimacy in the interchange—but the overwhelming sense she brings to me is confusion to the point of speechlessness.

"No one ahead until the box," she says, "there . . . churr-whoo?"

The box, I know, is how she sees the elevator. Taking her word that the next stretch of corridor is clear, I advance, unable to find words to ask her what has so baffled her. But as I round a corridor, I begin to understand.

What I had taken for shouting is a voice over the station's intercom system. A chorus of voices old and young, melodic and cracked, are yipping and howling—a cacophony that should have chilled me but instead warms me with noisy promise. What I hear is the cry of the full Pack and that means that they have come for me.

Near the elevator doors, Holly is shaking her comlink as if that will clear the channels. Angrily, she switches it off.

"Jammed, damn it, jammed and useless." She gestures to the wall speakers. "I wish someone would turn that racket off—they've got to have figured that it's no help to us."

"What do you figure is going on?" her companion asks, a young fellow with a red five o'clock shadow.

"Don't know," she shrugs. "I was having coffee and waiting word to bring Sarah back from Comp-C when the shift boss races in and tells me to get up here, pronto."

"Good," Rusty says. "I thought I was missing something. I'd been off shift asleep when I got called."

Crouched behind an ornamental plant, I wish they knew more. All they've done is confirm my suspicion that the Pack has come. However, since the only stairwell that I know of runs beside the elevator, the guards are effectively holding both.

This doesn't seem the time to go and try doors at random. I'm in as much danger from my Pack as from anyone else if I open a door unexpectedly. With my shaved head and patient's clothing, I'll too quickly seem a stranger.

Not wanting to be spotted by the guards, I move back along the corridor to Comp-C. The door is still ajar when I get there and, driven by some impulse, I return inside.

Nothing has changed. In the annex, Eleanora still sprawls, stiffening now, in her restraints. The computer banks twinkle, grunting slightly as some demand is made of them. I stare at them, stretching my hearing and catching little fragments of Jersey's joy as he built them, echoes of Dylan's fear as he saw himself being enslaved.

With sudden insight, I realize that Eleanora had been wrong when she believed that Dylan's growing addiction to the interchange had been mainly a result of the drug overdose she had been giving him. Certainly, that had played its part, but the real addiction had been to speech—to communication that would let him bridge the gap that he had created. He could refuse to write, but when given the chance to speak, the temptation was too great.

Wondering, I study the thing. Opening the hall door, I set Betwixt and Between in the corridor where they can see both ways. Then I set Athena on a high doorway, where she can see farther down the corridor and warn the dragon.

"Why let the stricken deer go weep, the hart ungalled play," I tell them. "For some must watch, while some must sleep: so runs the world away."

"We'll watch, Sarah," Between promises. "But how can you sleep now?"

I don't waste time hunting for an answer, but duck back inside Jersey's office before either my resolve fades or I am discovered. In what I plan to do, I suspect that my allies and my enemies would unite to stop me. Indeed, I realize that what I am doing is crazy by most standards, but at least I am comfortable with that thought. Being crazy is not new to me.

Too much time would be wasted if I were to seek out specific codes and processes, so I decide to be direct. First, I search along the walls for power cables—I have a few bad moments when I realize that they run straight into the walls and so cannot be easily unplugged. Then I check where they connect to the computer itself. After a few experimental jiggles, I decide that I can loosen them at this point. When I do so, with a groan that is almost like a person, the computer whirs and most of the lights on its panels go off.

But some of the lights tell me the thing still lives and I

search for a quick way to ruin it for good. Knowing only the vaguest details of how such machines work limits me some, but I start by blocking up various drives with any card or slip that fits—or better—that almost fits. Any exposed wire gets jerked loose. After a severe shock that leaves my arm tingling, I put on a pair of oversized gloves and appropriate a set of wire cutters from a tool kit in Jersey's office.

Rapidly, the remaining lights go off and as they do, I smash the little eyes of sparkling glass or plastic with the head of my wire cutters. I am rooting through a panel that has fallen open, strewing chips on the floor and grinding them under my foot, when I hear Betwixt calling.

"Athena says that someone is coming, Sarah. Wake up!"

I want to reply, "I am awake, as you must know from the noise in here" but I settle for "Yes."

Feet come pounding down the hall, heavy and hurried upon the carpet. Voices reach me. "There's her dragon! She must be in there!"

The door is flung open, just as I am moving to open it and as I reel back to avoid it, I am temporarily blocked from the sight of my rescuers.

"Shit! Someone's trashed the place real good," Grey Brother curses.

"Sarah?" Abalone begins to call.

Her voice breaks off suddenly as she sees the limp figure on the other couch. The lights are dim around Eleanora's body, masking the brighter gold of her hair and for a moment as though through Abalone's eyes I see myself sprawled there dead. The vision chokes me, but I manage to swing the door back and step forward.

. . . .

"We be of one blood, ye and I," I whisper and when Abalone turns, the smile that lights her face seems to burn away the tears that streak her painted cheeks.

"Sarah!" she cries, leaping past Grey Brother to squeeze me. "I thought we were too late. The message only came a few hours ago and it took us time to find the place."

"Whose hand the message writ?" I ask, squeezing her in return.

"I don't know," she admits. "It was weird, so weird that I almost missed it. It just said, 'I've found the Brighton Rock girl!'"

Grey Brother cuts in, "We've got to move now. Midline and the rest won't hold the guards for long and there may be reinforcements coming in."

The guards. I remember Margarita, Jersey, my only friends in this place. Questions claw my throat. Scooping up Betwixt and Between and summoning Athena to my shoulder, I follow my rescuers out. Abalone, however, will not be turned from the question of the message sender so easily.

"Sarah, you couldn't have sent that. Who did?"

Puzzling for a way to answer, I see as we pass through Jersey's office a series of framed documents on the wall. Guessing, I point to one.

"Jersey R. Kravis, Ph.D. and all the rest. Enough degrees to make a thermometer break." Abalone grins. "This Dr. Kravis is the one?"

I nod, feeling odd that I never considered Jersey by any other name than the one. With a sweeping motion of my hand, I mimic cutting my throat. Grey Brother sees the gesture and halts.

"You think he'll be in trouble for doing it?"

I nod, biting hard on my upper lip, remembering that Dr. Aldrich is still missing, wondering where he is.

Outside of the elevator, Abalone links her tappety-tap to a wall unit and starts sketching commands. With a triumphant chortle, she reads off a line of data.

"Jersey Kravis, Floor Three, Rooms 323–324." She glances up at the elevator, then at a wall sign. "That's this floor, just down there a ways. C'mon."

We pelt down the hallway, Abalone in front muttering off room numbers as we pass. She brakes in front of a closed door.

"This is it"—she looks uncertain—"Sarah, you'd better knock. If he has a scan, he'll know you."

I step forward and rap my knuckles on the hard white plastic. Then I notice a buzzer and thumb that too. There is no answer and a blazing tension makes my stomach begin to roil. After I bang repeatedly, Grey Brother pulls me back.

"Little Sister, he won't answer. I need to check with the Four. Perhaps one of the guards we've captured has a pass."

I reluctantly agree to follow, my fears for Margarita returning in an icy wave. My Pack can be brutal if they feel the need and these were the people who had kidnapped both me and Head Wolf, who had chased us from the Jungle. Would they see them as any better than Mowgli's wolves had seen the Red Dogs of the dekkan?

My feet cease to drag and I hurry after. Grey Brother and Abalone lead the way down the stairs to the ground floor, the recorded cry of the Pack beating at us from an open intercom we pass. I have never been here before and yet I hurry along without a glance as we pass various offices. The air smells of artificial scent and is without any trace of humidity. The corridor ends in a set of heavy fire doors, and when Grey Brother opens them, I hear many voices.

I hardly know whom to greet first and stand frozen with a stupid grin on my face. They are here—my people—Peep, seeming a foot taller since last time I saw him, a new grimness etched about his dark eyes; Midline, lean and arrogant, allowing himself the faintest smile. But two tear my heart: Professor Isabella, strangely militant in camouflage fatigues, and Head Wolf, paler, thinner still than he should be, but his dark eyes as mad as ever.

Unable to do anything, I pause, seeing them assess me, the shaved head, the strained, wild expression that I know remains for hours after any interchange session.

Abalone breaks the awkward reunion by being briskly businesslike.

"Sarah says the fellow who got us the message is a Dr. Kravis. She's afraid he's in trouble for doing it. We checked his rooms, but there wasn't an answer, so we need to find if the guards have a key."

Professor Isabella nods. "Are you sure we don't have him here? Chocolate and Edelweiss scared up a few people who weren't in uniform."

My pulse leaps hopefully. Professor Isabella squeezes my shoulder.

"We've got them this way, Sarah. Come along."

I take her hand and we go to another set of double doors, which are opened from within when Professor Isabella rhythmically knocks. The air in this room is even drier than without and smells heavily of herbs and spices.

From her seat on a stool by the door, Edelweiss grins tightly at me. "We put 'em in the larder—nice and tidy. Wonder whether they'll take the seasoning?"

I try to smile back, but my eyes are busy searching the cluster of guards. I see neither Jersey nor Margarita and as my anticipation is turning into dread, a sharp voice calls out.

"Sarah, *amiga*, what is all this? These people your friends?"

I almost laugh in my relief, but cannot find an answer for all her questions. Settling for a nod, I look at Abalone.

"Yes," she says. "We've come for her. You're calling Sarah 'friend,' lady. You friend enough to give us some help?"

Several of the guards glower at her, but Margarita ignores them and nods. "You get what you want, anyway. I see that, Blue Mouth. If I can get it, she can have it."

"We want the key to Dr. Kravis's rooms."

"Dr. Kravis?" Margarita looks genuinely puzzled. "I don't know what you asking."

"Don't screw around . . ." Abalone growls, but I grasp her arm and put my finger to her lips.

Looking at Margarita, I rub a hand over my bald scalp, then motion a taller, overweight figure, ending by holding my nose and grimacing.

Margarita watches my mime anxiously, her expression shifting from confusion to relief.

"Oh, Jersey—why didn't you say so? I don't have the key, but I can show you where one should be."

Abalone studies her closely. "Okay, but no funny stuff."

Margarita nods and only squares her shoulders when there is a rumble of anger from the prisoners behind her. Edelweiss shuts them up by examining the clip in the tranq pistol she holds.

"Full. And I got another. Understand?"

Once we're out of the larder, Margarita turns to Abalone.

"Look, Boca Blue, you gotta get outta here fast. When they not get an answer, they be here pronto. We keep near hundred-percent communications silence, but there are checks. When they not get an answer, they be here faster than a cheetah with a bee on his butt, *comprende*?"

"Got you," Abalone replies, letting Margarita through to a room that smells of men's socks and is decorated with video monitors and a computer terminal. "Why do you care?"

Margarita opens a panel by touching it with her thumbprint. "Maybe I like her. Maybe I just don't like what I've learned about here. Maybe both. Don't worry about me ratting. If you let me, I'll take one of the gravs and get outta here when you do. If I stay, I'm gonna be dog meat, first by my 'chums' and then by the boss."

"Okay," Abalone says. "If Head Wolf agrees."

She takes the key card Margarita gives her. "You come and wait with the Pack, lady. Sarah and I will go and get this Jersey."

Head Wolf only gestures and Midline comes with us. Professor Isabella turns and joins us without requesting the permission which Head Wolf grants anyhow with a fond smile and a royal wave of his slender hand. Apparently, they have reached an agreement of sorts.

We run back to the third floor, Margarita's warning giving us new urgency. I send Athena soaring ahead, but the caution is unnecessary. No one meets us and once Abalone has cut off the intercom, only silence greets us.

Snatching the key card from Abalone, I unlock the door, but Midline shoves me back before I can open it, a low growling warning me not to cross him. But when he cautiously opens the door, nothing comes out after us but a wave of acrid body odor.

Midline enters first. I listen for Jersey's indignant cry at the invasion, but the only voice is Midline's.

"Sarah, come quick."

I hurry in, knowing that the others follow. Midline motions me to a side door and steps back to let me pass him. When I cry out, a wordless, inarticulate thing, his hand is on my shoulder and somehow I find in it courage to advance.

Jersey lies sprawled on his bed, sheets and blankets neatly folded over a chest that no longer rises or falls. His eyes are closed, but I doubt that his death was peaceful, for his expression is twisted in a rictus of dismay.

On the bedside table are a few sheets of paper and a computer disk. As I bend to touch Jersey, as if somehow I can change what has happened, I see an ampule and an injector on the floor.

"C'mon, Sarah, you can't help him," Midline says, then his hand leaves my shoulder. "Hey, these got your name on them!"

I straighten then with a first and last kiss for Jersey. Midline has gathered the papers and disk and handed them to Abalone.

I look down. "Good night, sweet prince, and flights of angels sing thee to thy rest."

Then I leave, ignoring the others' comforting gestures, running as soon as I reach the hallway. When we reach the room the Pack is using as a command center, only Head Wolf, Margarita, and Edelweiss remain. A kit bag leans against Margarita's leg and she holds my aquarium clasped in her arms.

She shrugs. "The Wolf let me get my stuff and I grabbed this from your room. Not even a carp deserves to starve to death."

I motion as if to take that tank and she seems pleased. "You want it? Good. Think of me sometime."

"Naked I came into the world," I answer. "A friend in need is a friend indeed."

When we get to the outer door, Margarita turns with a wave and climbs aboard a small grav cycle.

"Better than severance pay," she says, then is gone.

The rest of us pile into a somewhat more cumbersome van. Peep raises us and sets a course, then he turns to us.

"I redid her vehicle registration," he says with a shy smile. "She can sell it with a clear record whenever she wants to."

Tense silence falls then, as if quiet will help make certain that we can get safely away. Only when we are out of the tropical zone completely does Professor Isabella recall the papers that Abalone still clutches.

"Sarah, may I see what Jersey left you?" she asks.

I nod, inordinately pleased that she has asked since she knows that I cannot read. Abalone hands them over and Professor Isabella skims them, her eyebrows rising slightly as she does.

"Sarah, do you wish to hear these now or later?"

I shrug, gesturing at those in the van. "We be of one blood, ye and I."

She nods and clears her throat. "Sarey, I thought a great deal about what you told me in the Comp-C and I've gotten a message out. If there are people looking for you as good as that girl you mentioned, they'll find you."

Abalone grunts as if acknowledging the compliment, but she looks puzzled, too. Professor Isabella goes on with the letter.

"I thought that my link wasn't detected, but I find I'm locked into my room—mechanically, so I can't override. What I told you about me is true, Sarey. I'm an addict and if they don't come with my fix, I'll start dying—have a breakdown first, though. So, when I know there's no coming back for me, I'll finish myself. The computers I built up in the Comp-C were a great idea, but I wish now I'd never pulled it off.

"The data disk contains what information I could scrounge on my employers. It also has what dirt I could find on Dr. Aldrich. That one scares me more than Dr. Haas—I don't think he even sees you as a person. Maybe this information will help you to stay clear once you get out of here.

"If I don't get to tell you myself, I'm rooting for you, and it was real nice talking to you. Yours, Jersey."

. . . .

Silence holds for a moment after Professor Isabella finishes, then Head Wolf asks softly, "He could talk to you?"

I nod, unwilling and glad to be unable to explain.

Head Wolf seems to appreciate that I have reasons for my silence.

"Lucky man," he says. "We'll keep you safe now, all of us."

"We've got a new Jungle now, Sarah," Abalone says, bouncing a bit, "better than the Cold Lairs under the highway. You'll see. Bet you'll like it."

I smile slightly.

"Sarah," Professor Isabella asks, her curiosity digging for the final pieces of the puzzle. "Did you ever find out about your brother and sister?"

I look at her, then pull Betwixt and Between close. "I am a brother to dragons, a companion to owls."

And that's all there really is to say.

SEVENTEEN

❦

BUT, OF COURSE, THAT'S NOT.

Head Wolf may be willing to leave unanswered the questions raised by Jersey's letter, but Abalone is all mongoose — eaten up from nose to tail with curiosity — and Professor Isabella isn't any better. Abalone saw enough of Jersey's office to have an idea of what he was doing with the Comp-C. Now she wants to recreate it.

I'm not so certain. I miss talking. I dream of conversations as once I dreamed of freedom. Yet, I am haunted by Jersey's swollen corpse, a specter that reminds me of the price I would pay for speech. Nor can I forget that the price would not be mine alone to pay, but would be extracted from any who gave in to the temptation to join me.

Still, despite my lack of enthusiasm, Abalone's pride has been piqued by Jersey's achievement. She delves into the library banks of a dozen networks, copying every article that he ever published, no matter what the subject.

"Weird man, your friend Jersey," she says, rubbing her eyes as she looks up from her tappety-tap. "I sure wish you hadn't busted up his machine."

"*Veni, vidi, vici,*" I reply, more calmly than I feel.

"What did you conquer?" she says with frustration. "I understand that there were drawbacks to his system, but I'm sure I could have worked them out."

"I am cabin'd, cribb'd, confined, bound into saucy doubts and fears," I answer.

"You doubt it?" She tries to smile and fails. "Sarah, don't you wish that you could just tell me what you want without all this roundabout hunting for words?"

"Even a fool, when he holdeth his peace, is counted wise." I pat her hand, pushing her tappety-tap away, offering her pipe.

"You really don't want me messing with this, do you?" she says, accepting the pipe. "Grab the dragon and come outside."

Our new Jungle is a burned-out high-rise which Head Wolf has outfitted with a new Web. Where a solid fragment of floor remains, Professor Isabella has set up her own residence, claiming that she is too old for ropes and hammocks. The Free People no longer rate her as one of the Tabaqui, not since she helped to free both Head Wolf and me. Since she refuses to let Head Wolf direct her, she is called Wontolla, the Outlier, and everyone is content.

When we pass by, she makes her way to join us.

"Going out for some air? Good, Abalone is looking pale. Some moonlight will do her good."

"Very funny."

Edelweiss smiles and waves as we head out. She's no longer antagonistic toward me, but she's still happier to see me heading out. Most of the other Free People are hunting.

We amble to a park that is little more than the overgrown rubble of a building destroyed in the same fire as our own Jungle. As we settle among the weeds and vines, Abalone distractedly draws her pipe to life.

"Late, late yestreen I saw the new moon," I comment, pointing upward, "wi' the auld moon in hir arms."

"Pretty," Professor Isabella replies. "Abalone, relax and take a look around. You're too quiet, child."

Abalone leans back against a bit of shattered cinder block and looks at the sky. Her smoke rings drift to join Athena, who snaps at them in lieu of moths. In my shoulder bag, Betwixt and Between grumble to each other about the possibility of a late-night snack.

"I'm a mess over Jersey's project," Abalone admits. "I've scrounged for every article I can, cross-referenced, plowed into obscure databases, and yet . . ."

"You do your job too well, Boca Blue," comes a voice from the darkness, "and now they looking for you. And for her."

Margarita steps out to where we can see her. She's dressed in a grey coverall that whispers uniform, but her sidearm is holstered and her smile is friendly.

"Hey, Sarah," she says, "bet you not plan on seeing me again. How's the fish?"

"Oh health! health! The blessing of the rich!" I reply, miming a swimming fish with one hand.

"It's fine," Abalone interprets dryly, "but I doubt that

you hunted us out to find out about Sarah's goldfish. Why are you here?"

"And how did you ever find us?" Professor Isabella adds.

"That's what I was trying to tell you," Margarita says, "before I stop to say 'hi' to my *amiga*. You've looked too hard after Jersey's stuff, Boca Blue, and now the Institute has got a line on you and they're going to use it to reel Sarah in."

I shrink back, my gaze darting into suddenly unfriendly shadows. In response to my fear, Athena wings out to survey the area.

"Easy, *chica*," Margarita soothes, "I'm more than a jump ahead of them, this time. You've got a day, maybe two before they come to take you. Plenty of time to get away."

"How did you learn this?" Abalone says suspiciously. "When we saw you last, you were running as fast as you could."

"*Sí*, I was running—or flying—but the money I made selling the bike gave me the means to clear my name"—she grins—"or at least to get the ears of the right people. I have a new employer who has set me to watch the old."

"And while you were watching," Professor Isabella prompts, "what did you learn?"

"Sarah probably couldn't tell you, but the Institute was being funded by an . . . economic concern called Ailanthus. They were using Sarah's talents, and those of her brother before that, to steal information that couldn't be had any other way."

"Yeah, we had some idea from Jersey's letter," Abalone

says, "but clearly we didn't understand just how things were."

"The Ailanthus company is run by dangerous people, who like getting their own way, but that don't mean that they're stupid."

Margarita perches on a rubble heap. "They've had people checking to see if anyone was showing too much interest in Jersey's research. Kinda a long shot, but they figured that the people who took Sarah might also be interested in talking with her."

"And then from that they were able to trace back to her," Professor Isabella says. "They won't stop, will they?"

"No. What she can do is worth too much money."

I listen, my illusion of safety shattered again. Yet, I am a different person than the woman who was sent away from the Home, a different person even from the one who surrendered to let her friends escape. I may be insane, but I value my freedom, and, Jersey was right, I do value being in control of myself.

"We'll have to hide her again," Abalone says, "maybe even fake her death. I can give up my research for now and pick it up once the heat is off. Wouldn't make much sense to push it if Sarah isn't around to share."

"We could go to the countryside," Professor Isabella says, "or perhaps back to the apartment near the park."

I put my hand on her arm, shaking my head in blunt refusal.

"Cowards die many times before their deaths; the valiant never taste of death but once."

"Sarah, what are you saying?" Abalone says. "We aren't running 'cause we're chicken. We're running to save you."

Again, I shake my head.

"Why should there be such turmoil and such strife, to spin in length this feeble line of life?"

"Sarah! You can't mean to kill yourself." Abalone turns pale beneath her paint. "That's craziness."

Weary with hunting for words, again I shake my head. Hearing my dragons sigh with relief, I lower my hand to scratch their heads as I search for a way to make my meaning clear.

"When the blandishments of life are gone, the coward sneaks to death," I reply at last.

"And you're not a coward," Abalone says. "Right, Sarah?"

I smile and Athena comes back to my shoulder. She bites my knuckle affectionately and reassures me that, for now, the night still belongs to us. The wind through the park ruffles my too-short hair, forcibly reminding me of my captivity.

"I have not yet begun to fight," I state firmly, my jaw set against any further protest.

"Fight!" Margarita says, her brown eyes wide with shock.

"What else can she mean?" Professor Isabella says. "She refuses to run and she certainly won't volunteer to return to those horrendous people."

I nod vehement agreement.

"What good will going after their mercenaries do?" Margarita asks. "That's all they'll send after her and there are always more to be bought. Your wolfy people won't last against them, even with the choice of battlefield."

"Into the jaws of Death, into the mouth of hell, rode the six hundred," I say.

"Six hundred? We're not six hundred." Then understanding awakens on Abalone's face. "Oh, you mean that we should take the fight to them."

I nod. "But be not afraid of greatness: some are born great, some achieve greatness, and some have greatness thrust upon 'em."

"Oh, my," Professor Isabella says. "Yet, this may be the way to end this madness, a strike into their black hearts."

"Black?" Margarita shakes her head. "No, *señora*. There's nothing as clean as blackness in their hearts. They're a messed-up swirling of all the colors of banknotes; the power at their heart is only what they can buy."

"We have no idea where they are or what defenses they might have or anything at all," Abalone says, but from how she toys with her pipestem I can see that she is merely listing research points, not admitting defeat.

"Some of this I may be able to give you," Margarita says after a thoughtful pause.

"No, we cannot expect you to risk your job," Professor Isabella says. "You have already given us a warning."

"She," Margarita says, touching my arm, "gave me my life. I want to do this thing and give her a chance to have her own."

I smile. *"Amiga, gracias."*

"Well." Abalone rises. "As Sarah would say, 'If it were done 'tis best it is done quickly.'"

"Isn't that from *Macbeth*?" Professor Isabella asks with a wry smile.

"Maybe once, but it's Sarah's now." Abalone turns to Margarita. "Are you free tonight?"

"And tomorrow," she replies. "I am visiting my sister and little niece and they will cover for me if anyone asks questions."

"Good," Abalone says. "Let's go to one of my safe houses and start planning. Best to bring this to Head Wolf as a reasoned-through plan rather than asking for support without an idea of what we'll need."

I nod agreement, but as I trail them to the hotel room, I resolve that support or no support, I will carry this through.

The conference proceeds smoothly—I realize that we are becoming something of old hands at this and that Ailanthus owes itself for our training. Margarita rattles off information which Abalone files. I know my Baloo well enough to realize that nothing will be taken on faith, but she has sense enough not to start cross-checking in front of our guest.

"Now, we've decided that you want the building where Dr. Aldrich has been set up. It will do you good—he stays there and does his work there and keeps his records there. The impression I got is that he is under sort of house arrest, maybe because he lost Sarah," Margarita says. "Not so good is that he is there because the building is in a well-guarded complex. There are a whole lotta sensors—heat and motion and plain old video. Human guards roam the place and some of them have dogs."

"Ouch," Abalone says, wrapping a fiery lock around her index finger. "Not very hopeful—rules out any frontal assault."

"Well, there is a bright spot," Margarita says. "The big

shots, they don't want to have to deal with all that every time they come to work, so there is a way in that all you need are pass codes and prints for fingers, eyes, and voice. Then you take a capsule trolley to whatever building you want and never cross the grounds."

"I may be able to do something about prints," Abalone says slowly. "Can you get us the codes?"

"They're changed on an erratic schedule," Margarita says. "You couldn't count on what I got for you being right. Sometimes they change every week, other times every couple of days, sometimes every couple of hours. The Security Chief didn't want to set up this entrance at all, so he's a bastard about avoiding patterns that could make it easier to get in."

"Clever," Professor Isabella says, looking up from the volume of Sun-tzu that she's been reading.

"We may have to blow the doors," Abalone growls, "and that means giving up any chance of getting in unnoticed."

Margarita looks surprised. "Hey, aren't you forgetting Sarah?"

Abalone tilts her head in puzzlement. "Sarah? She can't read or even tell left from right all of the time."

"Yeah, but things talk to her. She's the sweetest little codebreaker in the world." Margarita wags a finger. "What you think they were using her for or why they so hot to get her back?"

"I . . . I didn't think," Abalone admits. "I knew, but I didn't think. I'm so used to looking out for her that I forgot what she can do."

Betwixt and Between blow her a Bronx cheer—in duet,

but I am content to look smug. Then uncertainty seizes me. What if I can't do it? What if the lock is impersonal or has nothing to tell me?

Tentatively, I stretch my senses in a way I have not since Betwixt and Between first mentioned Dylan in my presence, but now there is a difference. Then I was not aware of my talent; now I know of it and to some extent have trained it. Within me, I turn a dial, move an imaginary volume control.

First, I hear only Betwixt and Between squabbling amiably with each other over some oatmeal cookie crumbs. Athena is asleep with her head beneath her wing and I can hear the rise and fall of her breath.

Turning up the imaginary volume, I hear Abalone's tappety-tap coaching her through a data heist. Louder still and Sun-tzu's words rise from the tattered book that Professor Isabella drowses over. Margarita's uniform giggles with pleasure over the kevlar threads in the apparently soft weave and her concealed sidearm announces its patient presence, as does the wicked tempered stiletto in her boot top.

Gleefully, I wrap my arms about my knees and rock back and forth. Soon. Soon we will go after those who have been hounding me and mine. I lick my lips and anticipate the battle.

EIGHTEEN

❧

WHEN WE MOVE, WE MOVE BY NIGHT AS THE CODE OF THE
Free People demands. This, however, is also best for our situation. We have decided that a very simple infiltration is
best. Once inside the Ailanthus complex we have three ob-
jectives.

First, we will find and destroy Dr. Aldrich's research material. Professor Isabella assures us that a scholar trained in
the competitive realms of science and academics will not
have published all of his work. In fact, he would probably
have published only the least significant elements. Once he
had backing, he would have published little. To share his
discoveries would only have reduced his opportunities to
benefit from them.

Our second goal is similar to the first. We will destroy any
experiments or materials he has accumulated. Thirdly, we—
or rather Abalone—will wipe the computers of any perti-

nent information relating to me and my abilities and then insert a virus that is tailored to contaminate any new efforts.

These are our basic plans, but Abalone has one other, one that she has not discussed. She plans to ruin Ailanthus financially, by stealing what of their funds she can access easily and then inserting rumors about their financial security into the electronic marketplace. Some creditors will be certain to call in debts and when Ailanthus learns that it lacks the funds to pay and tries to call in debts of its own, it will fuel the panic. Her tappety-tap shares her confidence that the company will not survive twenty-four hours.

It's okay with me that she keeps her secret, though, because I have one, too. I plan to kill Dr. Aldrich.

This isn't just vengeance—although I know that the Free People will see it as such and that Head Wolf will exonerate me as one who was killing to pay a blood debt. No, simply, I realize that Jersey's warning about Dr. Aldrich is true. The man is responsible for the deaths of my brother and sister and perhaps for those of my parents as well. Yet, he felt as little over these deaths as another researcher might over the deaths of as many lab rats. His death is the only thing that will stop him and I plan to give him that death.

Despite the many things we hope to achieve, our plan for gaining entrance is simple. The Ailanthus compound has self-contained power, so we cannot simply disrupt their operations from outside. Therefore, we will go in as if we belong. Margarita has assured us that we don't need to worry about being strangers. A suit is a suit to the guards and as long as we move purposefully and don't trip any alarms, we should pass.

Once inside, we should be relatively unchecked and hope to do our jobs and escape.

Now, as the sleek sedan hums Abalone, Professor Isabella, Midline, and me to our goal, I concentrate on testing my "volume" control in preparation for the challenges to come. I have been practicing in the time since Margarita's warning and now I can tune out the emotions of my companions and focus on the near-inaudible voices within the sedan itself.

Concealed in my sleek executive's briefcase, Betwixt and Between grumble about the lack of a window. From Professor Isabella's purse, Athena readies herself for what will certainly be her most dangerous flight.

"We should be there soon," Professor Isabella says, pulling back the sleeve of her dove grey suit to check her watch.

"Then we will," Midline assures her.

His business suit makes him look more ferocious rather than tamed, the perfect image of an Ailanthus executive. The sweet lines of its tailoring snigger over the weapons they conceal. Even his golden skin job fits with the image of decadent sophistication. Abalone and I are dressed in a similar fashion with briefcases to hold our tools. Peep is our chauffeur, natty in a navy blue uniform and matching cap.

"Outside checkpoint coming," Peep announces, his eyes busy with radar screens and sensors. "Looks like only one human guard."

"Stay icy," Abalone reminds him, "and don't even speak with him. Margarita says that the executives usually let themselves in, despite the warmbodies at the gate."

"I remember," Peep says, flourishing the scanner card, "and here's our invite."

We are all holding our breaths as Peep inserts the card into the scanner, but Abalone's forgery gets us through with barely a glance from the guard. He is so intent on his monitors that I am certain we are forgotten a minute after we pass.

Within the walls, Ailanthus has built a small city. Professor Isabella sighs when she sees the buildings and I do not need to question why. Here are all the technological advances that the city outside the walls lacks. The glass-and-steel buildings are interwoven with solar grids to capture cheap power, decorative ponds serve as emergency reservoirs, the trolley capsules run on superconductors to race the people from building to building with a minimum of delay. The grounds are elegantly manicured to soothe and inspire without distracting.

I can feel her envy, but do not let myself be distracted. Peep is steering us into the parking field near to a trolley terminus. No one drives within the compound and Dr. Aldrich's building is too far for us to reach without running afoul of guards and dogs. Here will be my first challenge and my heart races as the car stops and Abalone motions for me to get out.

Abalone has fitted her eyes with contacts and her fingertips with false prints to fool those scanners. A track to fool the voice scanner has been easily obtained, but Margarita could do no more. My job will be to find the code that voice must speak.

The trolley station provides sufficient cover as I press my

ear to the doorway. Abalone's breathing is nervously loud, but louder still is the grumbly voice of an executive reading from his latest security memo.

I listen carefully and then recite softly into the tappety-tap. "Aloe, geranium, clematis, iris, lily." Abalone strokes a key and the voice synthesizer repeats confidently. "Aloe, geranium, clematis, iris, lily."

The trolley door slides open and Midline and Professor Isabella hurry to join us. We are rushed, but I do not miss the admiring looks they spare me.

Peep immediately drifts the sedan over to parking, where he will conceal himself and await our return.

When the trolley door slides shut, a flat but pleasant voice asks, "Destination?"

Finger to her lips, Abalone keys her tappety-tap. "Aldrich's Lab" it informs the trolley importantly.

Unquestioning, even to my hearing, the trolley capsule glides forward. The ride is nearly without the sensation of movement, even when we go around curves, and is so swift that we do not have time to wonder about the lack of seats before the pleasant voice announces, "Aldrich's Lab."

We step out and I kneel before the code pad. I barely need to listen before Dr. Aldrich's clipped tones snap, "What nonsense!" I jump, realize that I am not hearing him, but merely a memory of him imprinted on the area and listen again. "What nonsense!" the doorway obligingly repeats, but nothing follows.

Hesitantly, I say to the tappety-tap, "What nonsense!"

Abalone stares at me and then, with a faith I don't feel is merited, signals the tappety-tap to repeat. "What nonsense!"

in the synthesized voice. At the words, the door slides open and I step in, my knees almost too weak to carry me.

Yet, once the door has shut behind us, I am needed again. Professor Isabella hands Athena to me and I send the little owl looking for security systems. From what Margarita had told us, the regions closest to the ceiling should be safe, since all of the detectors are set to look down for human-sized targets.

The owl returns and rests on my outstretched wrist.

"Humming eyes," she reports. "Two and then two again. Then no more."

Abalone has prepared for this. When I tap my eyes in our agreed upon signal for cameras and then make the sign for "nothing else" she fishes out her tools. Even before she has them in hand, I have found the concealed service panel and begin to work it free. While I do so, I am aware of Midline, weapon in hand, frozen into a watchful readiness.

The section of the wall comes free in my hands and Abalone reaches inside. The tiny light she wears on one finger like a ring illuminates only her work space. Still, almost as if I can see her face, I feel her astonishment at my initiative.

I smile. My dear Baloo, I went to the same hard schools as you. Did you think that I would learn nothing?

Once she has carefully inserted the chip that will fool the cameras into seeing only a dark corridor, she replaces the panels. Margarita has assured us that no human guard is ever posted in Aldrich's labs at the doctor's own request. Security had consented because his building was so deep inside the complex and "because Aldrich is such a nasty bastard under all that highbrow pose."

Abalone gives thumbs-up to the others and a squeeze on the shoulder to me. Then she flourishes something she has removed from within the work cubby—a floor plan so simple that even I can grasp it.

"This plan matches what Margarita got for us pretty closely," she whispers. "Aldrich's quarters are there. His labs are here. We'll be able to work in there undisturbed if we're quiet."

Midline swats her gently. "We know the plan and I'll cover the hall. Now, go!"

"Right."

Even in the dim-lit hall, I can feel Abalone blush.

Leaving Midline lounging against a wall in the corridor, Abalone and I let ourselves into the labs. As planned, Professor Isabella and Abalone awaken the computers and begin to scan and destroy data. My job is simpler; I am simply to collect any paper I find and stack it by a shredder that Professor Isabella has removed from her briefcase.

"I've got a secure outside line," Abalone announces softly, the first voice in many minutes, "and I'm going to start removing any knowledge of Sarah from the files and planting my virus. How are you doing with Aldrich's research stuff, Professor?"

She gives her head a birdlike tilt. "No trouble, but I am finding some very frightening things. There is no doubt that Aldrich was continuing his work. There's a great deal of new material about negative recessives and reinforcing traits interworked with material about memory, empathy, and magical thinking."

"Bastard," Abalone hisses, most of her attention on her own work. "I'm glad Ailanthus forced us to move now."

I roam between clean white counters and listen to the strange songs of the devices that stand regimented along them. Something in their songs makes me pay attention to one wall and, turning to examine it, I hear soft tittering.

From where I hold them, Betwixt and Between answer without my asking, "It wasn't us, Sarah. It was the wall."

I turn to examine the wall, noticing for the first time that it is the only one not cluttered with shelves or heavy gear. The few carts drawn up in front of it could be easily moved. Doing so, I listen again and quickly find the concealed release. There is no sign of alarms, so I palm it, just as Professor Isabella notices what I am doing.

"Sarah?"

I ignore her and, when the opening is large enough to admit me, slip through.

My motion brings up soft lighting illuminating a small, sparsely furnished chamber. A low dresser, a cabinet, and a box of transparent plastic are the only things the room holds, but what the box holds makes my throat tighten with rage.

A nude baby boy, no more than a year old, is slowly awakening in the box. His eyes are green, tinged with infant blue, and his hair is a shade more golden than my own. I don't need to be able to read the listing on the box to know that this child is a member of my family.

Putting Betwixt and Between on the dresser where they

can watch, I start flipping the fastenings on the box. The baby shows no interest in what I am doing and my rage grows with his indifference.

"Dear God! A baby!"

Behind me, Professor Isabella's voice rises in shock, but the soundproofed walls of the little room swallow the sound.

I nod, my attention still on the baby. When I move to lift it, she hurries over, sniffing the air suspiciously.

"Let me, Sarah. You need to support his head and cradle his body like so."

She demonstrates and I nod curtly. There is more rage in me than I knew was possible, but I struggle to conceal it.

Abalone comes to join us a few minutes later and freezes in the doorway when she sees my discovery.

"Who?" she squeaks.

Professor Isabella, now efficiently diapering the boy, actually has an answer.

"I believe that he is the child of Dylan and Eleanora, test-tube bred by Aldrich and carried by a surrogate mother. I thought that what I was reading over was a planned-for project, but obviously I was wrong."

Under Betwixt and Between's watchful gaze, she fishes a white jumper from the dresser drawer.

"I can get him dressed, but I don't know for how long he'll stay quiet. Already he's the most passive baby I've ever seen."

Abalone steps closer. "Drugged. Look at his eyes."

While they are distracted, I stalk from the lab and into the hall. Midline's dark eyes meet mine.

. . . .

"Finished in there?" he asks softly.

I nod, narrowing my eyes. "I must be cruel, only to be kind."

He studies me. "What do you want?"

I point to the door that leads into Aldrich's suite.

"We were going to leave him alone," he says.

"No."

There must be something in my expression, for he doesn't try to stop me when I move toward Aldrich's suite.

The door is not even locked and seems to leap open at my touch. Once I am in the room, I disconnect his comm. Then, deliberately, I turn on the lights and shake him awake.

"Silence is golden," I warn him, showing him the hunting knife I have carried since my return to the Free People.

He swallows his yell and says very softly, "You!"

"Vengeance is mine; I will repay," I growl.

" 'Saith the Lord,' " he replies tentatively.

"No," I say. "Vengeance is *mine, I* will repay."

He quivers under the bedclothes. "What do you want?"

My face is hard. "One fire burns out another's burning; One pain is lessen'd by another's anguish."

"Sarah." He struggles into a sitting position. "You never would have been born if not for me. You owe me your life."

"Life can be bitter to the very bone, when one is poor, and woman, and alone."

"Your life hasn't been bitter, Sarah," he says. "You have talents of which other people only dream. Surely you have enjoyed your abilities."

Slowly, I turn the knife so that the room's dim light plays

off the blade like will-o'-the-wisps over a marsh. My reflection in Dr. Aldrich's mirror shows me the incongruity of my tidy business suit and the steely blade.

"All ambitions are lawful," I say, testing the blade edge against my thumb, "except for those which climb upward on the miseries or credulities of mankind."

Dr. Aldrich is awakening to an awareness that this is real, not a nightmare—that he is about to die. Behind me, in the hall, I hear Professor Isabella and Abalone talking with Midline. I wait until they join me and carefully take the baby from Professor Isabella.

At the sight of his latest creation cradled in my arms, Dr. Aldrich bites down on his lower lip until blood beads forth from the thin flesh.

"You've found him," he says. "Give him to me! He's my last hope. They'll kill me if you take him. He's my property!"

His voice is tight with an edge that I have heard many times before in the Home. Tears overflow his eyes and mingle with the blood from his lips. A sour smell taints the air. Fear brutally breaks his mind in a way that neither guilt nor pity could.

Yet, despite the noise, the baby in my arms stirs only a little.

"Sarah," Professor Isabella says, "we've done what we came for. Come away."

I hand my nephew to her and motion for them to precede me from the room. In his bed, Dr. Aldrich burbles chaotically. I move as if to follow the others and then dart back into the room.

. . . .

With one hand I grab his hair, twisting his head so that he is forced to face me. His eyes are mad, but not with the clean madness of Head Wolf or Jersey. This is self-interest so acute that it has driven him mad with horror.

Grasping my knife firmly, I thrust it into the pulsating hollow below his Adam's apple.

"How sharper than a serpent's tooth it is," I say as I twist the blade, "to have a thankless child."

Beneath my hand, blood runs bright. Aldrich convulses once and then is still. The pulse fades as suddenly.

A hand—Midline's—draws my hand away and the knife falls free.

"The bone is cracked," he says gently. "Aldrich is dead. Not just from the knife wound, I think. His heart stopped from the terror. A good killing of one such as him."

Aware of the drumming of my own racing heart, I retrieve my blade.

"There will be fingerprints," Abalone says, "but that shouldn't matter. Right after we found the baby, I set up the heating system to screw up and start fires all through this building. Aldrich's research materials must be completely destroyed or someone else may try to duplicate his work someday."

"If we're finished here then," Professor Isabella says, "I think we should leave. The baby isn't likely to stay quiet forever, especially now that he's disconnected from that box."

As if to confirm her words, the baby kicks against his blanket. Taking Betwixt and Between from Abalone, I put them on his chest and the chubby hands reach to grasp my dragon.

"Sing a song of sixpence," I tell them, "a pocket full of rye. Four-and-twenty blackbirds baked in a pie."

"I always thought that was a really sick thing to sing about to a kid," Betwixt comments.

"Oh, shut up," Between replies. "You know what she wants."

"Yeah, I do. 'Rock-a-bye-baby'?"

Together they begin to harmonize sweetly on the lullaby. The baby's hands tighten and his expression brightens for the first time with something like delight.

Professor Isabella looks thoughtfully at him.

"I wonder," she says, "if he can hear the way Sarah can? The records seemed to indicate that Aldrich was trying to create the same talent."

Abalone looks at him and then starts shoving us down the hallway toward the exit.

"Of course, he can, can't you see? But, in case you've forgotten, we are in enemy territory and these"—the toss of her head indicates both the baby and Aldrich's corpse—"complicate things somewhat. I've called for the trolley capsule and signaled Peep and we really should be leaving."

Midline sniffs the air. "And the fires are starting. We want to be away before they are noticed."

"I did have the sense to cut the fire alarms," Abalone retorts. "Sarah, put your suit jacket in your briefcase. It has blood on it."

I obey, finishing before the trolley arrives. My hands are steady and, to my surprise, so am I. All my rage, frustration, and misery died when I struck out against Dr. Aldrich.

Despite Abalone's concern, our escape is easily managed.

Peep arches an eyebrow when he sees the baby, but his only comment is to tint the windows rusty brown. We speed by the attentive guard, but his attention is for his monitors, not for a single sedan.

Professor Isabella looks at me, her expression alive with concerns she won't admit.

"How are you, Sarah?"

I gesture to the receding Ailanthus compound, a wry smile bending my lips.

"Hating people is like burning down your own house to get rid of a rat."

"Well, I didn't figure that you loved him"—Professor Isabella tries to smile—"but I didn't expect you to murder him."

I reach out and touch the baby. He coos and with one hand lets go of Betwixt and Between to hold my finger.

"If slavery is not wrong, nothing is wrong," I reply after a minute.

"I see," Professor Isabella says, looking between the baby's face and mine. "You saw what Aldrich was doing to this child. Dylan was a slave all his life and, for all her apparent freedom, so was Eleanora."

I nod, content to see some of her confusion leave, even if she does not completely understand.

"Don't forget what he did to Sarah," Abalone adds. "Aldrich bred for her like he did for the others and so he created the block between her and true speech. She'll never escape his touch on her, no matter how good we treat her."

"Maybe," Professor Isabella says, a thoughtful look on her face. "I saw this child's files before we purged them.

Aldrich was working to negate Sarah's negative traits. Perhaps the baby will be able to talk both to us and to her."

"Or at least hear what she does and share it more easily," Midline agrees. "I like that."

"Whatever the child may do in the future," Professor Isabella says, patting the baby's rump, "we had better stop and get diapers before we return to the Jungle. He's wet himself."

"Mowgli, the Frog, I will call thee," I say, giggling. "He shall live to run with the Pack and to hunt with the Pack."

"Mowgli, the Frog! That's good—he's all wet!" Abalone laughs and the rest join in. "I have money to get Mowgli diapers. I emptied Ailanthus' petty—well, not so petty—cash accounts while I was mucking around in the system. There's money enough for diapers and more."

"After we get rid of this car," Peep promises cheerfully, "we'll stop at a store for stuff for the *niño*. Will that be soon enough, Professor Isabella?"

"I suppose that it will have to be," she answers.

The diaper, however, complains loudly. Only I—and Mowgli—hear. Smiling, I pat my dragons and they sing enthusiastically enough to fill our ears with silent song.

Looking over Peep's shoulder, I see the lights of the city spreading before us like a sea of diamonds. The sedan dips, angles, and we begin our descent.